Welcome to Shady Gulch, Dakota Territory.
Savannah: Book One
Lottie Mae: Book Two
Freedom: Book Three

Freedom

Silver Dollar Saloon

Paty Jager

Windtree Press
Hillsboro, OR

FREEDOM: SILVER DOLLAR SALOON
Copyright © 2019 Patricia Jager

Contact Information: info@windtreepress.com

Windtree Press
Hillsboro, Oregon
http://windtreepress.com

Cover Art by Christina Keerins
CoveredbyCLKeerins

Published in the United States of America
ISBN 978-1-950387-25-0

Disclaimer and Thank You

Shady Gulch is not a real town in North Dakota nor was it a town in the Dakota Territory at the time of this book. I took information about railroad towns along the Northern Pacific Railroad and made my own town and populated it with the ethnic groups that traveled to the area to set up new lives.

Because I believe in depicting races or cultures other than my own the best I can I use sensitivity readers.

Thank you to C. Morgan Kennedy for being my sensitivity reader and making sure I portrayed Freedom as would have been correct for the time period.

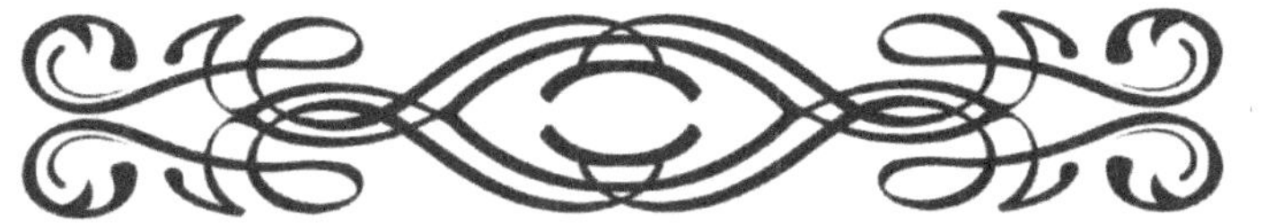

Chapter One

North Dakota 1880

Excitement buzzed through Freedom. The last time she and the other women of the Silver Dollar Saloon attended a Pie Social, she'd sold her pie to a handsome man dressed in buckskins. Ben Hogan.

He'd visited her half a dozen times since the last pie social. Every time he'd been a gentleman and she'd been reserved on the outside while hoping and dreaming he would take her out of the Silver Dollar Saloon.

She owed Beau Gentry, the owner of the saloon, for her very life, but she was tired of singing, dancing, and delivering drinks even though the Silver Dollar was a much different saloon from the others in town. Beau and his partner didn't allow the men to touch the girls or say anything nasty. Even though they, the girls, were treated more fairly than others who worked in saloons, she still hadn't been able to write her parents and tell them where she was and what she was doing.

If her parents knew she was hanging her hopes of becoming respectable on a white man, they'd be locking her up and tossing the key in the privy. But there were no colored men in Shady Gulch other than Jules, the co-owner of the Silver Dollar Saloon. While she was thankful Jules had been with Beau Gentry the day the two found her near dead alongside the Fargo train depot, she felt the same toward him as she did Beau. They were like big brothers. Something she missed. Her family lived in Chicago. Or at least they had five years ago when she'd been run out of town by her employer.

She'd dried her homesick tears two days after her employer put her on a train bound for the west. She couldn't go back to her family disgraced. She'd sent them a letter saying she'd found employment as a nanny with a family headed west. And that was the last time she'd communicated with them.

Freedom shook off the memories of five years ago. She'd learned then that a colored woman traveling alone was fair game to any man looking for trouble. Two men had beaten her, taken what little money she had, and tossed her off the train. She'd crawled to the nearest train depot hoping someone would help her. She'd lain in the cold for a day and a night before Beau and Jules came along.

That was the past. She was looking to make a future, one that she could hold her head up and look everyone in the eye. Freedom focused on the way her new dress brought out the golden shimmers in her eyes. Her eyes were her best asset. Drawing a brush through her thick hair, she pulled it into a bun at the back of her head. While no one in Shady Gulch made much of her being colored, she tried her hardest to fit in and not stick out. Allowing her curly hair to go willy-nilly as it liked was a sure way to be seen as different.

A knock on the door was followed by Belle peeking in the room. "Are you ready?" Her gaze drifted up and down Freedom's new dress. "That looks wonderful on you. You are becoming a very good seamstress."

"It's all because Mrs. Polzin allows me to work with her. I could barely sew a stitch before she needed help." Freedom was pleased with her results and the fact the seamstress in town was willing to let a saloon girl help her for a couple of hours each day.

"You keep helping her, and you could start up your own dress making business." Belle waved a hand. "Come on. We don't want to be late."

Freedom grinned. Belle had taken years to get over her hatred of men and though she still didn't trust any, other than Beau and Jules, she had started socializing more. Mostly due to Beau's sister Savannah, the preacher's wife.

She grabbed her hat, stabbed a pin through to keep it on her head, and left her room.

Down in the kitchen of the boarding house, where all the ladies who worked at the Silver Dollar Saloon lived, Mrs. Dearling, the wonderful widow who ran the place, was handing everyone's pies to them.

"Remember to smile when you are holding your pie and people are bidding. We not only want to raise money for the church, but you never know when you might catch a young man's eye." Mrs. Dearling thought of herself as a matchmaker. Once the battered women who came to live in the house and work in the saloon became comfortable around people and realized their problems could be overcome, she started taking them out into the community, introducing them around.

The women from the saloon usually found a husband within a few years of being taken under Beau Gentry's wing.

Freedom hugged Mrs. Dearling before taking her shoofly pie. It had been her lucky pie over a year ago when Ben purchased it. She hoped he made it to town today. The last time he'd come a calling, she'd reminded him about the pie social. Her mind wandered to the visit.

They'd sat on a bench in the city park. They'd talked about books they'd both read. She'd asked how someone living as he did, wearing buckskins and traveling about, was so learned and well-spoken. A veil had dropped over his face before he'd said his mother had made sure he had the best learning before she passed. Her heart had gone out to him that day, knowing he'd lost his mother. Then he'd asked about her family. He'd cared enough to ask and when he'd discovered she'd not had contact with them, had suggested she send them a letter. Very few of her friends even knew she still had family. That he'd asked and urged her to write showed he cared about her. And family.

Her insides fluttered thinking about his feelings toward family. She wanted a large family. Did she dare hope Ben felt the same? It was rare that a woman of color married a white man, but she could hope he cared enough for her, and didn't mind what others thought. It appeared that way the times they'd walked around town and ate at the café. He lived alone out in the woods. They would be alone, just the two of them. *Until they started having children.*

"You look lovely today child." Mrs. Dearling held her at arm's length. "You are going to fetch good money for that pie of yours." The woman winked at her.

Freedom wondered if Mrs. Dearling knew that Ben was here. "Thank you. I'm hopin' to fetch more than money for my pie."

"Don't go doing anything that will reflect badly on Beau," Mrs. Dearling scolded. She acted as if Beau were her offspring rather than her boss.

"You know I won't. I'm just hopin' a certain person will buy my pie and we'll go for a walk." Her chest tightened at the thought of asking Ben if he might be having thoughts about the two of them marrying. Up till now they'd talked about many things that she'd not have talked about with someone not like her.

"We'll see. We'll see. Come along, ladies." Mrs. Dearling, with a basket over her arm, led Freedom, Belle, Darie, and Liesa through the boarding house and out the front door. The back door exited into the alleyway behind the Silver Dollar Saloon. They used that door when going to work and the front door for all other outings.

"You look pretty and excited," Liesa said, walking beside Freedom.

"Thank you. I am. Do you think Ben will be here?" She knew she sounded more like a love struck fifteen-year-old than a twenty-year-old woman. But her dream since her family moved from the backbreaking work of farming in the south to the north, had been to marry and have children. She knew she'd be a good mother. Look at how well she'd taken care of the McCluskey baby…Her mood sobered. Until the fire. The one that took the baby's life and ended her job and the life she'd believed she'd been put on this earth to do.

Liesa's soft voice interrupted her thoughts. "Even though this man shows interest, be careful."

Freedom shook off the past and studied her friend. "What do you mean?"

Liesa was a small fragile woman. Her German accent was slowly getting less noticeable. She was the most timid of the women working at the saloon, but also the one who saw the most. "He does not always watch you with a smile on his face."

"You mean at the saloon?" She couldn't think of anywhere else Liesa would have watched the two of them.

She nodded. "Be careful."

Freedom glanced down at the pie she carried. Her friend wouldn't tell her lies. Could she maybe have seen him thinking this wasn't the place for Freedom to be? He'd told her several times she wasn't like other women who worked in saloons. He said it as if he were surprised. Ben wasn't like the other whites. The ones in the south who forced the slaves and former slaves to do their bidding or die. She shuddered remembering the stories told by her parents and other adults when they still lived in the south.

She shook her head. All she'd seen of Ben she couldn't see him being that mean or callous. Perhaps, when Liesa had seen him he'd been thinking about something else while he stared her direction. She did that all the time. Even when she was singing at the Silver Dollar. Her mouth would be open and the song coming out, but her mind was thinking of putting children to bed and getting ready to slip under the covers beside her husband.

But to make her friend happy, she said, "I will."

At the church yard, Savannah Webster, the preacher's wife and Beau's sister, presided over the pie table. "I'm happy y'all fetched your tasty pies." She smiled bright.

Freedom placed her pie on the table and whispered, "You are glowin' like a star." She was the only one who knew about their friend's condition. Savannah was with child. She and Lark, her husband, were keeping it quiet until it was noticeable. Savannah wanted to be active and there were some in the congregation who believed a woman should lie down and not lift a finger while with child. Especially, someone as delicate as the preacher's southern wife.

Freedom had helped Dr. Nolan with several of the births in the area, tending to the baby for a couple days when the mother was young or first-time.

Savannah had come to Freedom asking questions. Mostly about what happened when the birthing happened. While her friend was excited about having a child, she was also scared, having heard of so many women who lost their lives or babies at birth.

"I feel fit as a fiddle." She winked and took Liesa's pie. "You look lovely today, Liesa."

They all moved off toward the other women in town. While the women of the Silver Dollar Saloon were saloon girls, they were treated with more respect than the ones who worked in the other two saloons in town. Beau and Mrs. Dearling were the reasons they were treated differently. They made sure the girls acted respectable when at the saloon and when walking around town. When working in the saloon, the women weren't allowed to make small talk with a man who caught their eye unless Beau was nearby. Out on the street and in the boarding house, they were never alone.

While they were more accepted, they weren't completely taken into the women's circles until they married.

Lottie Mae, a past Silver Dollar girl, walked away from the other school teacher and gave them each a hug. "You all look pretty today." As she hugged Freedom, she said, "He's here."

Lottie Mae and her husband, Manfred, had talked Ben into dancing with Freedom at the Fourth of July dance.

"I was hopin' he would come." Freedom's heart beat against her ribs. Would she have the courage to speak to him about them maybe having a future? Was her racing heart love or excitement that she might be changing her life?

"When do you think you'll finish the house?" Belle asked Lottie Mae.

"Manfred said I can start measuring for curtains in a couple more months." Lottie Mae's smile stretched across her face. "I can't believe I'm going to live in a house and not the backend of a blacksmith shop."

"You deserve the house and the good man," Liesa said.

They all knew one another's stories. How each had ended up at the Silver Dollar Saloon because of men.

"We all deserve a good man." Lottie Mae's gaze landed on each one. Even little Darie, who helped Mrs. Dearling with the household chores since being attacked, violated, and thrown off a train a year ago.

They chatted for another twenty minutes before

Reverend Webster, Lark, as they all knew him, raised his hands and asked that they all bow their heads in prayer before the bidding began to start the pie social.

Freedom peeked at the crowd as everyone bowed their heads. Where could Ben be? Knowing the pies were auctioned off in the order in which they sat on the table, Freedom had made sure her offering was near the beginning.

Several pies were auctioned and bid on by husbands and Lark, who always made sure each pie received a bid, even if he started the bidding himself. Beau also made sure no woman left the social with her head hanging because her pie wasn't purchased.

"What have we here?" Lark raised Freedom's shoofly pie in the air. "I do believe this is one of Miss Freedom's shoofly pies." He glanced over at her. "Come on up here and let everyone know who baked this pie."

Freedom grasped her skirt, raising it just enough she could walk briskly over to where Lark stood. Once there, she dropped her skirt, clutched her hands together in front of her, and studied the crowd. Her heart leapt into her throat. There he was. Ben. Standing in the back of the crowd. He was easy to spot because of his height and he always wore buckskins, unlike the farmers who lived in these parts.

"Who'll be the first bidder on this—" Lark sniffed the pie, "—tasty smelling pie?"

"Ten cents," Beau called out.

Freedom smiled at him. He always bid on their pies. She glanced toward Ben. He was hesitating. Why?

"Fifteen," Jules shouted.

She heard Beau raise it to twenty cents, when Ben

finally raised a hand. "Two bits."

Her heart fluttered until Beau hollered, "Thirty cents." She turned a glare on him. He only nodded his head. What was he doing? He knew she wanted Ben to get her pie.

Returning her gaze to Ben, she saw him talking with another man, dressed like him but older. The older man walked away and Ben hollered, "Thirty-five."

Lark studied Beau before saying, "I have a bid of thirty-five cents for Miss Freedom's shoofly pie. Do I hear forty?" He asked three more times if anyone wanted to pay forty and pointed to Ben. "Sir, you have purchased a delicious pie." Lark handed the pie to Freedom. "Don't give it to him until he pays," he said in a low tone.

Why were her friends being so critical of Ben? Was it because he wore buckskins like an Indian? She understood being different and he'd always shown her nothing but kindness. He'd even helped a kitten out of a tree and handed it to the little girl who'd been crying the last time he visited and they were on a walk. She knew to be cautious of men and particularly white men, but her friends hadn't seen the way Ben treated her, the kitten, or the little girl. They barely knew him.

While she'd grown up being leery of anyone not family, her instincts had told her to trust Beau and Jules when they found her. And she'd used that instinct over the years to avoid trouble. She didn't have any wary feelings about Ben. He was a kind, considerate man.

She stood at the end of the table near Savannah, who wrote down the prices and took the money. "Your pie always sells for good money," Savannah said.

"I'm glad I can make money for the church."

Freedom

Freedom stood on her tiptoes, waiting for Ben to come up to the table to claim her and the pie.

Three pies sold while she stood by the table watching others claim their prizes. Finally, Ben walked up to her.

Freedom's heart was no longer racing with excitement. She was annoyed. Ben had made her stand there waiting for him with all the townsfolk glancing over and knowing her pie and presence wasn't being claimed. She didn't like being the center of attention, and she didn't like being treated as if she didn't matter.

Chapter Two

Ben strolled over to where Freedom waited. She was about ready to let loose on him when he said, "I'm sorry I kept you waiting. One of the men I travel with kept catching me up in conversation." He dropped the money in Savannah's upturned palm and reached for the pie.

"I was gettin' ready to tell Reverend Webster to resell it." She couldn't stop the irritation she felt from flowing through her lips. That was one of her downfalls, according to her mother, and the employer who'd put her on the train. He'd been fearful Freedom would tell his wife, he'd caused the fire that killed their child.

The crestfallen expression on Ben's face had her wishing she'd bit her tongue. "I'm sorry. It felt like the whole town was laughin' at me standin' here waitin' for you to claim the pie." She glanced up at him. "I was also hopin' you'd like me to keep you company while you enjoyed eatin' it."

Ben held out his crooked arm. "I'd like that."

Her heart hummed at how casually he offered his arm. They strolled away from the noise of the social to the side of the church that was shaded this time of day.

"That's a pretty dress you're wearing. I wish I had something to put on the ground before you sit." Ben looked around as if a blanket would appear because he'd wished it.

"I'll just sit easy." She slowly lowered to the ground with the help of Ben. His easy grip on her hand belied the power she felt in his arm under the buckskin as she grasped it to help her ease on down to the grass.

"We forgot something to eat it with." Ben strode back across the space between them and the others and picked up two plates and two forks. He returned quickly.

Savannah had cut the pie when Freedom handed it to her before the auction. All they had to do was scoop out a piece with their forks.

Freedom put a piece on a plate and handed it to Ben. He took the plate and started shoving the dessert into his mouth. She put a piece on her plate and picked at it with her fork.

"Are you goin' to stay long this trip?" she asked, holding her breath, waiting for his answer.

He glanced up from the pie and studied her before a smile crept across his lips. "I could stay a day if you've a mind to keep me company."

"I can when I'm not workin'." She thought a minute. "Or sleepin'."

"Would that be enough time to go for a buggy ride?" he asked.

She would make the time for a buggy ride. Even if she had to suffer lack of sleep. "Yes."

He glanced around at the people pairing off and in families sitting around the churchyard. "What about this afternoon?"

Her heart raced. "That would be perfect. We don't work on Sundays."

His eyelids lowered a bit, but he nodded. "That's right, the Silver Dollar is closed when other saloons stay open."

"Beau doesn't treat the saloon like others. He treats it like a proper business." She'd stick up for her boss and protector until her dying breath. He'd saved her and many other women and asked little of them. Just that they worked in the saloon until they were ready to step back into society.

Ben put a hand on her arm. "I know. I wasn't talking bad of him. I like knowing you don't bed men."

Her gaze shot to his eyes. What was he thinking behind those dark blue orbs? Did he think she was worth marrying?

He stacked his plate under hers. She'd only eaten a bite of pie. "We'll take these with us. Come on. Let's go see if anyone is working at the stable and get us a buggy." He helped her to her feet and handed her the pie.

"I should tell someone where I'm goin'," she said, glancing around to see if anyone from the saloon was close by. She didn't fear Ben, but she'd been taught from birth to not trust any white man fully. Having someone know where she'd be would make her feel better about the ride. She spotted Lottie Mae and Manfred at the end of the church. "I'll be right back."

Freedom clutched her skirt in her hands and hurried over to her friend. "Ben and I are going for a buggy ride." She didn't even try to hide the happiness in her voice.

Lottie Mae smiled. "Take him to our place. It's pretty and quiet there."

"Thank you!" She strode back to where Ben waited patiently.

"You didn't have to tell anyone. We'll be back before they miss us." He grasped her hand in his.

"If someone other than my friends see us walking away together, they may get the wrong idea, this way Lottie Mae can say I told her where we were going." Freedom felt better having told someone.

Ben led her away from the church and down the street toward the end of town where the livery stable sat.

The warmth of Ben's hand holding hers gave her a sense of comfort. It had been a long time since a large, warm, male hand had held hers. It brought back memories of her father and the security she'd felt with him. She glanced at Ben. He'd proved he would be a good father the way he'd treated the little girl with the kitten.

The contrary and vulgar Mr. Montgomery was at the stable. He didn't participate in anything that had to do with the church.

"Well, lookie here. You brung me a pie." The livery man reached out as if to take her shoofly pie.

She pulled it back, and Ben stepped between her and the man. "That's my pie. I paid for it, and I plan to eat all of it." His voice had a menacing tone she'd never heard from him before.

Freedom took a couple of steps backwards. Was this a side to Ben he showed often when she wasn't around? Maybe she should rethink going for a buggy ride alone with him. Then again, he was protecting her. She knew how important it was to have a man who would protect you. How many times had her father put himself between her mother and white men threatening her or their family? In those times her father had shown a side she didn't see at other times.

"Here's fifty cents. Harness a horse to a buggy." Ben put his arm around her shoulders. "And if I hear you've been giving Miss Freedom trouble, you'll be hearing from me." Ben's voice didn't hold the menace it had moments ago. His arm around her shoulders was light, comforting.

She didn't glance at Mr. Montgomery, but she had a pretty good idea what he was thinking and she didn't like it. Going for a buggy ride with Ben could tarnish her reputation. Especially, if Mr. Montgomery made up one of his lies.

"Maybe we shouldn't," she said, moving out of Ben's arm.

His gaze wandered over her face. "Why not?"

"It's not proper for me to ride off alone with you." She couldn't quite meet his eyes. Her heart pounded in her chest. She wanted time with Ben. To get to learn more about him. However, her mother's voice in the back of her head, saying she shouldn't do this, had her second guessing the buggy ride.

"Do you want to go back and get one of your friends to come along? You want a chaperone?" he said it softly, as if he cared about her reputation and her feelings.

She peered into his eyes. He was willing to take someone along if it made her happy. "No. I trust you."

She glanced over his shoulder. "It's what Mr. Montgomery might say that gives me second thoughts."

Ben shook his head and grinned. "Anyone who knows you won't think you'd do anything that wasn't proper."

Mr. Montgomery led a dark red horse forward. It was hitched to a one seated buggy.

"Thank you. I'll have it back before dark." Ben took the pie from her hands, set it on the seat, and put his hands around her waist, lifting her into the buggy.

Heat scorched her sides and up her neck at the familiar way he lifted her. Freedom quickly settled her skirt and picked up the pie, holding it in her lap.

Ben climbed up in the seat, took the reins, and walked the horse out into the spring sunlight.

"Which way?" he asked.

"North." She waited until they were clear of the town and said, "Lottie Mae and Manfred are buildin' a house on his property out by the spring."

Ben glanced at her. "Is that where you want to go?"

She scanned the barren landscape of sagebrush and few trees. "Yes. We'll have shade and could walk a bit."

"Then the spring is where we'll go."

She waited a few minutes, expecting him to start asking her questions. When he didn't, she decided to break the silence. "You told me your mother is gone, but where does your family live?"

He glanced over at her. "What do you mean?"

"Your father, sisters, brothers. Where do they live?"

"I don't have any. I lost my ma and brother when sickness came to our town. Pa and I never saw eye to eye. I lit out at thirteen and come across a man headed west to find gold. I tagged along and discovered I was resourceful enough to go out on my own." He held the reins in one hand and pried her left hand away from the pie plate. Holding her hand, he smiled. "I've been thinking though, that I'd like company at night. Gets lonely in the winter with the long dark hours."

He squeezed her hand. She glanced up into his eyes. Her insides squiggled. Was this what being in love felt like?

"I see. And what kind of person were you thinkin' about spendin' time with?"

"One that has strength to be alone a few days at a time when I'm working the trap line. Someone who can cook."

She started to wonder if all he wanted was a housekeeper.

"But most of all, I'd like to come home to your big smile and welcoming arms." His gaze searched hers.

"Me? You want to come home to me?" Her heart bounced around in her chest, making it hard to breathe.

"I've been thinking on it ever since we first met. You always have a smile, you make friends easily, and…" He raised their linked hands to his lips and kissed the back of her hand. "There's something about you that keeps you in my mind."

"Really?" she said, in a breathy way that made her sound like a smitten girl. She swallowed and vowed to not let him know how excited she was that he was thinking the way she wanted.

He grinned and his eyes sparkled. Ben pulled back on the reins, stopping the buggy. He placed a hand under her chin, lifting her face up as he lowered his head. Their lips touched briefly. He leaned back, gazed into her eyes, and lowered his head again.

This time he brushed her full bottom lip with his before kissing her. She'd never kissed anyone other than family and wasn't prepared for the sensation that trickled through her body at his intimate touch.

Ben leaned back, his face only inches from hers. "What do you say? Want to come with me when I leave in two days?"

"Yes," she said, before her mind kicked in.

"I was hoping you'd say that." He kissed her again briefly and started the buggy in motion.

As the horse moved forward, Freedom realized what she'd just agreed to. Or thought she'd just agreed to. "We can have Reverend Webster marry us tomorrow."

Ben glanced over at her. "We can get married by the traveling preacher who comes through once a month."

She stared at him. "I can't leave with you if I'm not married to you."

The trees that grew around the spring and would give Lottie Mae and Manfred shade, appeared ahead of them.

"Let's discuss this when we're at the spring." Ben clucked to the horse, moving it into a trot.

Freedom clutched the pie in her lap and wondered if she cared enough for this man to travel with him before marriage. She knew she'd do anything to leave the saloon but live with a man without marriage? That she couldn't do.

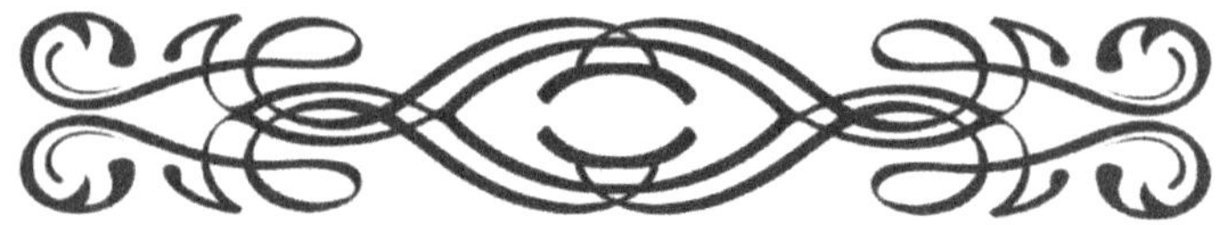

Chapter Three

Freedom studied Ben as he ate another piece of pie while they sat on a makeshift bench, he'd made from the lumber for the Albrecht's house. "Where do you live?"

"About twenty miles south of the Yellowstone River along the Powder River in Montana." He held a bite halfway to his mouth. "It's the prettiest country I've ever seen."

"Do you farm?" Freedom didn't mind farming. It was what her family did in Georgia after the war before moving to Chicago.

Ben shook his head. "I trap in the winter and this time of year I wander around trading goods."

She studied him. "Tradin' goods? Do you mean you're a peddler? You don't look like any peddlin' man I've seen." Every time she'd seen him, he wore buckskins and had a knife hanging from his belt.

"I trade items I pick up from reservations and sell them to people at the forts and railroad towns." He scooped up the last bite of his pie. "And I sell the furs I trap."

"It sounds like you do a lot of travelin'." She wasn't sure she wanted to be married to a man who was never home.

"You'll come with me. At least when the weather is good." He bestowed a charming smile on her. "You can still come when we have kids, that will be up to you."

Her hand covered the flutter in her belly. If he was talking kids then he wanted to bed her. Wanted to make them a family. He loved her. Joy burst in her heart. Her friends were wrong. He wanted her and loved her. She'd have the family she always wanted.

Ben set his plate to the side and grasped her hands, skimming his knuckles across her body. Her cheeks heated at how she allowed this man to touch her in ways she would not have tolerated from another. But he wanted her for a wife. He cared about her.

"Freedom, from the first moment I heard you could bake shoofly pie, to meeting you and looking into your eyes that shoot rays of sunlight, I haven't been able to get you out of my thoughts." He tugged her closer, looping her arms around his neck. "You are the woman I want beside me."

She stared into his eyes, feeling his strong arms around her. He would protect her from danger and take her away from the saloon. Both things she'd dreamed about the last few years.

"I'd be proud to be your woman," she said, hoping he'd kiss her again.

He did. This time his hands held her head, and he kissed her much more thorough than before, making her lips throb.

He eased his mouth away from hers. "Want to leave with me tomorrow?"

Her mind was still absorbing the kiss. "What?"

"Tomorrow. We could leave tomorrow. There's no sense in hanging around here when we could be headed home."

Tomorrow? She could wear this dress when they wed. But would Lark be available. And Mrs. Dearling would want to make a fancy meal. "What about the weddin'? I'd like to have my friends see me marry."

"We can grab the first preacher we come to."

"But I'd like to have Lark, Reverend Webster, marry us before we leave. It will make my friends feel better about my goin' off with you."

He stared at her. His jaw twitched a couple times. "If you can get them to do it tomorrow. I don't want to be gone any longer than that."

"Thank you." She kissed him on the lips. Then Freedom leaned back, afraid she might have been too forward.

He grinned and pulled her into another mouth numbing kiss.

The horse nickered and they parted, gathering the nearly gone pie and the dishes. Ben held her hand as he led her back to the buggy.

He set the pie plate and dishes on the floor of the buggy and put his hands around her waist. "This time tomorrow we'll be husband and wife."

The sparkle in his eyes had her insides galloping. He desired her.

He kissed her on the mouth and placed her in the buggy. She settled on the seat but not as far as on the way out. After all, they would be married tomorrow.

The buggy lurched forward as the horse started off at a trot. Ben placed his hand on her leg. Her cheeks and ears heated. She would have to get used to his touch. They were to be married. She pinched herself that what she'd wanted for a long time was finally coming true.

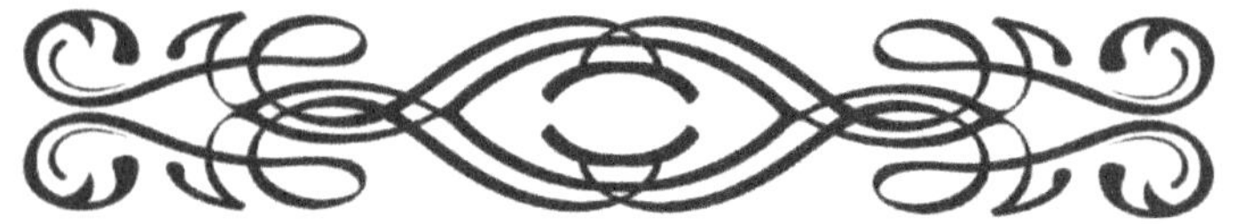

Chapter Four

"You're what?" Beau roared.

Freedom had seen Beau upset before, but this was the first time his anger was aimed at her. Well, not her. He was glaring at Ben.

"We are getting married tomorrow. Here, or Freedom will go with me and we'll get the first preacher we see to marry us," Ben said, standing up to Beau.

Jules stepped forward, peering at her. "Is this truly what you wish?" His Creole accent at times made him hard to understand, but she understood his words and his meaning.

"Yes. We want to get married." Freedom held her hand out to Ben, and he grasped it.

Both men stared at their linked hands.

Mrs. Dearling stepped around Beau. "If you are in love and want to marry, then I think it's wonderful. But tomorrow? There is so much that needs to be done. If it is love, you can wait until everything can be done properly.”

"I can't remain here any longer," Ben said.

"What is your hurry?" Beau asked.

"Perhaps, Freedom and I should wander over to Savannah's and see if Lark will be able to marry these two tomorrow." Mrs. Dearling turned Freedom around and shoved her out the front door.

"I don't want to leave Ben alone with Beau," Freedom said, trying to get around the short stout woman.

"They'll be fine. Jules is there to keep things civil." Mrs. Dearling linked her arm with Freedom's and tugged her down the street. "Tell me about your man."

Freedom forgot about the two men. She liked that Mrs. Dearling called Ben her man. But she'd prefer husband. "He travels for his work. He wants me to go with him. Even after we have children."

"Oh, so you did talk about that?" Mrs. Dearling stopped on the Webster's porch.

"Yes. He really cares for me. I can see it in his eyes." She smiled.

"Then he didn't say he loved you?" Mrs. Dearling held her hand in mid-air as if to knock on the door.

"Not the words, but with what he said, I know he cares."

The older woman shoved her hands on her hips and glared at her. "If he didn't say the words, you don't know for sure. A man who is in love is vulnerable and will tell you." She stared at Freedom. "And you? Are you in love?"

She shrugged. "I think so. I mean, I've never been. But I feel things, I've never felt before."

The woman stomped her foot and the door opened.

"Mrs. Dearlin' and Freedom. What caused you to stroll on over here?" Savannah asked.

The older woman put up a hand. "I'll tell you in a moment." She shifted her gaze to Freedom. "You don't marry a man because you feel a bit different or because he says nice things about you. There has to be love."

"What's this talk about marryin'?" Savannah asked, pulling them both into the house.

"Ben and I would like Lark to marry us tomorrow," Freedom said. She didn't care what Mrs. Dearling thought she knew about love. There were many kinds. What she felt for Ben could be love and what he felt for her could grow into love. They respected one another. That was half the battle, her mama always said.

Savannah grasped her hands and pulled her over to the kitchen table. "Honey, are you sure this is what you really want to do? You barely know the man. We barely know the man." She gently pushed Freedom onto a chair. "A cup of tea and visitin' is what needs done."

"I agree." Mrs. Dearling pulled out a chair and sat.

"I don't need a visit. I need you to say Lark will marry us. If he doesn't, I'll leave with Ben and be sad because my friends didn't care enough about me to be at my weddin'." Tears burned behind her eyeballs. It hit her that she would leave these people tomorrow. People she'd come to call family, and may never see again. Just like her real family. Maybe Ben traveled as far as Chicago? Her hopes soared. If he did, they could visit her family, and she could tell them face to face about her life since she'd left.

"Oh darlin', we'll be at your weddin'." Savannah put her arms around Freedom. "We aren't goin' to let you go off without bein' married."

"Married?" Lark walked through the door. "What's this about being married?"

"You tell Freedom her notion is as crazy as a cow with milk fever," Mrs. Dearling said.

Lark walked over to her chair and looked Freedom in the eyes. "What's going on?"

"Ben and I would like you to marry us tomorrow." She stared up at her friend, her preacher, and willed him to go along with uniting her and Ben and not argue.

"I see." He pulled out a chair and sat facing her. "What do you know about this man?"

"He likes the way I bake, my smile, and that I've a strong constitution."

Lark shook his head. "I didn't ask what he likes. I asked what you know."

She shrugged. "That he always treats me like I'm special. He has a job that requires travel, but asked me to go with him. He lives in Montana country twenty miles from the Yellowstone River."

"That's a long distance. When will we see you?" Mrs. Dearling asked, tears welling in her eyes.

"I'll write. I don't know if we'll travel this way as much as Ben has been lately or if he only did to come see me." The thought he'd traveled so far from home extra to see her, helped her see he did care for her.

She studied Lark. "Will you please marry us tomorrow?"

He nodded. "I prefer you leave this area as a married woman than travel about in sin."

Her cheeks heated. All the years working in the saloon Beau, Jules and Mrs. Dearling had worked hard to make sure the women were treated with respect. Her running off with Ben without properly getting married would not only sully her reputation but that of the Saloon and everyone who worked there.

"Would mornin' work, then? I'm sure Ben is goin' to want to get headed out as soon as possible." She had learned from her few talks with the man, his work meant a great deal to him.

"Is ten too late?" Lark asked.

"That should work."

"I should say so!" Mrs. Dearling said. "I'll have a fine dinner ready for everyone after the ceremony, and if you insist on leaving, you'll have full bellies."

She hugged the woman. "Thank you!"

"What are you goin' to wear?" Savannah asked.

"This dress. It's the best one I have."

Her friend shook her head. "It's pretty, but you'll need somethan' that will work for travelin'. I have a travelin' outfit that should fit you with minor changes."

Freedom shook her head. "I don't think we'll be travelin' by train. I'm pretty sure it will be by horse."

Savannah smiled. "Then I have the perfect outfit. Where is Ben?"

"We left him with a seethin' Beau at the boardin' house." Freedom realized it may not have been a good idea to have left the two alone. She didn't want her husband to be bruised and battered for the ceremony.

"Lark, would you go tell the men the weddin' is at ten tomorrow mornin' and then send the other ladies over. We'll need to do some work on my old ridin' outfit."

Lark kissed his wife's cheek. "I will gladly go save Ben." He laughed and left the house.

By the time Belle and Liesa arrived at the Webster residence, Freedom was tucked into Savannah's riding outfit and pins were being poked down the sides and in the hem.

"I think Ben has gained Beau's respect," Belle said, helping Freedom ease out of the pinned jacket.

"Why do you say that?" Freedom had hoped Beau didn't bully Ben into leaving town without her.

"He stood up to all of Beau's questions and didn't back down when Jules also asked if he was willing to stand up for you with others of his kind." Belle and Mrs. Dearling sat down at the table, each one beginning to sew the garment up a side.

The more she learned about Ben, the happier she was about her decision. She'd get out of the saloon and finally have a family. "I told everyone he wants what's best for me."

Savannah unfastened the skirt and dropped it to the floor. "Get into your dress. Liesa and y'all can start hemmin' the ridin' skirt, one each leg. I'll rustle up a cake."

Freedom scanned each woman in the room. Mrs. Dearling had become a beloved aunt and the other women who had gone through harrowing experiences to end up at the Silver Dollar had become sisters.

The door opened and Lottie Mae burst in. "I heard the news! Congratulations!" She hugged Freedom and plopped her hat on the coat rack by the door. "What can I help with?"

Mrs. Dearling stood. "You can take over here, and I'll go to the boarding house. Darie and I'll get busy on the food for dinner tomorrow after the wedding."

Lottie Mae and the older woman changed places.

"I'll expect you all in for a light supper at six." Mrs. Dearling glanced at the newest arrival. "That includes you and Manfred."

"We'll be there," Lottie Mae said, bending her head over the jacket.

Once Mrs. Dearling left, Lottie Mae and Savannah started in with all kinds of questions.

Freedom held her hands up, smiling and shaking her head. "I can't hear a thing with you both talkin'."

"How did he propose to you?" Savannah asked.

That was a hard question to answer. "Well, he said, he'd like to take me with him."

All needles stopped. Savannah marched over to the table a wooden spoon in one hand and her other hand on her hip. "He said he'd like to take you with him?"

Her mind started twirling. What was wrong with that? "Yes. I told him we'd have to be married and he agreed."

Lottie Mae's eyes blinked fast. "Did he kiss you?"

Freedom's cheeks heated. "He sure did."

Savannah laughed. "From the blush on your cheeks, it was heart stutterin'"

"You could say that." Freedom had the knowledge of two happily married women who were deeply in love to ask questions, but she wasn't sure how to ask, and if they'd find fault with her. Best to keep her questions to herself.

Belle leaned forward. "That doesn't sound like words of a woman in love." She shoved her side of the jacket onto the table. "I know what it's like to be in a loveless marriage. You'll be kicked aside as soon as you are of no value to him." She stood. "I'm not working on this anymore. I'll come to the wedding because I'm your friend, but you aren't getting my blessing." She walked out of the house.

Freedom's mouth dropped open. She slapped it shut and glanced at the other women. Liesa didn't make eye contact. "Are you thinkin' the same thing, Liesa?"

"Ja, you know little about this man. Maybe he kiss you, but that doesn't mean he love you." Liesa glanced at Lottie Mae and Savannah. "Their faces, they glow when they look or talk about their man." She shook her head. "I too, will be at the wedding. But *liebling*, be careful. I do not trust this man. He may wish to marry you, but I do not think it is for love."

Freedom's heart sunk. She wanted out of the saloon. The idea of living far from others and taking care of a family was what she'd yearned for since leaving Chicago. Alone, just she and Ben, there wouldn't be anyone to stare or treat her different.

Tears burned her eyes.

"Shh," Lottie Mae put an arm around her shoulders. "What do you feel in here?" She tapped Freedom's breast bone.

"That he will take care of me. That we will have fun together." She glanced at Liesa, then at the two who knew the freedom of getting out of the saloon. "That I'll be out of the Silver Dollar and livin' a real life."

They both nodded. But they didn't look as elated as they had earlier.

"If you believe in Ben, then we'll pray he is the one for you." Savannah turned back to mixing the cake.

Chapter Five

Freedom stood at the front of the church dressed in the beautiful riding outfit the others had helped her make smaller. Ben stood beside her. His eyes twinkled as he smiled and held her hands. She'd batted around all her friends' comments during the night and had walked into the church with a knot in her stomach. But the moment Ben smiled at her, she knew she was making the right decision.

"Do you Freedom Meade take Ben Hogan Litchfield for your husband?" Lark asked.

Freedom stared at Ben. He'd only told her his name was Ben Hogan. Where had the Litchfield come from? She shook her head.

"You don't want to marry Ben?" Lark asked.

"No, I mean, yes. I just didn't know there was more to his name." She stared at Ben. His gaze remained steadfast on her.

"I don't like to give people my full name. I'm not

proud of my pa, but in this case, it's a legal business, I figured I needed to use it." He squeezed her hand as if reassuring her.

She studied him. What about his father didn't he like? There were so many things she didn't know.

He smiled and squeezed her hands reassuringly.

But I'll have years to find them all out. "Could you repeat the vow," she said to Lark.

"Do you Freedom Meade take Ben Hogan Litchfield for your husband?"

She nodded. "I do."

"Do you Ben Hogan Litchfield take Miss Freedom Meade for your wife?" Lark asked and Ben didn't even hesitate with his answer.

She didn't hear the rest of the words Lark said as she gazed into her husband's eyes. They had a lot to learn about one another. Being alone on their travel to his home was a great way to discover their likes and dislikes.

"You may kiss the bride."

Before the words had escaped Lark's lips, Ben pulled her into his arms and kissed her as thoroughly as he had when they'd gone on the buggy ride. When he released her, it was a good thing his arm remained around her waist. Her legs barely held her up and her head was swooshing from lack of air.

They walked down through the pews where her friends all stood.

Lottie Mae hugged her and whispered, "That was some kiss. I think you made a good decision."

Hearing the words eased her apprehension as she hugged each person present and finally found herself in front of Beau.

"Come along everyone. I have dinner all ready for us," Mrs. Dearling said.

"Ben, you go along, I have some things I want to say to Freedom," Beau said, when Ben walked over.

The two men studied one another.

"Go ahead, Ben. Beau doesn't want others to know he has a heart." She smiled at her husband and waved for him to go after the others.

He nodded and walked out of the church.

Beau drew her over to a pew and they both sat. "I remember the day I found you at the train station." He cleared his throat as she nodded. "You were reluctant to go anywhere with me. Even Jules had to do some fast talking for you to understand we wouldn't hurt you."

She nodded. She'd thought her life would end right there in Fargo.

"You've been our shining light at the saloon since you arrived and started singing. We'll miss you." His eyes softened. "Don't tell the others, but I looked forward to hearing you sing every night."

She laughed. "Darie has a good voice if you can get her to even step inside the saloon."

He nodded. "I'm happy you found someone to take you away from the saloon. But I hope you made the right decision."

"Why is everyone tellin' me that!" She was starting to get annoyed with everyone warning her about Ben. He had shown her nothing but kindness and caring.

"Because he isn't the same as you."

"I know he's not a colored. It's as plain as my brown skin and his white skin. But what does that matter if we care for one another?" She knew they would meet hostile people who didn't think they should be married. Just her color made her a target. "If he's willin' to marry me because of his feelin's for me, shouldn't we have a chance at happiness?"

"You've been treated like everyone else in Shady Gulch. I don't want you to get away from here and discover not everyone can ignore your skin color." He put up a hand. "You say Ben will stick up for you. I hope he does prove me wrong. But to make me feel better…" He reached into a pocket inside his jacket "This is money for you to hide. If you discover you aren't happy with this man, I want you to use the money to come back to us. You will always have a home and be safe here." Beau handed her a small leather pouch. "Sew it inside of a dress or slip it into your boot when he's not looking. I don't want him to know you have money."

She studied him. "Isn't that lyin' to my husband?"

"No. It's having a plan if things don't work out. If they do work out then use it to buy something nice for yourself. Kind of a dowry of sorts." Beau held her hand and stared into her eyes. "Please, keep it for an emergency."

Freedom nodded. She knew his mother's story. It was the reason he took in battered women. It was his way of making sure she stayed safe. "I'll not tell him until we have been married years." She shoved the leather pouch into the top of her lace-up boot. "This will do until I have a better place to put it."

"Thank you." Beau stood, drawing her to her feet. He pulled her into a hug. "I want this to work, but we know so little about Ben."

She stepped out of the embrace. "I'll write and you will all hear what a wonderful life I'm havin'."

Freedom hooked her arm in Beau's and they left the church and walked down the street to the boarding house.

Her few belongings and the items her friends gave her as wedding gifts were packed in a canvas bag that Ben would tie onto the packhorse when they finished eating. The bag sat on the front porch of the boardinghouse. Knowing her things were in the bag, made the whole wedding and change in her life real.

She walked into the kitchen and everyone cheered. Ben walked over to her side. They sat at the head of the table. Beau, Jules, Mrs. Dearling, Lottie Mae and Manfred, Savannah and Lark, Belle, Liesa, Darie, Dr. Nolan and even Sheriff Blake sat around the table that had always felt huge. With so many people gathered around today, it felt small. But her heart was filled with love and gratitude for everyone sitting there.

Gazing around the table, a lump formed in her throat. These were all wonderful people who had graced her life. She didn't know when she'd see them again, but they would be in her heart and her memories forever. Tears welled in her eyes. She swiped at them with a cloth napkin.

"What's wrong?" Ben asked quietly, as the rest of the people carried on about how lovely the wedding had been.

"It's goin' to be like leavin' my family all over again," she whispered.

"You'll start a new family." He spooned potatoes onto her plate.

"Yes, I will." She sniffed back the tears and poked at the food he'd dished. She'd not had someone fill her plate since she was big enough to do it herself. She wasn't sure if she liked it because it showed he was considerate, or didn't like it because he thought she couldn't take care of herself.

She shoved a potato in her mouth to keep from saying something.

"Where exactly will you be taking Freedom to?" Mrs. Dearling asked.

"I have a homestead twenty miles south of the Yellowstone River." Ben put a bite of roast in his mouth.

"Any towns close by?" Lottie Mae asked.

"There's a couple within a day's walk, half a day by horse." Ben shoved more meat in his mouth.

"Any we might have heard of?" Lark asked.

Freedom held up her hands. "Why are you askin' him all of these questions? I'll send you a letter when we get settled and tell you all about where we live."

"How long until you'll arrive there?" Beau asked.

Ben studied him and glanced around the table. "I don't like how you are all treating me like I've done something wrong. I married Freedom, she is my wife, and I'll take care of her." He pointed to her plate. "Finish up. I'd like to get on the trail soon."

Freedom understood his desire to get away from her friends. They were treating him like the enemy. She smiled at the others and ate the food on her plate.

Savannah stood. "Y'all can't wander off until you've had a piece of my cake." She and Darie passed out slices of a sweet, tender cake with cooked butter frosting.

"This is delicious," Freedom told her friend. "Did you happen to write up a recipe for me?"

"I did. It's in the gift we gave you." Savannah

smiled at her husband.

"Thank you!" Freedom finished her slice of dessert at the same time as Ben. They stood.

Everyone else stood and followed them to the porch. She hugged everyone, promised to write and followed her husband as he carried her canvas bag down the street to the livery.

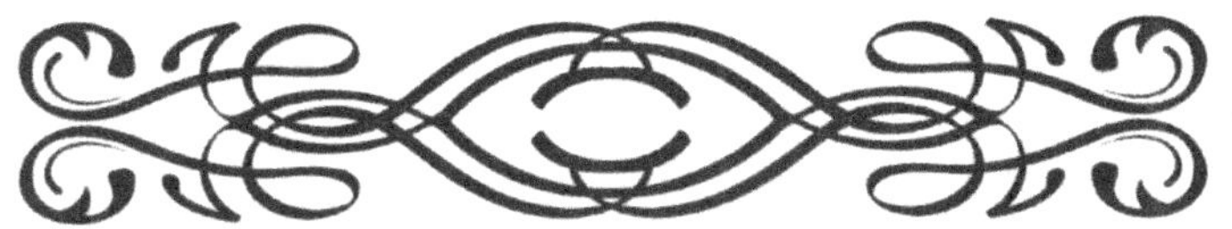

Chapter Six

The rocking of the horse had become second nature to Freedom after six days, but the points on her backside that ached from sitting in the saddle all day were hard to ignore. She not only had a sore backside, but her new husband had an appetite for her body. Each night after the horses were tended and she'd cleaned up from their evening meal, he undressed her and entered her body whether she was too tired or not. She received no pleasure from his bedding. She didn't understand how Savannah and Lottie Mae had glowed the days following their weddings.

She was beginning to dread the evenings. Tonight, they were to stay with a friend of his. He said the man had an Indian wife. At least she'd have a woman to talk to and perhaps ask about being newly married.

At noon, they stopped long enough for them to both relieve themselves and eat biscuits lcft over from the night before. To her relief, she discovered her monthly bleeding had started. This would keep him away from her for a few days.

She walked back to the packhorse and untied her bag.

"What are you doing?" Ben asked, hurrying over and grabbing her hands.

"I need to get a rag from my bag." Her cheeks heated. While they were married, they hadn't really become close. Not yet, and she didn't know how to tell him she was having her monthly.

"What do you need a rag for? No one can see if your face is dirty."

She stared at him. "What did you say?"

"Your dark skin. No one can tell if you're dirty. I like that."

She shoved her hands on her hips. "You like not bein' able to see dirt on me? Do you think I'm filthy all the time?"

"No. You're the cleanest darkie I've ever seen." He put a hand up to touch her cheek. "That's what I liked about you at first."

She slapped his hand away.

"Hey, you're my property and I can touch you." He grabbed her wrist, pulling her up against his body.

"I am not your property. I am your wife." Her body shook. She remembered the stories her ma and pa told about being slaves. How they had been property. She'd vowed to never be anyone's property.

"The church made you my wife and that makes you my property." He grabbed her bun, holding her head, and kissed her until her lips hurt from the assault. She shoved him away, gasping for air.

He released her. "Get on your horse. We'll be at Foster's by late afternoon."

"I can't get on the horse."

"What do you mean? You've had no trouble till now." He grabbed her by the waist.

"I need a rag. I'm bleedin'." She unbuttoned her riding skirt and let it drop, revealing her bloody drawers. "You do know about a woman's monthly curse?"

He nodded and looked the other way. "Get a rag and get decent." He stalked over to his horse and mounted.

She found a rag, tied her bag back on the pack, and walked behind a bush to hide while she did the best she could to secure the rag.

The curse had never caused her pain or fatigue like some women. But she hated the inconvenience of it.

Back on her horse, she stared at the back of her husband, wondering if she should have heeded her friends' warnings.

~*~

They walked their horses up to a sod house that sprang up out of the grassy landscape alongside a small stream. There were few trees for miles, but she didn't understand why the soddy had been built out in the open.

Ben dismounted and came back to help her down. Moments like this she wondered about his vulgar moods she'd witnessed at other times.

A small Indian woman dressed in buckskin, stepped out of the door.

"Foster, no here," she said, not smiling.

"It's Ben, remember me?" He walked up to the woman, leading Freedom by the hand.

She went willingly, hoping to have a chance to

visit with the woman.

"Foster, no here," the woman said again, this time backing up as if to enter the soddy.

"We'll wait." Ben put his hand out, stopping the blanket that was the door, from falling into place.

The woman scurried over to a small cookstove. Freedom had seen small coal burning stoves like these in the apartments in Chicago. But where would they get coal? She spotted a bucket by the stove filled with wads of dry grass.

"We won't hurt you," Freedom said, taking a step toward the woman. "I'm Freedom. What's your name?"

The woman slid her gaze from Ben and studied Freedom. "My man call me Mary."

Freedom saw the fear and tension in the woman. "Mary, is there a chance I could help you make coffee?" She reached a hand out to the coffee pot on a narrow table, that appeared to be used for preparing meals.

"No coffee." The woman pushed the pot out of Freedom's reach.

"I was only bein' helpful," Freedom said, glancing around for a place to sit.

The woman glared at Ben who walked over and picked up the pot. "That's no way to treat guests." Ben looked into the pot. "Freedom, grab that bucket there and go to the stream behind the soddy and get some water."

She started to say something but felt the need to leave the small confines of the soddy. She hoped they didn't sleep inside tonight. Sleeping under the earth would be a little too much like being in a grave.

Freedom picked up the bucket and headed for the

door.

"No go!" the woman called out.

Freedom glanced over her shoulder at the woman. Fear widened the woman's eyes and pinched her mouth. She was afraid of being alone with Ben. Shivers raced up Freedom's arm. This woman knew him and feared him.

"Come show me where to get the water," Freedom said, motioning for the woman to come with her.

"She's fine. She needs to get the coffee ready," Ben said, putting an arm out as if to keep the woman in front of him.

"No! She needs to help me." Freedom motioned again and the woman ducked under Ben's arm and hurried to the door.

Freedom didn't say anything as she followed the woman to the small stream with a six-inch trickle.

Mary walked to a spot that had a hole dug down to dip a bucket.

"Has Ben hurt you before?" Freedom asked.

The woman glanced at her and then back down at the hole. "He not nice man. He hit and call names." She grasped the bucket from Freedom and dipped it into the water.

Freedom retrieved the bucket from her and clutched the handle with shaking hands. What had she done? She was six days from Shady Gulch and her friends. Could she get away from Ben and back to them? Did she even know which way to go?

She glanced at Mary, wondering how long they could stay out here to prevent going back to the soddy. Swishing sounds in the grass, swung her gaze toward her husband, stomping their direction.

He ripped the bucket of water from her hand and held it out to Mary. "Take this in and start the coffee."

The woman scurried off with the bucket.

Freedom licked her lips and faced her husband.

"Don't you ever disobey me again." His eyes narrowed, and his voice had a menacing growl.

"I won't stand still and let you hurt someone." She clenched her hands at her sides. As much as she didn't want to see just how violent he could get, she wasn't going to let him hurt anyone. "You were goin' to hurt her, weren't you?"

"All women need to be put in their place. Especially squaws and darkies."

She gasped and his hand whipped up, slapping her across the cheek.

Freedom cradled her cheek under her hand and stared at the man she'd thought cared about her. "Why did you marry me when you surely don't care about me?"

"I knew you wouldn't come with me without marrying. I've seen how much work Foster gets out of his squaw and figured you're a sight better to look at than a squaw. I could also tell you were desperate to marry."

Her heart shattered. She'd fell for the first man to show her attention. And he didn't even like her, it seemed. She should have heeded all her friends' warnings and the teachings from her parents.

He grabbed her by the arm. "Get in there and help Mary make supper. I'm sure Foster will be hungry when he gets back." As he pulled her back to the soddy, Freedom's mind raced with how to get away from him. She didn't care if their marriage had been in a church and in the eyes of God, she wasn't staying with a man who thought she was property and hit her.

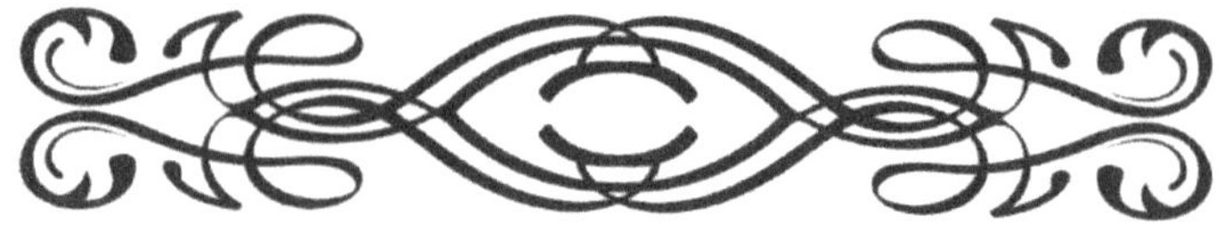

Chapter Seven

The man, Foster, did arrive right as the sun set and the prairie became a dark abyss. Freedom didn't like how he greeted her. He held onto her hand too long and his gaze never rose above her chest. She wasn't as well-endowed as most women, but her breasts were larger than his wife's.

His hand landed on her backside as she helped Mary clear the table after the meal. Freedom spun around, holding a pot in her hand. The metal container connected with his head.

She didn't apologize, but did glare at the man and then her husband who didn't seem to care the other man was taking liberties.

On her trip to use the hole in the ground that was the outhouse, Freedom studied the landscape lit by the half moon. As she'd noticed when they'd arrived earlier, it was open country for as far as she could see. She'd have to remain with Ben until they came to a settlement or they entered wooded land. Out here, she could be spotted for miles. Getting away would be impossible.

As she walked back to the sod house, Ben emerged. The way he moved his head, she could tell he'd thought she'd run off.

He caught her upper arm when she started to move by him. "Where you been so long?"

"I was enjoying the fresh air. The soddy is stuffy and smells." She waved a hand toward their belongings. "I'd rather sleep out here tonight."

"You're sleeping where I can keep an eye on you." He pulled her into the small, stuffy, earthy smelling enclosure. Ben undressed to his long drawers and settled down on a blanket in the corner.

Freedom settled down next to him, having taken off only her boots.

The lantern was blown out. The rustle of clothing meant the couple were undressing. The cot along the wall creaked as they settled in for the night.

The heat and odors didn't allow Freedom the relief of sleep. Making as little noise as possible, she slipped out of her riding skirt and blouse, sleeping in her chemise and drawers, hoping this would cool her down enough to drift off.

She slept little, between the snoring of the men and whimpering of the woman. What was the man doing to her? Or was she dreaming about horrors that had been inflicted on her?

Freedom knew the nightmares of reliving past horrors. The night she'd been attacked on the train and tossed off the moving conveyance like trash with only the clothes she was wearing. She shuddered remembering her first night with Ben. His hands ran back and forth over the scars on her body. He'd questioned her, but she could tell he didn't feel indignation for what the men had done to her. It had been after that night, he'd started treating her differently.

The cot creaked.

A hand grasped her shoulder.

She sat up. Her head thunked something. The hollow sound and hardness told her it was another head. The sour smell wrinkled her nose. *Foster*.

"How about you and me go outside and get friendly?" he whispered.

"I'm married to Ben. I'll not bed another," she said, hoping she sounded faithful.

The man chuckled. "It's all right, Ben said I could try you. I've never had the likes of you before."

Disgusted with the man and her husband, she shoved him away. "I don't care what my husband told you, I'm not a whore."

This time the man cackled, and Ben stirred beside her.

"He said he found you in a saloon. Don't tell me you ain't a whore." He grabbed her arm. "Come on outside."

Seething at this man's suggestions and her husband's disregard for her, she slapped him as hard as she could.

The sound rang through the small room.

"Why you, darkie whore!" The man kicked her, connecting with her side.

"Ben!" she screamed, hoping her husband would save her.

He sat up. "What are you yelling about?"

"H-he k-kicked me." She could barely get the words out it hurt so bad.

A light went on. Mary stood by the table in her buckskin dress, holding the kerosene lamp. Her eyes were wide.

"You told me I could have a go at her and she slapped me," Foster said, sitting back on his heels. All he had on were his long, stained underdrawers. There were dark stains at his armpits and his bulging belly nearly popped the buttons.

Disgust burned in her throat. Freedom leaned into Ben, praying he would support her in this one thing.

Ben shoved her away from him and stood. "Damn Foster, if you can't get the job done on your own, don't expect me to help." He walked out the door in his long drawers.

Freedom couldn't believe what her husband said.

Foster leaned toward her, his hand reaching out toward her breast clad in only her chemise. She used all the strength she could muster with her hurting ribs and back-handed him in the face.

"Damn you!" He yelled and shot to his feet. He stumbled over to where his boots sat next to his cot and pulled out a knife. "You're goin' to do what I say or I'll start slicing' you."

She stared back at him. "I'd rather die than have you put your hands on me."

His eyes widened and he swore under his breath, before stalking out the door.

Mary set the lantern on the table. "They will hurt you."

Tears burned behind Freedom's eyes. Pain,

humiliation, and fear were all factors for the tears. What had she done?

Mary hurried over to the cot and then over to Freedom. "I have knife. You take." She held out a knife with a bone handle and small pointed blade in a leather sheath with a rawhide tie. "It go on leg."

Freedom understood what the woman was offering. A weapon to protect her. "Thank you." She glanced at the door. "Will they come back and…" She couldn't say it. The thought of having the two of them force her to take them made her stomach churn.

"I not know." Her eyes held sorrow.

"Why don't you leave?" Freedom asked.

"I disgrace family if I return. I am gift to Foster from my father."

Freedom stared at the woman, she now realized was no older than herself. Foster was old enough to be her father. "Couldn't you find somewhere else to go?" She thought of the Silver Dollar Saloon. Of Beau who would take her in. "If you ever do leave, go to Shady Gulch, Dakota Territory and to the Silver Dollar Saloon. Tell Beau, Freedom sent you. They'll take you in."

"You know this place?" Her voice held hope.

"I do. They helped me when I needed it."

She frowned. "You need them now. Your man kill you."

A shiver slithered up her spine. Freedom hoped to get away from him before he had the chance. "If I get away, I'll come back here and get you. We'll go to the Silver Dollar together."

Hope glistened in the woman's eyes. "Yes."

The blanket swished open.

"Get away from her!" Foster bellowed.

Mary scurried across the room and sat on the cot.

"The only reason I'm leavin' you be this time is Ben says you're bleedin' and that's why you're so ornery. Next time. I'll have you." He lowered onto the cot, told Mary to take her dress off, and right there with the light on he entered her.

Freedom rolled with her back to the cot. The grunts and whimpers were more than she could stand, forgetting she wore only her underclothes, she shot to her feet and ran outside.

The cool sweet air, stopped her several feet from the door. If only she could sleep out here…

Ben caught her in his arms. "How about you and me lay down in the grass."

She didn't want him as a husband any more. Learning how horrid a man he was, she didn't wish to be a compliant wife.

"I'm bleeding, remember?" she said as politely as she could muster.

"I already have a bucket of water drawn to clean us off afterwards." Ben grasped her by the arm and led her over to a grassy spot near the well.

She held her arm over her hurting ribs and grit her teeth, vowing the first chance she had, she would run away from him.

~*~

The next morning, Freedom was thankful to climb onto her horse and follow Ben away from the sod house. She felt for Mary and had whispered to the woman she'd try to come back for her as they embraced.

After Ben had his way with her, she'd remained

outside, sleeping curled up next to their belongings. She'd felt safer under the stars, knowing the two men were in the house asleep.

When they stopped at mid-day, Freedom asked, "When will we come to a town or your home?"

Ben studied her before answering. "We'll stop at Milestown for supplies."

"Is it the closest town to where we'll live?" Freedom didn't plan on living with Ben. She hoped to find someone in the town who would help her get away from her husband. She'd head back to Shady Gulch and tell Beau about Mary.

"It's not far from Fort Koeugh. It has plenty of supplies for the fort and surrounding area. The closet town barely keeps enough food and supplies for the people who live there." Ben handed her their canteen. "We'll keep going until after dark. I want to get to Milestown tomorrow by dark."

She nodded. If he were too tired to want to bed her, the better she liked it. Freedom raised the canteen to her mouth and barely wetted her lips before Ben took the water vessel away. "I didn't get a drink."

"You'll have to drink faster." He swung up on his horse and started out.

Freedom had half a notion to not follow. However, they were still in prairie with only small swells of ground changing the scenery. She didn't know if her horse could out run Ben's, and she preferred not being easy to find once she made her break. She put a foot in her stirrup and swung her leg over the rump of her horse, thankful Savannah had insisted she take the riding outfit. It made riding a horse and doing the chores Ben heaped on her easier than in a skirt with yards of fabric.

They traveled by the light of moon for several hours before Ben stopped his horse. The last mile, Freedom had nearly fallen off her horse twice. The slow pace and rhythm of the horse's walk had rocked her to sleep.

"Make camp," Ben said, taking hold of her horse's reins as her feet touched the ground.

"There are still biscuits left over and a can of beans," she said, believing they would eat and go to sleep.

"I don't want cold biscuits and beans. Make a fire. Cook the beans. Make fresh biscuits." He glared at her.

"We've been riding those horses since early this morning. I'm tired." She turned her back to walk away.

A hand slapped her back and grabbed her clothing, causing the neck of her blouse to strangle her.

She put her hands up, trying to grab at the hand holding her.

"I said I wanted a fire, cooked beans, and fresh biscuits," he growled in her ear and shoved her forward.

She landed on her hands and knees, gasping for air.

A boot caught her backside. "Get goin'."

Her face landed in the dirt and bunch grass. She pushed to her hands and knees and slowly stood. Tomorrow in Milestown, she would leave him.

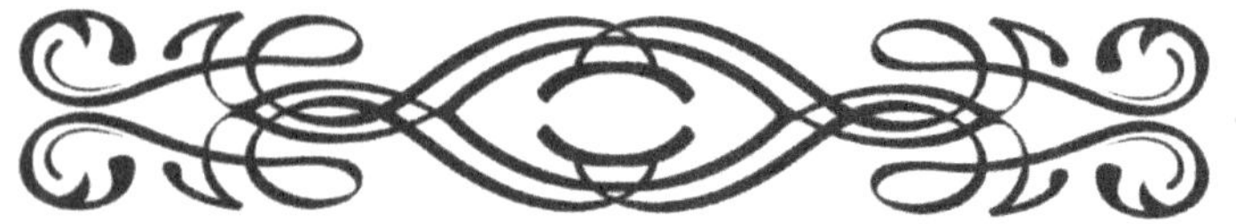

Chapter Eight

Milestown sat alongside a river. Freedom had become antsy the closer they rode to the town. This was her chance. She'd made sure to wash her face and shake the dust out of her jacket and skirt this morning. She'd even attempted to wash the sweat from her body before the sun came up and Ben had stirred. She wanted to be as presentable as possible when she talked to someone about getting her away from her husband.

Every time Ben glanced over his shoulder at her, she had a feeling he knew what she was planning. She'd smile and try to hide her nervousness.

The town was two to three times larger than Shady Gulch.

She noticed the stares the minute they entered the busy main street. Studying the townsfolk, she saw a Chinaman duck down an alley but no one with skin as brown as hers.

Ben stopped in front of a mercantile and

dismounted. "Get down. You're coming in the store with me."

She dismounted, studying the street. They'd yet to go by a church. She was hoping to tell her story to a preacher and have him help her.

"Come on. We aren't staying here any longer than getting supplies." Ben grabbed her by her upper arm and hauled her into the building.

"Mr. Hogan, good to see you again," a stout bald-headed man behind the counter said. His gaze landed on her and his eyes widened.

Freedom glanced at her husband. He didn't introduce her. She moved a foot to step forward, and he held her back.

"I'll take my usual supplies, Otis." He drew her back toward the door. "You wait by the horses," he whispered, having changed his mind about her being in the store. "And if you aren't there when I come out, and I have to find you, I'll make you walk the rest of the way."

She glared at him and walked out to the horses. When he was out of sight, she scanned the people walking by. A woman in an everyday dress, glanced at her and then away.

"Ma'am," Freedom stepped up on the boardwalk in the woman's way. "Could you tell me where I'd find a church?"

The woman's eyes met hers. "Your kind believe in God?"

She had to hold back her anger. It had been years since she'd been treated as if she didn't think or behave as everyone else. "We believe as strongly as you. I really need to find a church."

The woman pointed farther along the street. "Three blocks up and then two to your right, there's a church." The woman stepped around her and hurried away.

Five blocks. Freedom glanced at the mercantile door. It was now or having to find her way to a town later. She hated having to leave her belongings, but it was a small price to pay for freedom from this man.

Rather than be seen running down this street, she ducked between the two buildings and ran two blocks over. Then she walked the three blocks to the church. It was small, simple, and sat on a corner.

She patted her hair to make sure it still laid flat and walked up the steps to the door. It opened, and she felt at ease for the first time since leaving Shady Gulch. She walked up the aisle to the alter and peered at the cross in the stained-glass window behind the pulpit.

Finding a preacher here this time of the day was unlikely, but his home should be somewhere nearby, probably out the back.

Saying a quick prayer for guidance, she walked to the door at the side of the alter and stepped back out into the sun. There was a small house behind the church. A clothesline with both men and women's clothing gave her more courage.

Freedom walked over to the house and knocked on the door.

It opened. A short, plump woman with gray hair stood in the open doorway. "What are you doing knockin' on my door?"

"I'm looking for the preacher and sanctuary." Freedom wanted to step into the house to not be seen, but the woman stood firmly in the way.

"Sanctuary from what?"

"My husband. He's cruel and allows other men to…" she couldn't say it.

"Marriage is sacred. You should do your best not to upset your husband." The woman started to close the door.

"You don't understand. I married him because I thought he cared for me. It turns out all he wanted was a…" it was hard to say the word. "Slave."

The woman looked her up and down. "What did you expect?" The door slammed.

Fear and anger warred. She wanted to beat on the woman's door and make her take her in. But at the same time if she couldn't find someone to help her, she'd have to hide and hope Ben didn't find her. But in a town of all white faces, where could she hide?

She had no money… Wait she did! She'd forgotten the money Beau had given her.

She'd head to the stage depot and get a ticket on the next stage out of here. It didn't matter which direction it was going. All she wanted was to get as far from Ben as she could.

Walking two more blocks, she came upon an older man sitting on a box behind a building.

"Sir, could you tell me how to get to the stage depot?" She wiped a hand across her sweaty brow. The heat had grown each day they'd traveled across the prairie. Today, with the town's buildings blocking what little wind had relieved them on their travels, her jacket and heavy skirt had made her overheated.

The thin, narrow-faced man stopped whittling and studied her. "Where are you headed?"

"Anywhere but here." She wasn't mentioning Ben. It was apparent she wouldn't get any help if she said she was leaving her husband.

He smiled. "This place grows on ya." He pointed back the way she'd come. "The stage is on Main Street. About two blocks down from the Steiner Mercantile."

Her stomach clenched. Directions she didn't want to hear. That was the mercantile that Ben had stopped at. "Do you happen to know when the next stage is leaving?"

"If it's on time, tomorrow morning at six." He glanced at her. "You can get a ticket today, but you won't get out until the morning."

She nodded. "Is there a cheap hotel that would take me in?"

He thought a moment and said, "Try the Blair House. It's more of a boarding house than a hotel, but Mrs. Dudley only cares about money. She won't care you're different as long as you put money in her hand."

"Where would I find the Blair House?"

"Go over one street and keep heading that way. You can't miss it." He studied her. "You running away from someone?"

Telling him could get her caught. He was the only person who knew she planned to get on a stage. And he'd know where she was staying. After having such poor judgement about Ben, she was hesitant to say anything.

The man's kind eyes glimmered with tears. "You can trust me. A fella I didn't care for but my daughter married, near beat her to death. If you're running to get away from a mean husband, I won't tell anyone."

The pain on the man's face and the tears in his eyes couldn't be faked.

"I married a man I thought cared for me. It turns

out he only bought me to beat up and bed. I want to go home."

The man nodded. "I won't tell anyone I seen you or where you are."

"Thank you." Tears trickled down her cheeks. She swiped at them.

"You want me to get you the ticket for the morning? That way you can wait until the stage is ready to pull out before you step up to board." He stood up, leaning on a cane. "I can bring it over to you at Mrs. Dudley's."

"T-that would be wonderful."

"Where do you want the ticket to take you?"

"Shady Gulch, Dakota Territory."

He whistled. "I can only afford to get you to the next town. I don't have enough to get you all the way."

She had to make another decision. Did she dare let this man know she had money or wait and purchase another ticket at the next stop? "The next stop will do."

She understood it would probably take most of her money to take the stage. Money Beau had told her to use to get back home. She studied the man. He seemed sincere. But she'd not been good at seeing through to Ben's real self.

"I can pay you for the ticket when you bring it to me," she said. She didn't want the man thinking she went around getting people to buy her tickets.

"Will that leave you enough for the boarding house, food on the way, and more tickets?" the man asked.

"I think so." She peered into his eyes.

"I had a daughter who needed help and someone helped her. I'd take helping you as a way to make up for that stranger's kindness."

The tears in his eyes made up her mind. "Thank you."

He nodded. "I'll get the ticket and see you at Mrs. Dudley's."

Freedom nodded and headed the direction he'd told her. With each step, she hoped she hadn't given her trust to someone who would use it against her.

Mrs. Dudley was a formidable looking woman who stood as tall as a man and had shoulders just as broad. She agreed to putting Freedom up for the night and had just shown her into a small clean room on the first floor when someone pounded on the door.

"Open this door!" Ben shouted.

Freedom grabbed the woman's arm. "Don't tell him I'm here. Please." She had put her trust in the old man and now she was putting her trust in this woman. The old man had to have told Ben where she was.

"Ouch! Stop pinching me. Go through the kitchen and out the back door. Hide somewhere until dark. Then come back." The woman waved her down the hall to the back of the house.

Freedom ran to the back of the house, glancing back as the woman walked toward the front door.

She hurried through the kitchen and opened the back door, holding the screen door to keep it from slamming. She pivoted to run and ran into a body.

Fear crackled under her skin as she looked up into the angry eyes of her husband.

"I told you to stay with the horses!" He grabbed her by her upper arm and dragged her to the front of the house where the horses stood.

There was no need for words. He wouldn't listen,

and she had nothing to say.

Ben grabbed her by both arms and slammed her onto her horse. "You stay there until I tell you to get off." Her horse was tied to the packhorse. He mounted his horse and they set off through town and out.

Her teeth chattered, knowing she would be in for a beating when he found an isolated place.

Chapter Nine

Water Runs Fast and six warriors had been off the reservation for three days hunting. The food promised them when they'd moved to the reservation hadn't been sufficient. The hunting party had found a herd of elk the day before. The other warriors were packing it back to their people, the Absarokee. Water Runs Fast had told them to go on. He'd wanted time to himself to think about the way the Whiteman's government had not followed through with their promises and be alone to experience a vision.

He traveled by the light of the moon filtering through trees as he followed the Mussel River. Water had always been his spirit. His journey was to find the perfect place to sit and listen to the water's voice.

A human scream scattered the birds in the trees and made his horse snort. He stopped his horse and listened. The whistle and crack of a whip was followed by another scream.

Water Runs Fast slipped off his horse and crouched, following the sounds.

His hands clenched at the sight of a man whipping a naked brown-skinned woman. He didn't care what the woman had done, she didn't deserve to have the flesh of her back laid open.

He worked his way closer. When he was within striking distance, he launched himself out of the trees, circling the man's neck with one arm, and pulling him backwards. Before they both hit the ground, Water Runs Fast twisted out from under the man and straddled him, grasping the whip and throwing it away from the man.

The man's eyes widened at the sight of his attacker, but they narrowed quickly, and he grabbed Water Runs Fast's neck in his hands. The man squeezed, cutting off his air.

Grabbing the knife from his belt, Water Runs Fast plunged it deep into the man's side.

His eyes widened.

His hands slowly released as his body went limp.

Water Runs Fast sprang to his feet, wiped his knife on the man's clothing, and turned to the woman.

Her eyes were closed, her body slumped over a boulder.

Walking closer, he noticed many darker spots on the woman's skin. Spots that had been caused by blows. He glanced at the man's body losing blood and life. He spit at the man and looked around for something to cover the woman with. Women in his tribe were treated with respect.

He spotted a bundle of supplies and started going

through them. They were all things his people could use. He found a smaller bundle with women's clothing. Pulling out a dress, he walked over to the woman.

She must have fainted from the pain. Her back was splayed open from the slicing of the whip. He wondered how a man could inflict such torture on a woman.

He didn't want to be found here with the dead body by another white man. Water Runs Fast put the pack on one of the horses tied to a tree, and saddled the other two horses. He wrapped the woman in a blanket, and holding her over his shoulder stepped into a stirrup and onto a horse. He settled her in his lap, with one arm around her, and headed back to his horse.

The woman cried out when he'd traveled an hour from where he'd found her. They were next to a stream. He could clean her wounds and make her comfortable.

"Quiet Brown Bird, I will help you," he said in a soft tone.

The woman's eyes opened. They were wide and filled with bursts of sunlight. She started to struggle, and moaned.

"You are safe. I will not hurt you." He stopped the horse and dismounted, holding her in his arms. A grassy spot not far from the water appealed to him. Water Runs Fast carried her to the spot and gently placed her on the ground.

She stared at him, then back the way they'd come. "Ben, he'll follow." She started to rise.

He placed a hand gently, but firmly, on her shoulder. "The man will no longer hurt you."

Her gaze locked onto his. They remained this way until a horse snorted.

"H-he's dead?"

Water Runs Fast saw disbelief and relief flash in her interesting eyes. "He is not of this earth."

"You?"

He nodded. "He tried to kill me. I fought back."

Freedom felt she owed this man for doing what she didn't have the strength to do the first night they'd left Milestown and Ben had "taught" her not to try to ever leave him. He'd kicked and beat her as if she were a dog. But even a dog deserved better treatment than he'd given her.

Tonight, her battered body had felt strong enough to carry her away from him. She'd thought he'd gone to sleep after stripping her and having his way. She'd crawled off the blanket he'd thrown down as their bed and had just reached her clothes when he'd grabbed her and thrown her over the boulder and started whipping her.

Her back stung like the devil, but she'd known pain before. It was the elation she felt at another's death that worried her more.

"I clean your back. Have medicine," the Indian said.

She studied him. He was as tall as Ben, broader shoulders. He wore only the leather trousers she'd seen in photographs. His hair was long, straight, black and hung about his broad shoulders and halfway down his body. She scanned his face. The chin was square, strong. His eyes weren't the hard blue she'd looked at for the last few months, they were brown, and questioning.

She swallowed and nodded, remembering he'd said something about tending her back.

He didn't smile, but his eyes blinked once before

he walked over to Ben's packhorse and untied the bucket.

She watched his long legs carry him to the edge of the stream where he walked in up to his knees, raised his face to the sky, chanted, and dipped the bucket. What tribe was he? One that didn't kill women, she hoped. She should be scared of him. He'd killed Ben and acted as if it was an everyday occurrence to kill someone who tried to kill him. But she was too weak and hurting to care if he killed her too. If he did allow her to live and didn't treat her as poorly as Ben, she'd owe him for setting her free of that monster.

A shudder started at her toes and worked its way up her body. She shivered uncontrollably by the time the man returned.

He placed the bucket beside her and stared. "I not hurt you."

She nodded.

He frowned. "Cold?"

She shook her head.

His brow wrinkled more. "Sick?"

Freedom didn't know what to say. She didn't know how to explain her body shaking. The cold was deep inside of her. "I-I don't know what's wrong."

He nodded and walked over to a horse that appeared to be his. He dug into a leather pouch and returned to her. Crouching beside her, he held out a small leafy bundle. "Eat."

Her hands shook as she took the bundle and opened it. The smell of meat was the first thing she noticed. The contents were mashed dried meat and berries. She'd been craving meat, having eaten only beans and biscuits since leaving Shady Gulch.

He smiled and made the motion of eating the food with his fingers.

She took a bite and was surprised at the taste. It was better than what she'd been eating. "Thank you."

He nodded and opened the back of the blanket, exposing her back to the cool night air. A shiver rippled across her skin.

"I try not hurt," he said softly as the cold water trickled down her back.

She tried to concentrate on eating the food, but the stinging couldn't be ignored. Freedom closed her eyes and realized the water no longer trickled. She opened them in time to see the Indian walking back to her with moss in his hand.

"What are you going to do with that?" she asked.

"Clean."

She closed her eyes once more as the moss scrubbed back and forth on her back. Tears trickled out of her eyes. She bit her bottom lip to keep from crying out or whimpering. It didn't hurt as bad as the whip slicing her skin, but enough to make her stomach churn.

"Done." The voice was soft and gentle.

If only Ben had been this caring. She stopped herself. He had been at first. Was this man only doctoring her to take her to his tribe to be a slave for them? She'd heard about tribes stealing people from other tribes for slaves. And stories of wagon trains raided and women and children taken to the Indian villages and made into wives and slaves. She clutched the blanket and packet of food to her chest. Was he only helping to sell her?

The man walked over to his horse and reached in the pouch again. This time he returned with a small earthen bowl.

"What is that?" She sniffed. It smelled like stale animal fat.

"Bear fat."

She twisted, keeping hold of the blanket and facing him. "You're not putting that on me."

"Heal cuts."

"I didn't have that on my other wounds and they healed fine." In fact, she hadn't had anyone to wash her wounds after the train beating. They'd become infected. That was why she was out of her head when Beau and Jules found her and took her to a doctor. She didn't want to become sick and not be able to get back to Shady Gulch.

"Why did that man hurt you?" the Indian asked.

"Because I tried to get away from him." She didn't want to add he was her husband. This man would think her a fool to have been married to such a monster.

"Did you run because he beat you?"

She studied the man. She barely knew him. He was an Indian and all she'd read or heard about them, they were dumb and savage. This man proved all those tales wrong. She changed the subject. "What's your name?"

"Water Runs Fast."

She studied him. His voice was soothing like a gurgling stream and his temperament so far was as calming. But the name was long when it could be summed up in one word. "Your name means swift. May I call you that?"

He nodded. "And you are called?"

"Freedom."

He tilted his head a bit and studied her. "Freedom? Is this new name because you get away from man?"

"It's always been my name."

Swift held up the vessel of bear fat. "This will heal you."

She sighed. "All right." And presented her back to him.

Freedom winced as the man gently rubbed the fat into the wounds. How he could stand the smell astounded her. Her nose twitched as the more he applied, the riper the odor became.

"You have scars that are old."

She knew he wanted to know about them, but when she'd told her husband how she'd received them, he had treated her differently. Why would a stranger treat her any different?

First light, she'd take a horse and head back to Milestown. She wanted to make sure the old man who had offered to buy her stagecoach ticket was still alive. Ben had told her he'd overheard the man asking for a ticket on the stage the next morning and how much for a ticket from there to Shady Gulch when he was in the depot looking for her. When the man hadn't told him at first who he was buying the ticket for, Ben had hit him. The man had handed over the ticket and told him where she was. She couldn't blame the old man. He'd been trying to help her and didn't owe his life to her. Ben had taken all of her money. She'd have to work at Milestown and save up money to get back to Shady Gulch. She wasn't going to send a telegraph asking Beau to send money.

A thought struck her. The money should still be in Ben's pocket.

"I need to go back to where you found me," she said, standing, holding the blanket over the top of her breasts.

"It is not good to visit one so evil." Swift crossed his arms.

"No. He took my money. Money I need to get back to my friends." She had to make him understand the money was important. Freedom narrowed her eyes as another thought struck. "Did you take his money?"

It was the first time she'd seen anger flash in his eyes. "I do not steal from the body. I took horses and supplies for my people."

She had to make him go back. "Money would help your people. You could buy more supplies."

He narrowed his eyes and studied her. "I will not go back."

She sighed. "I can go back by myself." They were brave words. She didn't want to go by herself. If Ben happened to still be breathing, she wouldn't be able to dig into his pocket and take the money, even though it was hers. She'd have to go back to her plan of getting to Milestown, working, and saving to get back to Shady Gulch.

"It better we go. Too close to body if found." Swift walked over to his horse. He put the bear fat away and stepped over to the pack horse. He put his hands on her bundle of belongings.

"Those are mine." She tried to walk, but the blanket caught her foot.

He didn't say a word, only pulled out her extra pair of drawers and ripped them.

"What are you doing?" She tried another step and had to catch her balance when the blanket caught her foot again.

"Cover cuts." He walked back to her. "Drop

blanket."

She stared into his eyes. "No."

He smiled. The tipping of his lips changed his whole face. She'd not seen a more handsome man.

"I have seen your body. I put blanket on you."

Her cheeks heated. Of course, he had. She'd fainted from the pain and woke while sitting on his lap on a horse.

He put a hand on the top of the blanket. "I only wish cover wounds."

She stared into his eyes. Concern and not a trace of mean shone in their brown depths. Freedom released the blanket and stood naked before Swift.

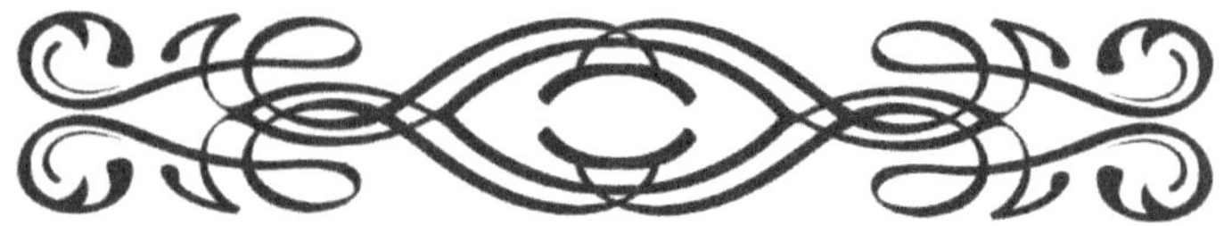

Chapter Ten

The woman, Freedom's, skin was the color of a buffalo. An animal that had sustained his people since they were born upon this earth. Water Runs Fast had promised he'd only cover the wounds, but as he'd washed her back and applied bear fat, he'd fantasized about what her firm, round backside would feel like in his palms.

She peered into his eyes, and he didn't dare let those notions show. He lowered his gaze to her more than handful breasts. They would suckle strong children.

Water Runs Fast placed a hand on her shoulder, spinning her around. He placed one strip of the garment he'd torn across her back, keeping his gaze off her backside. "Arms up." She raised her arms out straight from her sides. He wrapped the cloth around, going above her breasts, then around the back and below her breasts and down her body until he had her cuts all covered.

He walked over to his parfleche where he'd shoved the dress he'd started to put on her before. He returned to Freedom with the dress.

"How did you have this?" she asked, not putting it on.

Her breasts were even more noticeable with the white bandages framing them. He didn't know her story, but when he did, he would determine if he should take her to the reservation.

"To put on you before. Your back…"

She nodded. "I need my undergarments."

He watched her. "Only dress. All women wear."

She shook her head. "I need my chemise and drawers."

"I not know these things." He held the dress out to her.

The woman gathered the blanket around her and walked over to the packhorse, her back, firm backside, and legs visible. She dug in the bag where he'd found the garment he'd used for a covering on her wounds and pulled out another garment liked the one he'd torn.

"I will at least wear drawers," she said, ducking behind a tree.

He stood where he was, holding the dress. What was she doing back there?

A hand appeared at the side of the tree. "Dress, please."

He walked over and placed the dress in her hand as he glanced around the tree. She had the white garment on her lower body, like he wore his leggings. She raised the dress, disappeared within the cloth and her head and front appeared. Her arms were covered in long sleeves.

This was good. His people respected a woman who only had her head and hands uncovered.

Freedom fastened the front of her dress, hiding her dark breasts from his view. Water Runs Fast smiled. He would have good dreams this night having witnessed her body.

She stepped out from behind the tree. "I didn't see my boots in the pack." She held up her skirt, showing her bare feet.

"I save you, not look for boots." He crossed his arms.

"Then I guess I'll have to go back. I can't be walkin' around barefoot. It's not proper and my feet have spent years in shoes. They won't be happy walkin' on rocks and stickers like when I was a child." Her riding outfit would be with her boots. Without it, she had this dress and one other set of clothing.

"No go back. Not safe." He grabbed her arm gently but with determination. Water Runs Fast had a feeling the Whites would feel just as angry about her killing the man as they would him.

She stopped and put her hands on her hips. "I need my shoes and would like my money. If you'll give me my horse, I don't care what you do with the rest of them and the supplies." She walked over to the smaller of the horses. Its brown color was a shade darker than the woman's skin. "I'll take my bag, my boots, and my money and you'll never have to see me again. I'm goin' home."

"Where is home?"

"Shady Gulch, Dakota Territory." She stepped into the stirrup and her skirt caught the back end of her horse as she swung her leg over its back.

Freedom

The horse shot forward.

The woman landed on her back. Air rushed out of her mouth moments before she moaned.

Water Runs Fast knelt beside her. He saw her chest rising and falling, but her eyes didn't open.

He put a hand behind her head to raise her up. Wet warmth covered his fingers. He stared at the blood on his fingers. She'd hit her head on a rock. Warriors and children who had falls and struck their heads didn't always return to the living. Why did she need money and boots?

He carried her to a boulder and leaned her back against it. At the pack, he once again dug into her bag and this time grabbing a garment that looked like a thin dress, he tore it in strips and returned to the boulder. Water Runs Fast placed these on the boulder before searching for more moss. Wandering from tree to tree he wondered about the time he wasted with this woman who only had money on her mind.

As an Absarokee, he had no need for money. All he needed were the food and shelter the earth, and now the white man's government, provided. Carrying the moss back to the woman, his gaze landed on her face. She had high cheekbones much like his people, but her mouth was fuller, her eyes, that startling mixture of earth and sun. She was a woman he wanted to know better.

Water Runs Fast placed the moss on the cut on Freedom's scalp and then wrapped the torn dress around to keep the moss in place.

After catching the horse that had startled, he made sure they were all tied together and mounted his horse, holding the woman. They had to get farther away from the dead White man.

~*~

Freedom's head ached. The pounding resounded in her head like an axe chopping wood. A cadence that she realized her whole body rocked with. Slowly opening one eye, she watched sunshine flicker through the tops of trees. She became aware of a strong arm wrapped around her body and her legs draped over a hard leg.

Both eyes sprang open. She focused on the strong chin, long black hair, and masculine nose of the man holding her. Swift, the Indian who killed Ben and cared for her injuries.

She put a hand to her head and discovered a bandage. "What happened?" she asked, not really meaning to speak out loud.

The horse didn't slow as the man peered down into her face. "Your horse did not like your dress."

Trying to remember what he was talking about made her head hurt worse. "Tell me later." She closed her eyes to go back to sleep.

Her body shook.

"Wake," Swift insisted.

"I'm sleepy."

The rhythm of the horse stopped.

She opened her eyes and stared into his brown concerned gaze.

"You must stay awake. You sleep, you not wake up." He grasped her body, slipping her right leg over the horse's neck, making her straddle the horse and look over the horse's head, not into Swift's eyes. A strong arm wrapped around her middle. She leaned her head back against his chest. His chin hovered over her head, tickling as it brushed wayward strands of hair.

"If you sleep, I will wake you," he said, and the horse started to walk.

Worried he could be right about not waking, having seen this happen to men who were hit hard in a fight or from objects while working, she raised a hand to feel where she'd hit her head. Before she could touch the sore spot, Swift captured her wrist and lowered her hand.

"Do not touch."

"Where are we goin'?" she asked, hoping conversation would keep her awake.

"To cave. You get better."

She thought about this. Alone with this man, somewhere she'd never be able to find her way back to Shady Gulch. "I don't want to go to a cave. I want to go home. Back to the Saloon, to Beau, Jules, Lottie Mae, Savannah, Belle, and Mrs. Dearling. And Liesa and Darie. Even Sheriff Blake and Dr. Nolan."

"All these people your family?" he asked.

"In a way. They took me in and didn't treat me different when I was sure I was going to die." She sniffed. It had to be her sore head that made her feel sorry for herself. She'd not thought much about how she'd come to Shady Gulch. She'd just arrived and felt at home with all the people in her life. Being married to Ben had reminded her of all the hate and hostility her family had left in the South and had encountered at times in Chicago. The hate Mr. McCluskey had shown when he'd thrown her out after the loss of his baby. A loss she'd had nothing to do with.

Swift's large hand cupped her chin. "Do not cry. Your man not worth tears."

She sniffed and wiped at the tears trickling down

her cheeks. "I didn't say he was my man, and I'm not crying for him. I'm crying for me."

The horse stopped. Gently, he leaned her a bit and turned her face up to his. "I not hurt you." The sorrow in his eyes that she would think such a thing, stung her conscience.

"I know. You have been a gentleman."

"What is gentleman?"

She smiled and peered into his confused eyes. "A man like you. One who respects a woman, helps her in her time of need, and doesn't expect favors for helping." Her cheeks heated at her last remark. He'd seen her bare as the day she was born and had only tended her torn skin. She knew many men who would have taken advantage of her distress.

His eyes had lost their confusion only to fog over again. "What is favors?"

Rather than answer his question, she straightened and stared forward. "Where did you learn to speak English?"

"English?" he questioned as he urged the horse back into a walk.

"What we are speaking."

"White man talk? Fort. Reservation agent. Scout for Army." He said it all as if it were normal.

She hadn't expected to find an Indian who spoke so well. "What tribe are you?" She'd heard stories about the fighting of the Sioux and how they had killed many cavalry soldiers in a battle over the Black Hills. Her heart thumped against her ribs. Maybe he was taking her to be tortured by his tribe?

"Water Runs Fast is of the Absarokee, Raven People." The pride in his voice settled her thoughts. He wasn't Sioux.

"Raven People?" She'd never heard of Indians called this.

"Whites call us Crow." Indignation fueled his words.

"That doesn't sound as pretty as Raven People."

His chest pushed against her back. He was proud of his tribe.

"Where do you live?"

"On the reservation." This time he wasn't as proud.

"Where is the reservation?" Maybe it was near Fort Keogh. If so, she wouldn't be that far from Milestown and could get a job and pay her way back to Shady Gulch. She'd been gone almost two weeks. Another two and everyone would be worrying what had happened to her when they didn't receive a letter.

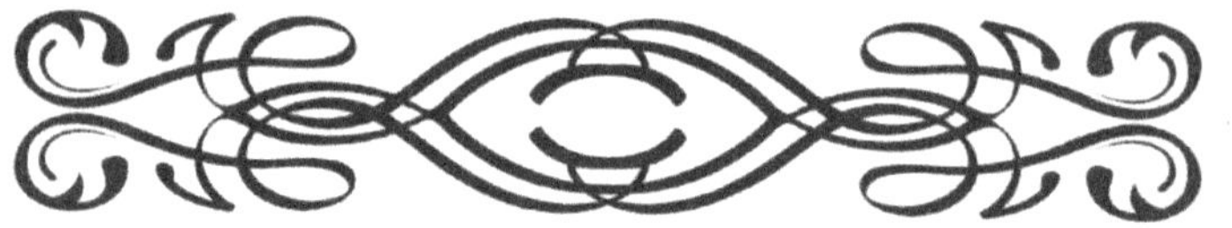

Chapter Eleven

Water Runs Fast liked the way the woman felt in his arms. He'd not married. Not because women didn't want him, but because he hadn't found a woman who interested him. He'd met a woman in one of his visions. This woman he'd saved was much like his dream woman. This woman stirred things in him. Things he'd not experienced from another woman. It made his heart strong to have her ask about the reservation. He wondered if his finding her was a sign. Afterall, her name was Freedom, something the Absarokee had been seeking for many summers.

"Where I live is two suns away."

"Two suns?" Her head tilted and half her face came into view. She had a pleasant face. One he wouldn't mind seeing each morning when he woke.

"White man call them days."

She smiled. "I see. Suns. Days. The sun is up during the day. That makes sense." Her body settled even more against his.

The woman had become comfortable with him, even though he'd killed the man she'd traveled with. Had they been husband and wife? She said he wasn't her man, but why else would they have been traveling together? He'd seen White men marry Indian women and a few Indian men marry white women but he'd not seen a White and one so dark as Freedom marry. Could she have been a slave? That would make sense of her scars and the whipping. But she was too strong a spirit to be a slave. She would have never broken, and would have always been trying to flee.

"Is there a fort near where you live?" Her soft voice broke into his thoughts.

"Custer. It is big." He didn't like going to the fort. While the White fathers said it was on the Crow reservation to help them, the soldiers made more trouble than they helped. They were to help the supplies for his people arrive at the agency, but many times only half of what they were promised arrived.

Freedom sat up straight and twisted, her captivating gaze studying him. "Do they have a place I could work. To get money to return to Shady Gulch?"

As far as he knew, only soldiers worked at the fort. And the only way to get back where she wanted to go, was by horseback or in an Army supply wagon.

"You come to my village. Get well, then I help you get home." Knowing how the soldiers treated the Absarokee women, he didn't believe Freedom would be treated much better.

She peered into his eyes, started to open her mouth to say something, then snapped it shut before facing forward.

What had she been about to say? They had only a short distance more to go to arrive at the cave, where he planned to stay for a few more days. Until the woman could sit on a horse by herself. Riding into the village with the woman in front of him on one horse would lead the elders to believe they'd coupled. He respected the woman and did not want to push her into something she did not want. She wished to go home. He did not know where Shady Gulch was, but he would help her find it.

Her body once again sagged against his chest. He jiggled his arm around her body, feeling the weight of her breasts on his forearm. His body came alive in a way it had not since he'd become a man and learned to control his body and desires.

Why did this woman do these things to him?

"*Áxxaashe Ishté*, Sun Eyes, do not sleep." The woman had no sleep the night before as she had been beaten and he had cleaned her wounds, but because of her fall and hitting her head, he wished her to remain awake. He did not want to have her drift into a final sleep.

He wiggled his arm again, this time cupping his hand to her side and shaking all of her body.

"What? Why?" Her hand touched her head and the cloth he'd wrapped to hold the moss in place. "My head hurts. Why did you shake me?"

"You should not sleep."

"I'm tired. I was awake all night." Her words faded.

The cave would have to wait.

He stopped the horse, lifted her leg over the horse's neck, cradling her in his arms, he swung his leg over, and slid down off the horse with her in his arms.

"Ow!" she cried out as his feet hit the ground.

He'd tried to land as softly as he could. But pain was good. It would keep her awake. He released her legs, lowering them to the ground. "We walk."

She swayed and pushed away from him. "Leave me here. I'll be alright."

Water Runs Fast smiled at the woman's funny talk. "You come." He put an arm around her waist and made her walk beside him. His horse followed, leading the others.

"Ouch! I wish you would have let me go back for my boots and money." She hopped on one foot and then cried out from the bouncing.

He placed her on a boulder and pulled two leather pouches from his parfleche on his horse.

"What are you doin'?" Freedom asked as she watched Swift dump the contents of two leather pouches into his larger one.

"Make foot covers," he said.

She rubbed the bottom of the foot something had pricked as they'd walked. Why did he insist she stay awake? Riding on the horse in his arms, she'd felt safe. The safest she had in a very long time. Sleep had been a welcome relief to the pounding in her head.

He knelt in front of her, placing one pouch over the foot she rubbed. "This will keep feet safe." He used the leather tie to wrap around her ankle twice and tie.

Placing that foot on the ground, she raised the other one and brushed dirt off.

Swift placed the second pouch on her foot, tying it around her ankle as well.

She stood. The leather between her feet and the

ground did feel better. "Thank you."

He gave one nod and put his arm around her waist, urging her to walk.

"I can do this on my own." She pushed against his side and took several steps ahead of him.

"You wobble like newborn horse," he said.

The world did feel as if it were moving. "All right. You can help me. Only because I want to get where you'll let me sleep."

Two strides and he had his arm around her waist, propelling her forward.

Thirty minutes later, her legs wobbled worse and felt as fragile as the thin stemmed wildflowers she'd been admiring. Before she could utter a word, her body swung up into Swift's strong arms.

"When will we stop?" she asked, staring into his concerned brown eyes.

"When stars in sky."

She had no idea what time it was, but night had to be coming soon. Even though he didn't want her to close her eyes, she couldn't keep them open any longer.

~*~

The woman had fallen asleep as soon as he picked her up. Water Runs Fast had wanted to keep her awake, but seeing how tired she was, he was compelled to let her sleep. He continued to carry her to the cave. He was tired of riding.

At the cave, he placed the woman against the entrance as he unloaded the horses and tied them out. Once he had a blanket spread on the ground inside, he carried her in and placed her on her side on the blanket, covering her with another one. The cave was cooler than the outside.

Freedom

The stars and moon arrived in the sky, darkening the interior even more. Water Runs Fast brought in dry limbs and started a fire. It would not only allow the woman to see where she was when she woke but would keep her warm.

With the fire glow, he dug into his parfleche and pulled out a meal of pemmican folded up in leaves. He sat across the fire from Freedom, eating and watching her.

She mumbled and moved her head back and forth before her face tightened in anger. What had happened to her that she had become a slave to the White man?

Her eyes opened. She slapped at the blanket over her as if fighting it off her. Her body jolted to a sitting position. The firelight made her big eyes glow like two suns in a dark world.

"I am here," he said softly to not frighten her.

Her gaze flew from the fire to where he sat. He breathed in once, and Freedom calmed, settling the blanket about her shoulders and watching him.

"How long have we been here?" she asked, licking her thick lips.

He picked up the pouch he'd filled with water and walked over to her. "The night will soon grow into day."

"Thank you." She took the pouch and drank.

He heard her stomach talking. He handed what was left of his food to her.

"Thank you, again." She stared at the bundle before peering into his eyes. "I will make you a meal tomorrow. There are supplies in the pack."

He nodded unsure what to say to her offering to cook. When a woman cooked for a man who was not family, it meant she had an interest in showing him she would be a good wife.

Water Runs Fast returned to his side of the fire. He pulled a blanket around his shoulders and leaned back against the wall of the cave. Now that the woman knew where she was, he could sleep.

"Are you goin' to sleep sittin' up?" her soft voice asked.

He opened his eyes slowly. "Only your side is long enough for me to lay."

Her cheeks darkened and her eyelids drooped. "I didn't know."

She didn't offer him a place beside her.

He closed his eyes and leaned his head back against the rock.

~*~

Freedom ate the food Swift had given her while watching him sleep sitting up. She knew he'd fallen asleep because his impressive chest rose and fell in even rhythm. This was the first time she'd been able to study him closely without him watching.

He was an impressive man. Wide shoulders, broad, muscular chest. His arms and legs as solid as a tree when she'd touched them. He was big and powerful, yet, he'd treated her as if she were as delicate as a flower. He reminded her of Beau. A man she considered a brother. Could this man be given her trust?

His body shifted slightly, but he continued to sleep.

How could he sleep sitting up like that? She glanced down at the space she had between her and the wall. She could scoot closer to the wall and give him plenty of room to stretch out. Or, she glanced at the area where he sat. She'd be fine curled up over there, and he could have the larger space. She'd suggest that in the morning. He'd said they would remain at the cave for a few days.

She fell to sleep thinking about the supplies they had and what kind of meal she could make for him. He had to be getting tired of that meat mixture he fed her.

Chapter Twelve

Sun shone in the cave as Water Runs Fast opened his eyes and stretched his arms. His knuckles scraped the side of the cave, and dirt rained over his head. His back, legs, and backside ached from how he'd slept. He needed to get out and walk to loosen his body.

A glance at the other side of the nearly dead fire revealed Freedom still sleeping on her side. Her blanket had slid down around her waist. The way her arms folded into her chest, she was cold. He walked over, pulled her blanket up, and placed his over the top.

He stirred the ashes, shoved a few smaller branches into the fire, and walked outside. The air held the moist thick scent of rain. It was good they had the cave to stay dry. Studying the sky, he spotted the gray heavy rain clouds moving their way. The sun would soon be gone.

Before it left and the animals huddled up out of the rain, he would gather meat. Water Runs Fast entered the cave silently, retrieved his bow and quiver from his belongings, and returned outside in search of a deer.

~*~

Rustling sounds lingered in Freedom's groggy mind. She woke, stared at the dim gray around her, the small glow of embers in a fire, and the glimmer of sunshine at the opening to the cave.

Memories came back to her: the beating, the whipping, Swift caring for her wounds, and then being carried in his strong arms.

Her gaze snapped to where he'd been sleeping. There was only the cave wall and his small bundle of belongings. The blanket on her felt heavier. A glance down, and she found two blankets over her. She'd never had a man treat her so well. Sure, Beau and Jules treated her with respect, but they treated all the ladies at the saloon that way. And she'd been treated well by Lark, the doctor, and the sheriff, but this was different.

Then her mind latched onto how thoughtful and caring Ben had been in the beginning. She glanced at the extra blanket and narrowed her eyes. Swift would turn on her, all men she'd counted on, except the men of Shady Gulch, had. Mr. McCluskey, who'd said she'd have a job with his family until the baby grew up, turned her out at the death of his son. Then Ben vowed to God he would honor and protect her and look what he'd done. No, she couldn't get soft for any man.

She folded the blankets back and pushed to her feet, still clad in the silly pouches Swift had put on her feet. But they had made walking easier. The cool air had her hurrying out to a bush not far from the cave and relieving herself. When she finished, she walked back toward the cave and peered up at the dark clouds quickly gathering overhead.

Good thing they had the cave. From the dark brooding clouds, she figured they were going to get a good downpour. She hurried into the cave, found the bucket, and followed the sound of gurgling water. Before bending to dip water from the stream, she put her hands over her head and stretched. Her back stung, but knowing she wouldn't be beaten for taking a few minutes to loosen her body and enjoy the water and fresh air, lightened the heaviness in her heart.

The dread of living the rest of her life with a man who had treated her poorly was lifting with each hour she realized he was dead and could no longer hurt her.

A quick glance confirmed here was no one around. She sat on a rock and untied the pouch shoes. Then she unbuttoned her dress and lay it on the rock by her shoes. She pulled the legs of her drawers up to her knees and waded into the cold water. She hadn't had the time or inclination to give her body a thorough scrubbing with her husband always watching her every move.

She pulled the bandage from her head, and using the bucket, poured icy water over her, scrubbing at her scalp everywhere but the injury. Her thick, curly hair, hung down around her shoulders. The bandages around her body drooped and slid down from the water splashing her body. She peeled the cloth strips off and walked out into the deepest part of the creek. The water now dampened her drawers. Her body shivered from the cold, but she gritted her teeth and floated on her back, hoping to wash away the stinky bear grease and cleanse the wounds.

The sky above her grew dark as she peered up, her body floated with the slow movement of the stream.

Tree limbs came into view.

Freedom dropped her feet, realizing she had floated downstream from where she'd gone in.

Her feet didn't touch the bottom. She quickly flipped onto her stomach and started paddling for the closest shore. When she thought she would float all the way to a settlement with nothing on but wet drawers, her feet found purchase and she stood.

Slogging through the water, her feet slipping on stones, she made her way to the creek bank and sat on the grassy edge, her feet dangling in the water.

How far had she floated? She stared up at the sky that was now cloud darkened and hiding the sun. Was she even on the same side as she went in? Yes. The river had been in front of her and running to her right. It was still the same.

She stood, drew in a breath, and hugged her arms over her bare breasts as she walked up stream, following the creek.

Rain started to fall. She was already wet, so it didn't matter, but when the wind picked up, her skin prickled with cold. Rippling shivers ran up and down her body. All she'd wanted was to clean up.

The pelting rain soon made it hard to peer across the creek. She shivered and thought about just leaning up against a tree and letting whatever happened to her, happen.

"Freedom!"

Her name! It had to be Swift. "Here!" She called back and faced the direction she'd heard the call.

"Freedom!" He sounded closer.

"Here! I'm here!" she called, walking carefully over the sticks, rocks, and thorny plants.

Within seconds, she spotted Swift dodging through the trees toward her. The moment he spotted her, his stride went from a run to a ground covering walk.

He walked straight up to her and put a hand on her shoulder. "Are you well?"

She nodded and shook her head. "I just wanted a bath. But I floated downstream."

He hugged her to his side a moment before sitting her on a log, cleaning her feet, and untying the pouch shoes from his leather belt. He tied those on her feet, then produced her dress from the quiver on his back.

Freedom held her arms up as he settled the garment over her shivering body. It was a welcome warmth though the rain wouldn't allow it to be dry for long. "You seem to come to my rescue a lot," she said, not looking at him.

He put a hand under her chin, raising it and making her rise off the rock and stand in front of him.

She still didn't peer into his eyes. She feared he would be mad at her for causing him to hunt for her.

"*Áxxaashe Ishté*, I wish you to look at me."

The name caught her off guard. She peered into his face. Concern wrinkled the corners of his eyes and forehead. However, there was a trace of a smile on his lips.

"What does, *Áxxaashe Ishté* mean?" She feared it would mean trouble woman.

"Sun Eyes. You have sunshine in your eyes. I wish to see this sunshine when you talk to me."

The name he gave her, and the reason behind it, warmed her from the inside. "I'm sorry I caused you trouble, again."

He continued to peer into her eyes a few moments

more, then dropped his hand from her chin. "I have meat. We eat good today." Swift put his arm around her shoulders, and they walked side by side back to the cave.

She was grateful he looked for her and even more grateful he had brought her clothing with him. From now on she would stick to washing from the side of the creek bank.

At the cave, there was a deer carcass hanging in a tree. She walked inside and found her bucket full of water.

"Why is the bucket here?" she asked.

"I found bucket and clothing. Thought you hid from me because no clothes. I fill bucket and bring." He pointed to the bucket of water. "You not return. I find clothes, no *Áxxaashe Ishté*. I call."

She smiled at his being respectful when she was floating nearly naked down the creek. "I'm glad you called. I was beginning to give up."

"No!" he said forcefully. "Never give up. *Áxxaashe Ishté* is strong woman."

His insistence humbled her to think this man who had known her a day had discovered more about her than a man she'd married. "I'll never give up, Swift. Just for you."

The smile, she seldom saw, appeared and her heart fluttered. A sensation she'd not had with Ben. It was a gentle flutter and warming in her chest. But she steeled herself from any thoughts other than staying free. "Cut meat off the deer, and I'll make you a meal." Freedom walked over to the pack and started digging out cooking utensils and ingredients to make biscuits.

Water Runs Fast walked out of the cave and into a

downpour. He quickly sliced a rump off the deer and took it back in to Sun Eyes. He was pleased she liked his name for her. He had told her about calmly returning to the cave with the bucket of water. While he had walked and had told himself she was hiding in the trees from him, his head told him the man had found her and was whipping her somewhere. When he'd encountered her the first time, she'd been bare and seeing her clothing and the strips of cloth, he'd feared the man had stripped her again.

When she'd returned his call, his heart had resumed beating. The woman with her sun eyes and strong heart had taken a hold on him. He wished to return to his village and ask the medicine man about this woman's strong medicine.

He placed the meat on a black pan Sun Eyes had placed on the ground next to the fire.

"Thank you. Do you want steaks or a roast?" she asked.

Water Runs Fast stared at her. He didn't know steak or roast.

She pointed to the pan. "Cook like this, which will take longer, or slice and fry. Then we can eat as soon as the biscuits are done."

His stomach talked.

"I'll slice and fry. Your stomach sounds hungry."

He grunted and went back out to tie the deer higher in the tree in case a bear smelled the kill. He'd left the guts where he'd killed the animal, hoping it would deter the large animals from following him back here.

The skin and brains were rolled up inside the cave. If they were here long enough, he'd show Sun Eyes how to prepare the hide.

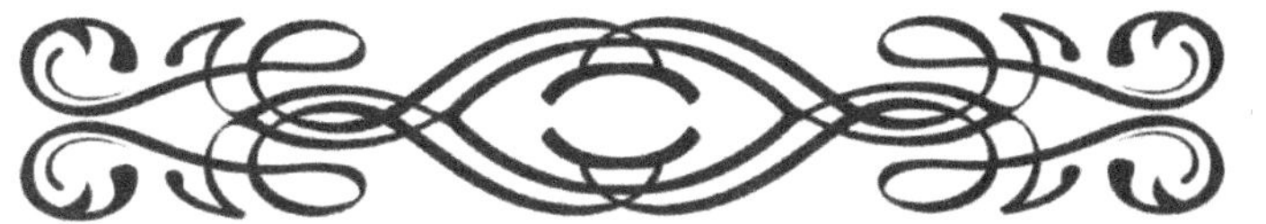

Chapter Thirteen

Freedom's stomach rumbled at the scent of the cooking meat. She'd not had a meal with meat, other than Swift's pemmican, since leaving Shady Gulch. Ben hadn't taken the time to shoot anything for a meal, saying beans and biscuits was good enough. She'd grown sick of them and had hoped for a meal when they visited the Fosters. But there they had a soup made of plants Mary had gathered and soda bread. It had been a change but not what she'd craved. She thought of Mary daily and planned to get her away from her husband.

She hadn't even discovered what tribe Mary was from. It made her sad she knew so little of the woman, but they had bonded over their aversion to their cruel husbands.

Freedom opened the lid on the Dutch oven to check the biscuits. They looked done. She picked up a plate, forked three slices of venison on and added three biscuits.

"Swift. Your meal is ready," she said to the Indian's back. He'd stood at the entrance to the cave, starring out at the rain, while she'd cooked.

He faced her and walked over, taking a seat on the other side of the fire.

She placed two slices of meat on her plate and one biscuit. Even though she made a fine biscuit, she was tired of eating them.

"You did not take much food," he said, staring at her plate.

"It will be enough to start." She cut the meat into bite sized pieces with a sharp knife.

Swift picked up a piece and dropped it. "*Tawée!*"

"Hot?" Freedom asked.

He nodded and poked at a biscuit with a finger.

"That is warm, too, but not like the meat. It cools off faster." She picked up her biscuit and tore it in half. Steam swirled out of the hot center.

Swift copied her movements.

She placed meat between the halves and ate it like a sandwich.

He placed meat in the biscuit, took a bite, and smiled as he chewed.

It appeared he thought what she'd made was very good. He continued eating one venison and biscuit sandwich after another. When he'd finished all three biscuits, his gaze landed on the open Dutch oven and biscuits still inside.

"You can have more. They're easy to make," she said, motioning for him to take another one.

He grabbed all but one out of the oven. Then he forked more meat on his plate and continued eating the venison sandwiches as if he would never get another meal.

Freedom finished her food and dropped her plate, knife, and fork into the bucket of water.

"For you," he said, pointing to the last biscuit.

"I'm full. You may eat it." She stood, to dry the back side of her skirt. She hadn't bothered putting on dry clothes and having sat at the fire cooking, the wet drawers had soaked through her already damp skirt, giving her chills when a breeze blew through the cave.

"Change clothes," Swift said.

She glanced over her shoulder at him. "What?"

"Put on dry clothes."

Freedom spun around and pointed to his still wet leggings. "You haven't changed."

He shrugged. "All I have."

Her cheeks heated thinking about him sitting where he was with nothing on while his leggings dried.

"I only wet here," He motioned with his hands. "You all over."

She had to agree with that. While her dress had been dry when she'd put it on, her skin had been wet and the rain had continued to fall as they walked to the cave. She was damp or soaked all over. The heat from the fire as she'd cooked had done little to dry her out. Her hair still felt heavy and wet.

Swift licked his fingers and dropped his plate into the bucket. "Change. I will stand at door."

His chivalry touched her, considering he'd seen her bare body almost as much as her dead husband. Though her husband had mostly witnessed it in the dark as if he couldn't tolerate seeing so much dark skin at one time in the light. That thought angered her.

"You don't have to stand over there and get a chill. I'll just duck into the shadows." She went to her pack and realized she didn't have another set of drawers. Swift had torn up her spare pair for bandages. Digging through her pack, she could only find one chemise.

She held up the one she found. "Did you rip up one of these?"

His eyes sparkled. "Dress too thin, but good for bandage."

"It's not a dress. It goes under a dress to help hide…" She couldn't bring herself to say nipples. "Things."

His eyebrows rose. "What things? If dress made of hide, it is thick, not need more dresses under."

She understood why Indian women didn't wear anything under their clothing if their dresses were made of the same leather as his leggings.

Freedom moved to the shadows with her chemise, a blouse, and skirt. The only other clothing she had besides what she wore. She'd have to go without drawers until her one pair dried. She hoped the fort carried women's clothing. Or at least linen to make a couple extra sets of underclothes.

She unbuttoned her dress and cried out as she tried to pull the wet fabric off her injured back.

"I help." Swift's voice was right behind her.

Accepting his offer was the only way she'd get her dress off without pain. "All right." She raised her arms.

The weight of the dress lightened on her shoulders and the cool air slowly touched her back as the garment slowly rose up over her head.

"You need more covering," he said, before stepping away and placing her dress on the pack.

"You can't rip up anymore of my clothin'. I'll be walkin' around bare." Her whole body heated at the notion of walking around all the time as she'd been when Swift found her lost beside the creek. It had been a freeing feeling. But there would always be someone else who could come along. She shuddered at the memory of her husband's rough hands; groping, squeezing.

"You are cold. Stand by fire. I have seen you." Swift led her over to the fire.

The light seemed as bright as the noon day sun. When she started to put her arms up to hide her breasts, he touched her arms.

"Do not be ashamed of body. It is as a woman should be."

She studied him, studying her. The glimmer in his eyes and the expression of awe on his face didn't make her feel ashamed. She'd witnessed a look like this on faces before when she'd gone to the art museum in Chicago. People stood in front of paintings with this same expression. She'd never considered herself beautiful. She was common. But seeing Swift's awe made her feel special.

"I think if I sit here, and let the fire dry my back, I can put my clothes on without a bandage." She hated to break the spell, but didn't want to stand here thinking things she shouldn't.

"Take off." He pointed to her drawers.

This was a problem since she didn't have anything else to put on down there. "I'll be completely bare."

He bent toward the folded-up blankets and picked one up.

She felt foolish. The blankets had been there the

whole time. She could have wrapped one around her as soon as the dress had come off.

She slipped the drawers down her legs and stepped out of them.

Swift placed the blanket around her front. She lowered her arms, holding the blanket over the top of her breasts. She stepped sideways to sit on a rock with her back to the heat.

He placed the ends of the blanket under her backside, but she could feel the heat directly on her back.

She grabbed her hair, trying to squeeze the little bit of water from it and wind it into a bun at the back of her head.

"No. Hair is pride." He nudged her hands away from her hair and it fell down her back.

He split the strands in half, pushing each half over a shoulder to her chest, then took the half on the side where he crouched and worked his fingers through it, raking out the tangles.

"I have a brush in the pack," she said, enjoying having someone fix her hair. Once in a while, at the boarding house, the girls had helped each other with their hair and before that her younger sister would play with her hair at times. But there was something different about Swift gently combing his long fingers through her tight curls. His fingers and the back of his hand touching her bare shoulder sent jolts of heat through her body, warming her from the inside out.

He only grunted at her attempt to have him use a brush. When his fingers no longer tugged on knots, his hands moved as if he braided her hair.

She put a hand up to feel and discovered he was.

His hands stopped, and he reached out to his pouch, pulling a rawhide string from it and securing the end of that braid.

He crouched at her other side and did the same with that batch of hair. Only it seemed his fingers lingered longer on her neck and shoulders as he worked as if he didn't want to stop touching her hair. She wondered at his knowledge of how to braid when his long straight hair, hung about his shoulders unbound.

Swift placed her second braid on her chest, skimming his fingers along the top of her breast.

Her gaze shot to his face. Braiding her hair had lit a fire in his eyes. And she had a feeling elsewhere. While he had been gentle and caring, she wasn't ready to have a man, even this one who had shown her nothing but kindness, bed her. She didn't understand how women put up with it. It seemed a harsh way to make a child. Not only did the mother suffer through the birthing, but the conceiving as well.

"How is my back?" she asked, to draw attention away from the thoughts.

He ran a gentle hand over the wounds. "Dry. Bear fat now."

She shook her head and stood. "I don't want that smelly stuff on me again. I'll dress."

Water Runs Fast took a step back. He knew when to not push a woman. He'd let his thoughts show in his eyes moments ago and that was why she wished to get covered. Her skin, smooth and dark, excited him in a way he'd not experienced before. He wanted to touch her, even if it was just a brief whisper of a touch. Her hair was thick and strong, just like her body and mind. He wanted to have her under him and feel her strength as she clung to him. From the way she now stood with her back to him, drawing the thin dress over her head, he knew it would take time for her to feel the same.

And he wondered at the man who had whipped her. Had he taken her without her consent? Men of such actions were not tolerated in the Absarokee. He was glad he'd killed the man.

Chapter Fourteen

Night settled around the cave entrance. Freedom watched from the dry interior as Swift moved the horses to more grass and retrieved a fresh bucket of water. She had batter made for hotcakes and planned to impress Swift with them for their supper.

He entered the cave carrying an armload of dry limbs. "We leave for my village tomorrow."

She liked the idea of getting closer to the fort. She could send a letter to Savannah to let the others know she was well. She wouldn't tell them about Ben's death just yet or that she'd been traveling with a Crow Indian. She would tell them about Mary and hope the woman could get to them.

Freedom followed him to the fire. He dropped the pile of wood in the area where he'd slept the night before. She ignored the thoughts bumping around inside her head and knelt at the fire. The pan was hot and ready to cook. "We're having hotcakes for supper."

Swift grunted and crouched beside her, watching as she poured the batter into the pan and flipped the cake.

She placed the cooked one on a plate and poured more batter in the pan. When she'd cooked all the batter, she placed two cakes on a plate for her and handed the other one to Swift.

He plucked a cake from his pile and put it on hers.

"I can't eat that much," she said, attempting to pick up the hotcake he'd placed on her plate.

"You will only eat pemmican until we get to village. Eat." He sat on his backside away from the fire and began eating the hotcakes.

She leaned back on the rock where she sat and ate two of the cakes. Her stomach couldn't hold any more. A glance at Swift's plate and she could see he would eat her last one.

She set the plate down within his reach as she stood to go relieve herself.

"Where you go?" he asked.

"To find a bush," she said, not glancing back. As she used this lull in the rain to take care of nature, she wondered at how comfortable she had grown with Swift. He'd seen her bare body and she'd said things to him, she'd not have said to her husband. And it felt right. Shame hadn't even crossed her mind all the times he saw her bare body or they talked of things women and men shouldn't talk about.

Entering the cave, she smiled at the empty plate. Both plates sat beside the water bucket. She wanted water to wash with in the morning. She used a piece of her torn chemise to dip in the water and clean the plates.

Swift sat with his back against the cave wall, a

blanket over his shoulders.

She sat down on her blanket and took off her pouch shoes. "Tell me about your village?"

He studied her for several moments and nodded. "My mother's family lives at the village."

"Your grandparents? Your mother's parents?" she asked.

"Yes, and her cousins, aunts, uncles and their families. When a warrior marries, he moves to the village of his wife's mother." Swift shrugged.

"None of your father's family is there?" She didn't understand how only one side of a family would be represented.

He shook his head. "My uncle, my father's brother, married my aunt, my mother's cousin."

"I'll go to a village that is all your family?" She wasn't sure she would be welcome to a place that was for family only.

"I wish you to meet my uncle the medicine man. He will take pleasure in your strong medicine."

"What do you mean?" She didn't like his comment. It sounded like he planned to give her to his uncle. As a slave to be bedded. Her instincts kicked in and she shot to her feet. "I'll not be given to a man to bed. I am not a whore."

Swift loomed in front of her. "What is whore?"

"A woman men pass around to use for their carnal pleasure." She crossed her arms. "I will leave tomorrow with one horse. I will not be used that way."

His eyes darkened. "What is this carnal pleasure?"

She groaned. How did she tell him what it was? "A man undressing a woman and putting his…his male part in…"

His eyes narrowed and then widened. He placed a hand on the side of her face. "Water Runs Fast would never let another touch *Áxxaashe Ishté* this way."

She peered into his eyes and saw the truth in their depths. He would protect her. "Then what did you mean your uncle would take pleasure from me?"

He urged her back down onto her blanket and he sat beside her. "My uncle will see your strength and tell me if our futures will be together."

She sucked in air. He wanted them to be together. She wanted to get back to Shady Gulch. "How will he do that?" Better to keep asking questions than to think about what he'd suggested.

Water Runs Fast picked up Sun Eyes' hand and held it in his. He'd wanted to clasp hands with her all day, but had not found a time that she wouldn't shy from him. His heart ached that she thought he would give her to another to enjoy her body. What had she endured that she would think that little of him?

"My uncle will meet you, chant, and speak to *Ah-badt-dadt-deah,* the one who created the earth." It all seemed natural to him. "He will know if you are the woman from my vison."

She squeezed his hand as she moved from her backside to her knees, facing him. "What do you mean vision?"

The golden sparks in her eyes fascinated him. They came alive when she was excited. He wished to see that when they came together.

She squeezed his hand again, drawing his thoughts back to the present and his gaze to her mouth.

"What do you mean by a vision?" she repeated.

"I have had visions. We go up the mountain for

days, not eating, and wait for our spirit animal and a vision." He thought back to a vision he'd had when he was young. He'd been sitting by a waterfall, listening to the roar of the water crashing over the edge and splashing into the lake below. A woman with dark skin had told him he would help his people. He studied the woman sitting in front of him. She had been the woman of his vision. "I had a vision that you would come to me."

She sat back, trying to draw her hand from his. He didn't let her slip away. "You told me I would help my people."

"I'm sure you are making this up." Her eyes didn't hold the excitement they had earlier.

"No. It is the truth." He had no proof other than his own mind.

"How was I dressed?" She didn't ask out of curiosity. Her voice held challenge.

He faced her, crossed his legs, and grasped her other hand. He closed his eyes and walked back in time to the vision when he was young.

Áxxaashe Ishté had been younger too. Not a child. Her body just starting to become a woman. She had a carefree smile and her sunshine eyes lit up at the sight of him. She wore a thin dress like the one he tore for a bandage. That was how he could see her woman body forming.

"What do you see?" Her whisper was inches from his face, her warm breath caressing his cheek.

"You are wearing your thin dress. You are just becoming a woman. *Áxxaashe Ishté* has a warm smile even in her eyes."

She leaned back and tugged on her hands, but he

held on.

He concentrated on their connection of hands.

"You will help the Raven People," Áxxaashe Ishté said.

"How," he'd asked, in awe of her beauty and buffalo colored skin. His body, also just coming of age of a man, heated as his gaze skimmed her body and face. Much as it had the last few days they had been together.

"You will know when I am by your side."

He'd reached out to her and she'd dissolved. Water Runs Fast remembered having heated dreams for weeks after that vision. Dreams in which he made many trips to the river to cool his body.

He opened his eyes and stared into the mature face of the girl who had kept him from looking at any other woman. His body had known his mate from his vision. He knew better than to tell Sun Eyes this.

Linking his fingers with hers, he held their hands up between them. "You came to me in a vision and told me when you were by my side, I would help my people."

Her mouth dropped open.

He stared at her pink tongue, amazed that he found her open mouth as body heating as her smile.

Water Runs Fast used their linked hands to push her chin up and close her mouth.

"You're makin' that up," she finally said.

"No. It is the truth. I had forgotten that vision until this night." He released one of her hands so he could touch her face. A face he'd dreamed of all those years ago.

She sat still as he ran the tips of his fingers over her forehead, down the side of her eye, over her eyelid as she closed her eyes, and across her long soft eyelashes. His body heated as he traced her nose, cheeks, and rubbed his thumb softly over her lips and down her chin. This was the woman, his vision. His heart, body, and mind remembered her as if he had traced her face in his vision.

"You are the woman of my vision."

Freedom's body heated and trembled from the delicate way Swift had traced her face. She closed her eyes for part of it but when her eyes were open there was no denying he was remembering something he'd experienced before. The thought she'd been in a vison he'd had years ago, stuttered her thinking. There was no denying she'd not been afraid of him and he'd helped her with no questions.

Her heart thudded in her chest like a galloping horse. Were they meant to be? Was her cruel treatment by Ben necessary for her to meet up with Swift? She didn't want to think that had been necessary to bring her to her future.

The hand that had traced her face now moved to her neck, skimming the length of it. She wanted to relax, enjoy his soft touch, but she'd learned not that long ago that a soft touch could turn hurtful in a blink of an eye. Leaning away from him, she opened her eyes.

His gaze locked with hers. Waiting for the softness and admiration in his eyes to fade to anger, she stared back.

When he remained still, not touching, only staring into her eyes, she did relax. Even gave him a shy smile.

He returned the smile, his eyes warming.

Her insides churned, not revulsion but with

excitement. Could he be a man who would only show her tenderness and caring?

She reached up with her free hand and touched Swift's face. Tracing his features as he'd traced hers.

The tips of her fingers heated as she skimmed them over his skin. A flutter low in her body surprised her and she pulled her hand away. What was this odd sensation?

She placed a hand on her belly and stared at Swift.

He smiled. "You may continue to touch me."

Freedom studied his features. His smile warmed his eyes. She saw no trace of anger or displeasure. Wondering if touching him would set her insides fluttering again, she cautiously slid closer to him and this time ran her hand down his bare chest.

The muscle bunched and rippled under her palm. Heat scorched her hand, coursing up her arm and swirling in her chest, making it hard to catch her breath. Propriety said to pull her hand back, but her curiosity swept her hand across the wide space between his shoulders, enjoying the heat and firmness. Ben had never allowed her to touch him. He'd only used her and turned his back to her.

She frowned thinking of him. How had she been so stupid to not see the signs her friends had seen?

Swift touched her cheek. "Are you displeased with me?"

She shook off her thoughts. "No! Very pleased." Her cheeks heated at her bold statement.

He smiled. "It makes me happy you are pleased." Swift grasped her hands. "You are like a day filled with sunshine. Your touch heats my skin and your smile warms me inside."

Freedom stared at the man. His words were exactly how she felt about him. How could she be so enthralled with a man she'd only known for a few days? Granted he'd saved her life, rid her of her abusive husband, and doctored her wounds. But it was more than his chivalry that made her wish to look at him and hear his voice.

Could a person fall in love in a matter of days? Was it possible after all she'd been put through by men to think she could trust and love a man?

Staring into Swift's dark brown eyes, she felt as if she'd found her home and herself. The thought shocked and warmed her. Was he the man she was meant to live out her life with? Or was she taking his caring for more than it was?

She thought of how the other women had asked her about Ben's kisses. Would kissing Swift help her decide if this was just gratitude for his kindness?

Freedom peered into his eyes. There was no condemnation or anger, only caring and a hint of something she couldn't put her finger on. But it wasn't malice. She leaned forward, pressing her lips to his. She knew little of the act as she and Ben had barely kissed after the wedding.

The sensation of their mouths meeting tingled unlike anything she'd experienced with her husband.

She separated her lips slightly, and Swift leaned away from the touch.

Horror that he didn't want to kiss her, straightened her back and pulled her hand from his grasp.

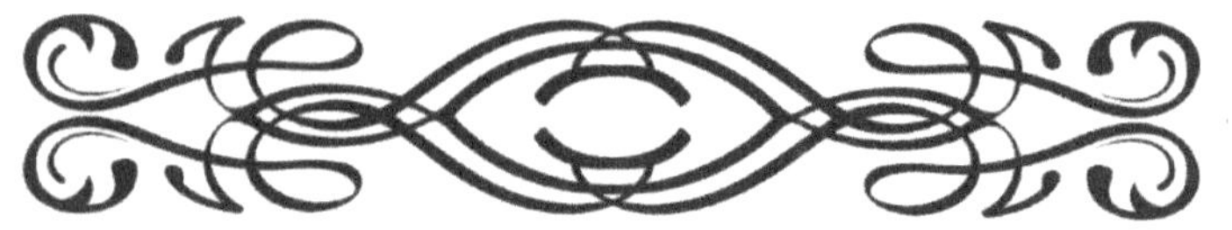

Chapter Fifteen

Water Runs Fast stared at Sun Eyes. He'd enjoyed how they'd touched mouths. Especially since he'd only moments before found her mouth enthralling.

"Why do you pull your hand from mine?" he asked.

"Y-you didn't want to kiss me."

He studied her. She was hurt. "What is a kiss?"

Her angry eyes softened. "You don't know about kissing?"

He shook his head.

"It's when a man and a woman press their lips together." She put up a hand. "But it's only if they like each other more than any other."

He smiled. "Does you touching my lips with yours mean you like me?"

Her cheeks darkened in color and her eyelashes covered her eyes. "Maybe a little."

He laughed. "You like me enough to press our lips together." His body heated. If they touched lips, there could be more touching, more of them coming together. "Can you show me more of this kissing?"

Her eyes lit up the way he loved. She leaned toward him and moments before their lips touched, she closed her eyes.

He wasn't sure what to do, but was intrigued. Food was a sustenance a body needed to stay alive. Could a kiss also be sustenance? He slid his tongue between his lips and tasted Sun Eyes lips. They were salty and not unpleasant.

She gasped. He smiled and nibbled on her bottom lip. Tasty. This was something he could come to enjoy very much. Her body relaxed against him. Yes, he would like this very much. While doctoring Sun Eyes, he'd dreamed of holding her in his arms. A man who had lived by taking chances, he slipped an arm around her, drawing her so close, her soft body molded to his.

Her head fell back and she gasped for air. "I need to breathe."

He loosened his hold and studied her long neck. It was a vision of beauty. Tracing his fingers along the silky skin, he felt her body shudder. A quick glance at her face and he understood it was a tremor of excitement and not revulsion. Her puffy lips from his nibbling were tipped in a smile that resembled a cougar with a full belly.

Pride had him asking, "You have kissed many men?" The thought of her pressing her mouth to others upset him. Since the vision he had been waiting for her, even if he hadn't realized she was real. He didn't like the idea of her being with men.

"I've only kissed one other, and only a few brief touches. Nothing like…this." She put her forehead against his and stared down at the blanket between them. "The man who-who you killed was my husband."

He raised her face with a finger to her chin to peer into her eyes. "He was your man? Why did he beat you?"

Her eyes flashed with anger. "He treated me like he cared, and I married him to live with him and have a family." She broke contact with him and settled onto her backside. "Only a day after our wedding, when we were on the trail to his place, he started treating me like a possession. Like a slave. He used my body, hurt me, and made me do all the work." She pulled her legs up to her chest and wrapped her arms around them. "I hated him within days and realized what I'd thought was love, was just me hoping to have found a way out of the saloon and to have the family I always wanted."

Water Runs Fast watched her face crumble and tears trickle down her cheeks. He pulled her into his arms, hugging her as tight as he could without hurting her back. "I am glad the Great One urged me to go on alone and find you. I saved you and now you will help me save my people."

She leaned her head against his chest. "You have proven to me you are more honorable than my husband. But can you promise you will never turn on me?" The sad whisper was like a thousand arrows to his heart.

"I promise." He pressed his lips to hers and enjoyed the feel of their mouths meeting.

Her body moved closer as her lips parted and nipped at his. The sensations coursing through his body were unlike any he'd ever experienced. His hands found her round firm backside. He leaned back, drawing her body over his.

Her breasts pressed against his chest, her hands slid down, feeling his shoulders, chest and sides. "Mmmm, you are firm all over," she said.

He had another firm body part. Water Runs Fast didn't want to couple with her. Not yet. But this running his hands over her and touching of mouths was as exciting as hunting bear or counting coup on the enemy.

Freedom's hands tingled with each area of Swift's body she touched. That he allowed her to freely roam her hands over him, made her happy. Ben hadn't wanted her to touch him. He hadn't kissed her or just held her as Swift did now. She liked the feel of his large hands cupping her backside. She could feel his need pressing between her legs. As much as she believed Swift would never hurt her, she wasn't ready to allow him to enter her body.

Right now, she found pleasure with him. She didn't want pain.

The way he held her and his hands massaged her back and rubbed away her misgivings, she could understand why Savannah and Lottie Mae glowed after they wed. This bliss of having a man's hands adore you and not hurt you would be something to look forward to each night.

Placing her hands on either side of Swift's face, she drew her body along his length and kissed him with all the heat and passion she felt that very minute.

His hands moved up her sides, skimming the sides of her breasts and she gasped.

He drew out of the kiss and asked, "Did I hurt

you?"

"No. I never thought I would think a man's hands could feel heavenly," she said on a sigh.

He grinned. "When you are ready, I could touch you all over. Just my hands on your bare skin."

Excitement skittered across her skin at the thought of his large hands skimming across her bare skin. However, she was still trying to make sense of the sensations his touch elicited in her body and how she wanted to deal with it. She would not rush into anything with another man, no matter how wonderful he seemed.

"I'm tired and would rather sleep." She smiled to soften her rejection. "I'll remember your offer."

He stood and tossed more wood on the fire. "We sleep now," he said, indicating for her to lie down.

"Are you going to sleep sitting again?" she asked, wondering if he would accept sharing her blanket after she'd just rejected him.

Swift shook his head. He placed his blanket next to hers.

She scooted over.

"I will lay with you this night." He helped her stretch out, then placed their blankets over her, and he slipped in behind her. His arm draped over her waist and he kissed her neck, all the while keeping his chest from pressing on her back. "Sleep Sun Eyes. We will go to my village tomorrow."

She closed her eyes. For the first time in a long while she was safe and truly cared for. He might not have been what she'd imagined her husband would be, but then he was closer to her imagination than Ben had been. And this time, she was in love. Her heart and mind were not at war, they were content.

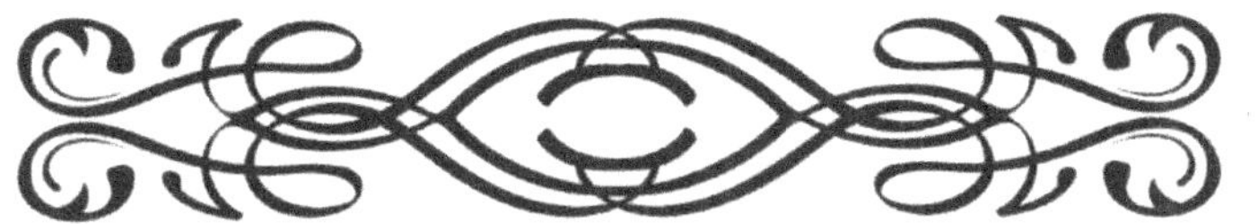

Chapter Sixteen

Water Runs Fast smiled as he and Sun Eyes rode toward his village. Waking next to her this morning had filled his chest with pride. That she trusted and cared for him as deeply as he did her, made his heart sing. She had listened to his vison and believed in their past meeting. She was his mate. They were meant to do good things for his people.

His family and village had to see she was his mate, and together, they would work to keep the people strong. That she was not white would be in her favor. While the Absarokee had always tried to get along with the whites, there were still those who did not trust them. He was one. Plenty Coup, one of the Crow Chiefs, had talked with many powerful white men and yet the Crow people still suffered from lack of food and clothing that was promised.

He stopped at a small stream and peered up at the sun. Mid-day. They would reach the village before dark. A glance over his shoulder and he smiled.

Sun Eyes had learned to bunch her skirt up when getting on and off the horse. She bunched her skirt now, showing her long strong legs. "Are we getting off?" she asked.

He nodded.

She climbed down from her saddle and dropped her skirt. During the night she had shed her shirt and bottom dress, sleeping in the thin dress. He'd been able to feel more of her curves and enjoy her small murmurings in her sleep as he'd skimmed his hand over her hips and cupped her breasts. At least he'd believed her to be asleep until she'd spun in his arms and kissed him, pressing her breasts to his chest and whispering, they needed to sleep.

He'd smiled, kissed her again and then tucked her arms between them and rolled to his back, allowing her to sleep on top of him while he cupped her backside in his hands.

The food she'd made before they left the cave had filled him. He'd noticed it gave Sun Eyes great pleasure to feed him. It was a good quality in a wife.

He slid off his horse and led all the horses up to the stream for a drink.

"Are we getting close to your village?" Sun Eyes asked, dipping her hands in the water and sipping.

"We will arrive before dark." He crouched and drew water into his hand to drink.

When he stood, Sun Eyes watched him. Fear dulled the brightness of her eyes. "What is wrong?" He put a hand on the side of her face.

"Will I get to stay with you? In your home?"

He'd been trying to figure out how to keep her with

him. But without them coupling, she would stay in the maiden's lodge and he with the other unmarried men.

"I do not have a home. I sleep with the other unmarried men. You will go to the lodge of the unmarried women."

Her eyes widened and her head shook. "I don't want to stay with the women. I want to stay with you."

He reached out and pulled her to his chest. "I will see what I can do."

Her face tipped up to him. "You are the only person I know out here. The only one I trust."

He understood her fear. It was much like when he joined the white man's Army as a scout. He brushed his lips across hers. "I will do what I can."

~*~

By the time they rode down the hill toward the village with thirty tipis scattered about the bottom of the small valley, Water Runs Fast could think of only two places Sun Eyes could stay that would not be with the unmarried women. With his mother or with his sister. His mother did not have a man right now, but his sister did. He would have to ask his mother to allow Sun Eyes to live with her and her sister and two children. His father had died from a wound suffered while hunting and his mother had moved in with her sister's family. Then his aunt, Woman Talks Softly, lost her husband and youngest child to sickness. Leaving her with a girl ready to go to the unmarried women's lodge and a younger girl.

Having Sun Eyes stay with his mother and aunt would give him more chances of being with her.

A rider on horseback raced out to meet them.

Water Runs Fast greeted his friend, Wolf Tracker.

His friend's gaze lingered on Sun Eyes. "I thought you were going on a vision quest?" he asked in Absarokee. He pointed to the horses and woman. "You counted coup instead."

While it would have added to his position in the band to have agreed he'd snuck into an enemy camp and took the horses and woman, it was not the truth. "She was in need of help. These are her horses and supplies." He would not tell anyone she was the woman of his visions, except his mother and the medicine man, Antlers On Wrong.

"What is this dark woman's name?" Wolf Tracker asked.

"*Áxxaashe Ishté*. Her eyes have rays of sunshine."

Wolf Tracker grunted and rode quickly back to the village.

Water Runs Fast groaned. Everyone in the village would be out watching their arrival.

Freedom rode up alongside Swift. "Who was that and what did he want?"

"He is Wolf Tracker. A friend. He came to see who I brought."

"He didn't look happy."

"He is hard Indian to please."

She studied the man she rode beside to see if he was making a joke. From the serious expression on his face, she didn't think so. "Are you sure this is a good idea? I could ride to the fort and find a way to get back to Shady Gulch."

"No. You will stay with me." He glanced at her. "You do not go to fort alone."

She hadn't wanted to go to the fort alone. A fort meant many men. She had enough good sense to want to stay away from trouble.

They walked the horses in between the first tipis. She had been in awe of the cone-shaped tents when they started down into the valley. There were also some long structures made of sticks and hides.

Men, women, and children with dogs scattered between the lodges gathered together, watching them like spectators at a parade. Some younger men raised their fists and did a strange yell. Swift shook his head at these men and nodded at others, but kept on leading the horses with her riding beside him. While the people didn't look mean, they didn't look as if they were pleased with her either.

"Why are they staring?" she asked quietly for only Swift's ears.

"You are different and it is not often I ride in with more horses than I left with." He smiled at her then stopped at a tipi. He dismounted and helped her down, before she could raise her skirt to dismount. Even though the smallest children ran around with nothing on and the young boys and men only had on leggings, the women and girls were covered with long leather moccasins and dresses that only revealed their heads, necks, and hands.

A woman stepped forward and talked to Swift. He replied in a language she didn't understand but did recognize the name Swift had given her.

He touched her arm and motioned for her to step closer. "*Áxxaashe Ishté*, Freedom, this is my mother, Moon Woman."

The woman was Freedom's height but more filled out in the face. Her leather dress hung straight down, hiding whatever plumpness there might have been in her body. Her brown eyes stared at Freedom. "My son says he wishes you to stay with my sister and I." She waved to the tipi behind her. "We already have four living here."

Freedom glanced at Swift. "Why do you want me to stay with your mother?"

"She will question everything you do. She will not ignore you. You will not feel alone here."

She studied the woman. While Moon Woman wasn't glaring, but also studying her, she wondered at five people in the small structure. "I don't want to be a burden. I could stay tonight and tomorrow you can take me to the fort so I can see how to get home." Even as she said it, the conviction she'd felt to get back to Shady Gulch, only a day ago, wasn't as strong.

"No go fort," Moon Woman said. "Bad things happen at fort."

Freedom peered into the woman's eyes. She had a real fear of the place. Freedom understood the woman's fear. It was how she, herself, had felt going to town before they moved to Chicago and she'd stayed in the colored part of town. At least she could try to get a letter to Savannah.

"Does anyone here go to the fort? I'd like to send a letter to my friend and let her know I am well."

Another woman stepped out of the tipi. She was a younger version of Swift's mother.

"*Áxxaashe Ishté,* this is my mother's sister, Woman Talks Softly," Swift said, motioning to the younger woman. "I will get your things." He left her standing in front of the two women and feeling the eyes of everyone else on her.

"It is my son's wish you stay with us. It will be.

Come." Moon Woman, pivoted and held the blanket across the opening to the tipi open.

Freedom glanced over her shoulder at Swift who was untying her canvas bag. She ducked through the opening and found the inside appeared larger than the outside had suggested. It wasn't big, but everything was in its place, making it appear roomier.

She stopped at the sight of a young woman sewing beads on a piece of leather and a girl of about ten playing with a stick doll. They both glanced up and shot to their feet.

"I won't hurt you. I'm a friend of Swift's." She held her hands out as if showing them she had no weapon.

"Who is this Swift?" Moon Woman asked.

Freedom spun to her as Swift walked through the opening carrying her bag. "He is." She nodded to the man who'd saved her. "His name Water Funs Fast also means swift. That's what I call him, like he calls me Sun Eyes when my real name is Freedom."

The two women shared a glance before Woman Talks Softly pointed to a spot for Swift to put her bag.

"I'd like to go through the supplies and bring some in here for your family since they are puttin' me up," she said touching Swift's arm when he spun to leave.

He glanced at her hand, then up into her eyes. "We may need these supplies to get you home."

She shook her head. The hungry people they'd ridden past needed the food now. She would find a way to get supplies when Swift could take her back to Shady Gulch. "Your people are hungry now. There isn't much, but see if you can share it with those that need it most."

His lips curved into a smile. He pressed his lips to

the top of her head. "You are a good woman."

His words filled her with pride, that a man with his bravery and kindness would say she was good.

"Come get what you would like to share with my family. Do you wish me to keep the horses?"

"If you need them, they are yours." She owed her life to this man. She would not deny him anything.

"*Ahóoh*, thank you." He grasped her hand, leading her back out to the horses.

Most of the crowd had dispersed but there were some young men and children still watching.

An old man with gray braids and a hat that had some kind of horns on it walked up, using a tall walking stick with feathers dangling from the top. "Ho!" he said.

"Ho," Swift replied and while he untied more of the pack on the horse and handed her packages, he spoke to the man in their language. Again, she heard the name he'd given her spoken.

The old man walked over to her, put his hand on her shoulder, said some words she didn't understand, smiled, and walked away.

"Is he an uncle?" she asked, using an empty cloth sack to mix flour and cornmeal into. She could make corn cakes for Swift and his family. She also gathered her cooking utensils and stacked them by the door of the tipi.

"He is Antlers On Wrong. He is a medicine man. He said he felt goodness when you walked into the village." Swift smiled.

She liked the old man because he liked her without even seeing her. "This is all I'll need." She headed to the opening of the tipi and stopped, glancing over her shoulder. "Will I see you before I sleep?"

He nodded. "I will come for the evening meal. Perhaps we can go for a walk."

Her heart picked up speed. "I would like that." She ducked into the tipi, carrying the sack of flour and meal. "Where should I store this?"

Moon Woman helped her place it in a leather vessel with a lid. She understood it was to keep the mice and other creatures out.

"I have my cooking and sleeping things outside," she motioned to the door. The young girl hurried out and back in carrying the heavy frying pan. She chattered in the language Freedom was wishing she knew.

When all the rest of her belongings were in the tipi, she saw that her living here would put them all in tight quarters. "I'm sorry for this. When Swift, Water Runs Fast, said I'd have to stay in a lodge with unmarried women, I was fearful."

The four women stared at her.

"Not that I thought anyone would hurt me, but because, I-I..." She didn't know what to say.

Woman Talks Softly stepped forward. "Water Runs Fast trusts you with family. You will stay."

"*Ahóoh.*"

Both women smiled at her use of their word for thank you. They all moved things around to make a spot for Freedom to sleep when the time came.

Chapter Seventeen

"Why did you bring that dark woman to our village?" Wolf Tracker asked, joining Water Runs Fast as he led the horses to the tipi of the chief.

"She has nowhere to go." What he wasn't admitting was he didn't want her to leave. Not only did he like the way she made him feel, he also had the blessing of Horns On Wrong to make her his wife. As the medicine man, he knew of Water Runs Fast's dreams and visions. All young men tell the medicine men of their vision dreams. The older wiser men help them to decipher what the dream means to their future.

"She wandered about alone?"

This was the hard part. He had to tell someone he'd killed a man. But he didn't want it to be his hot-headed friend. He would tell the chief and the medicine man only. Tonight, when he saw Sun Eyes, he would ask her not to tell his family. They did not need to fear white men coming to harm them.

"No. But the person she was with came to harm. She is alone now." He stopped at Chief Red Bear's tipi and called out.

The Chief stepped out of the structure, his eyes scanned up and down Water Runs Fast. "You have returned long after the others."

Water Runs Fast motioned to the tipi. "I would like to talk to Chief Red Bear alone."

The Chief's gaze landed on Wolf Tracker and then back to him. The older man nodded. "What of your horses?"

"I will take the pack off here. Wolf Tracker can put them with my other horses." He studied his friend. The man nodded, but his lips were in a firm line. He planned to ask more questions later.

Water Runs Fast and his friend untied the pack and placed all the supplies on the ground by the chief's tipi. Wolf Tracker led the horses away and Water Runs Fast entered the home of the village chief.

Sad Starling, the chief's wife, knelt by the fire, stirring their evening meal.

"Why do you need to speak with me?" the Chief asked, indicating Water Runs Fast sit down across from him with the fire between them.

"You have heard of Sun Eyes, the woman I brought to the village?"

"Yes. She has brown skin, different from ours."

Water Runs Fast smiled. "Yes, her skin is the color of the buffalo. An animal who sustained us for many winters." He wanted to make sure the chief understood the woman was good for their people. He couldn't tell the man of his visions or how Freedom had been one of the people to speak to him in the vision. Visions were sacred and only spoke about with a medicine man.

The chief bowed his head understanding the significance of the words.

"She has offered her supplies to the Absarokee of our village."

The Chief's eyes lit up. "That will be good. The soldiers have not delivered the supplies they promised."

He nodded. "I must tell you, I found her being beaten by a white man."

Chief Red Bear turned his concerned eyes on Water Runs Fast. "How is she with you?"

He stared the chief in the eyes. "I killed him."

The chief studied him for what seemed like half a day before he spoke. "This man, did he have reason to beat her?"

"No. He was cruel to her. She wished to leave him. That is why he was whipping her." Remembering the sight he came upon, curled his hands into fists.

"There was no one else around?"

"No. We left quickly, stopping only long enough for her wounds to heal."

Chief Red Bear stared at him. "I see. Is she your wife?"

"Not yet. But I wish to make her so."

The chief grunted. "If white men come looking for her, what will you say?"

"The truth. I tried to stop him beating her and he tried to kill me. I killed him first."

A quick nod from Chief Red Bear. "It is done."

Water Runs Fast stood as did the chief. They clasped arms over the fire. He walked out of the tipi, knowing he had told his chief all that had happened and what was in his heart. Now to go see how his mother

Freedom

was getting along with Sun Eyes.

~*~

Freedom waited impatiently for Swift to return. Even though Moon Woman had said he would return soon for the meal, she was worried he'd found trouble for bringing her to the village. She stood inside the door of the tipi listening for approaching footsteps.

"My son will come. Standing at the door as if to pounce is not good." Moon Woman motioned to a blanket that had been folded to seat two people.

She started to give in when she heard footsteps. A word was called out and Swift appeared through the opening. Without thinking, she wrapped her arms around his waist and hugged.

Opening her eyes, she noticed the two older women's brows were furrowed and the younger women were hiding giggles behind their hands. She peered up into Swift's face.

His eyes twinkled. "I did not run away, *Áxxaashe Ishté*."

Foolishness relaxed her hold on him. Her arms dropped to her side. She'd made a spectacle of herself. Something she'd worked years to never do.

"Come, we will eat and I will tell you what I did." He led her to the blanket for two and they both sat down, side by side.

Her heart thudded in her chest as he crossed his legs and his knee bumped her hip, as she'd sat with her legs folded under her, like the other women present.

Moon Woman handed her a bowl of soup. She sniffed. While the smell wasn't off-putting, it didn't smell like anything she'd eaten before.

She waited for a spoon but the others raised the

bowls and drank.

Swift lowered his bowl and motioned for her to eat as he did.

She raised her bowl and sipped. The broth had a bit of an onion and meat flavor. Once the liquid was gone, she noted the others dug the meat and vegetables out with their fingers.

The last time she'd eaten with her fingers had been as a child. She picked up a piece of meat and popped it in her mouth. And chewed. And chewed. She secretly spit the piece back into her bowl and tried another one. It wasn't as tough and she eventually was able to swallow the smaller pieces that ground off.

The others finished and watched her. She smiled and set her bowl down in front of her.

"I'd like to make breakfast for you tomorrow."

They stared at her as if not understanding what she said. "The morning meal? I'll make corn cakes." She glanced at Swift. "You'll be here for the morning meal?"

He nodded. "I take all meals here. I only sleep in the unmarried men's lodge."

"Good." She smiled at him.

Swift stood and held out a hand. "*Áxxaashe Ishté* and I will take a walk."

Freedom's insides fluttered as she took his hand.

"Is that a wise thing?" Moon Woman asked.

"Chief Red Bear and Horns On Wrong know my story," he said, drawing her to the opening.

Freedom wondered at his mother's question and Swift's response. What did he mean by they knew his story?

Outside, it had grown dark. The stars glittered in

the dark blue sky. She loved being outside at night, always had. The sparkling stars and the glowing face of the moon always made her happy.

Swift continued to hold her hand as they walked slowly through the village toward what appeared to be a cluster of trees. Did he plan to kiss her? Her body tingled at the thought.

A man stepped out of the shadow of a tipi. He talked to Swift in the language of their people.

Freedom wished she knew the language. She was getting tired of not knowing what was being talked about but she could tell by the firm grip on her hand, it was her.

"Come," Swift said, tugging her hand and walking briskly away from the man and the village.

"Why did he stop us and why are you angry?" she asked when he finally stopped inside the trees where it was darker.

"What was your man's name?" he asked.

She shook her head. "Why? What does that have to do with the man stopping us?"

"Dead Horse say a man come to fort, tell Major Litchfield his son was knifed by a darkie woman."

Freedom stared through the darkness at Swift. "Major Litchfield?" She strangled on the words. There would be no way to get a letter to Savannah or Beau or anyone through the fort if the person in charge was Ben's father.

Hands pressed on either side of her face. "What was your man's name?"

She clasped his wrists in her hands. "He told me Ben Hogan. Then at the weddin' Lark called him Ben Hogan Litchfield. He, Ben, said he didn't like his father so he never used his name." She shook her head the best she could with him holding it. "I didn't know his father was…was a…" She peered through the darkness at Swift. "They're lookin' for me. I'll bring trouble to your village. I have to leave. I have to go back to Shady Gulch. People there will know I tell the truth."

"You did not kill him." Swift said.

"No, but if they think so, they won't be lookin' for you." She tried to see his handsome face in the darkness. "I could have been happy here. With you."

"You will be." His arms encircled her, drawing their bodies close.

Tears seeped out of her eyes. "No, I can't stay. I can't put you or your family in danger."

"No one will say you are here." His hands kneaded her back, drawing her closer.

"I don't want them knowing I could bring the army down on them at any moment. I have to leave." Even as she said the words, her body wouldn't move away from his.

"I will take the matter to council. A decision will be made." His hands moved up her arms and captured her head. Only this time, he placed his lips on hers.

She liked he was a quick learner about kissing. She wasn't an expert but he'd learned exactly what made her body tremble.

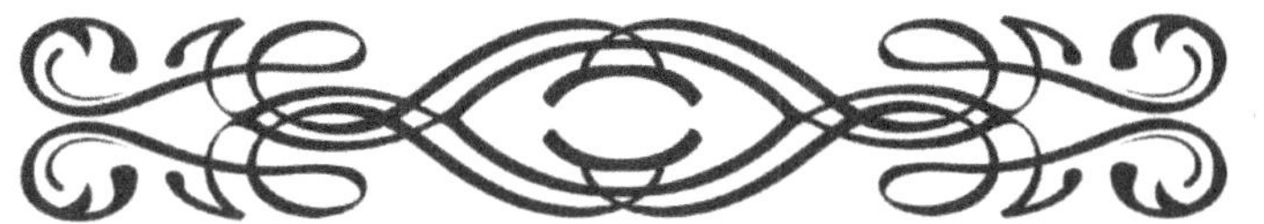

Chapter Eighteen

Her body came alive under his hands as Water Runs Fast massaged her. Now, touching his mouth to hers, her body, leaning into his, vibrated, and he knew, she was his. He opened his mouth to better taste her lips. She did the same and their tongues touched. The heat that ripped through his body at such an intimate action had his hands dropping to her backside and pulling her tight to his throbbing maleness.

Her arms circled his neck. Her fingers tangling in the hair at the back of his neck.

When their mouths parted, they both panted as if they'd climbed to the top of the highest peak.

He wanted to lie her down here, among the scent of pine, earth, and flowering elderberry. He no longer wished to sleep in the unmarried lodge. Having spent the night before with his arms around her, he wanted that every night.

"I need to go. I can't bring trouble to you or this

village." Sun Eyes pressed her hands on his chest, pushing out of his arms.

He grasped her hands, drawing them up to his chest. Water Runs Fast held them there. "I do not want you to leave. I wish you to be my wife."

Sun Eyes' mouth dropped open before snapping shut and she said, "If I became your wife, I would bring trouble to the village. You would make me stay. Not let me get help from my friends." Her voice held conviction. As if she knew what he would or would not do. No one but he knew his heart and his thoughts.

He did not want her to think being his wife meant she would be ordered around. "No. I would not tell you to stay. I would say we must talk to the council. They will help us make decisions. And I would not keep you from your friends."

"You would let me make decisions?"

The awe in her voice made his chest hurt. His people had always used the wisdom of both the men and women of the village to keep everyone safe. "We will make decisions together. You do not tell me and I do not tell you. We talk it over and decide what is best."

"And my friends? They would help us prove I didn't kill Ben and that you did to stay alive."

"I will take you to your friends." It would not only make Sun Eyes happy, it would give him a chance to tell them she would be treasured with him and get the two of them away from Major Litchfield's army until things settled down.

"But they are many miles, days from here." She put her hands on either side of his face. "You would make such a long trip for me?"

He shifted his head and brushed his lips across the

palm of her hand. "For us."

She lowered her head and her soft lips nibbled at his. Just as he engaged in the nibbling, she drew back.

"If you stay true to your word, I would be honored to be your wife." Her voice was husky and her hands skimmed up his chest, reawakening the need in his body.

"We should do the normal courtship," he said through gritted teeth as her hands made a lazy trail up and down his arms.

"What is the normal courtship?" she asked her lips only inches from his.

He thought on that. She did not have family for him to give horses or gifts. His mother had been after him to find a woman from the Big-lodges clan. "Usually the mother of a man who has counted coup or has seen twenty-five summers will choose a wife for him from another clan. It is how we keep our people strong." He knew his mother would be unhappy he had chosen his own wife, but she would be satisfied it was not from their clan.

"Which are you?" her hands stopped moving up and down his arms. They now rested on his chest. Her breath warmed his face when she talked. From the weight of her hands, her head must rest on them.

"We are the Whistling Waters clan."

"Is that why you are Water Runs Fast?" A finger traced the bone that ran from the middle of his chest to his shoulder.

"I am a fast runner and they wished to name me for the clan. My mother's family is of high standing."

"Will you someday be chief?"

He shook his head. "No. There are others more

favored. I only wish to help my people remember the past and not be torn apart by the whites."

Her lips barely touched his. "I would like to help you do that," she whispered across his mouth before she pressed her lips to his.

Freedom dove into the kiss as Swift took control, pressing his lips to hers, his mouth moving, tasting, and taking her breath. Her body began humming. His touch, his lips, his words all made her understand he would not hurt her. He would treat her with respect.

He had asked her to be his wife. Her heart stuttered at the thought. Swift would never turn on her as Ben had. She knew with all her heart Swift was the man who would care for her until she died.

He pulled out of the kiss, holding her head. His desire for her pressed against her lower body. Knowing him as she did, she didn't fear he would take her body without her consent.

The flutters and chirps she'd only barely heard while they talked disappeared, leaving a startling silence.

Swift leaned down and whispered in her ear. "Someone is about. Stay."

His warmth retreated. She wrapped her arms around her and listened.

It felt like hours she stood still, waiting. She had a good idea how to get back to the village, but didn't want Swift to return and worry because she wasn't here. He might think someone had taken her as he'd done at the creek by the cave.

A bird squawk, crickets chirping, and rustling of leaves reignited the evening sounds. She drew in a deep breath. Whatever had caused the unease in the woods was gone. But where was Swift?

As if her wondering conjured him up, a movement to her right caught her attention. She recognized the way the shadow moved.

He stopped beside her. "We must go back. It seems there are some who do not wish us to be alone. They believe you will bring us bad times."

She groped in the dark for his hand. His large one captured hers. His touch comforted and showed her, he was the man she wished to grow old with. "If you can help me return to Shady Gulch, we can get my friends to help. I don't want to cause you trouble with your family. But I do believe we were meant to be together."

He raised their clutched hands and rubbed the back of her hand on his face. "I will not give you up. My vision said you and I will help the Absarokee. We will sleep this night apart and set out for your people tomorrow. When you are ready we will become husband and wife the Absarokee way."

Her heart stuttered in her chest. "What is the Absarokee way?"

He brushed his lips across hers and whispered. "We become one. We share a bed and our bodies."

"What if I fear that…part of becoming your wife?" If she had met Swift before Ben, she was sure she wouldn't even have hesitated. Surely the act of coupling couldn't be as bad as it had been with her husband. Lottie Mae, Savannah and all the other happily married women she knew wouldn't have always had smiling faces if that were true.

But she cringed at the thought of the act.

"We will talk of this as we journey. Now we must get back to the village." He squeezed her hand, leading her back to the village, hand in hand. At his mother's tipi, he entered.

There was a colder greeting than before. Word of Ben being related to the major must have reached Moon Woman.

Water Runs Fast instantly knew his mother had heard about the dead man. He had planned to work out the details for the next day without having to defend Sun Eyes. That would not happen now.

"What has this woman done?" his mother asked.

"Nothing." Water Runs Fast stepped between his mother and the woman he loved. "She was beaten and treated badly by the major's son. I came upon them when he was whipping her." He thumped his chest with a fist. "I tore the whip from his hands and he attacked me. It was him or me."

His mother's gaze dropped to the knife handle sticking out of his moccasin. "It was your knife that killed him?"

He nodded.

Her face fell and her eyes filled with tears. "I do not wish to lose you, too."

Sun Eyes stepped around him and put her arms around his mother. "I don't want to lose him either. My friends in Shady Gulch will help us. But we have to go there so I can explain it all to them."

His mother studied Sun Eyes, then him. "You would go with this woman. To her friends?"

He took two steps to stand beside the two women he loved. One for giving him life and the other for making his heart happy.

"I will go. To tell them we are to be husband and wife and they do not need to worry for her. And for their help to keep the army from hunting her and our people."

His mother held Sun Eyes from her. "When will you become husband and wife?"

"We have talked. On this journey, Sun Eyes will make the decision if she wishes to be my wife." He stared into the golden eyes of his woman and saw she agreed to it being her decision.

His aunt stepped forward. "There is much she must learn." Woman Speaks Softly's face glowed with happiness as she put a hand on Sun Eyes' shoulder.

"I will pack supplies to carry on two horses. And I must speak with Antlers On Wrong." Water Runs Fast grasped Sun Eyes' hand. "I will be here when the last of night slips away."

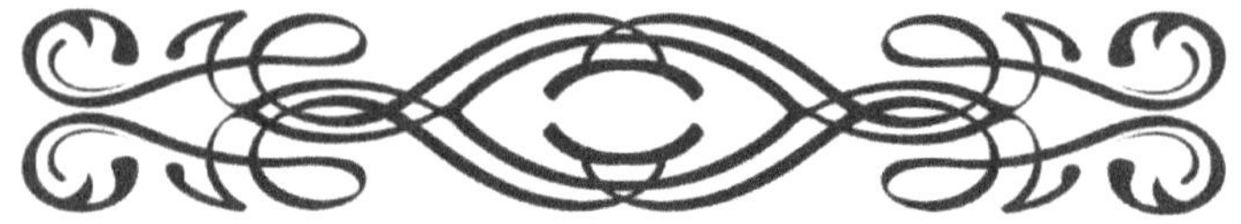

Chapter Nineteen

Even though she'd only met Swift's mother and aunt the day before, she was sad to leave them again so soon. They promised there would be a tipi with gifts waiting for her and Swift when they returned. The thought she would finally have a home and in a village with people who treated her like an equal made her as happy as knowing she would become Swift's wife by the time they returned. She'd have Lark perform a Christian marriage when they arrived in Shady Gulch.

True to his word, Swift swept into the tipi as soon as others began stirring outside. She'd barely slept thinking about traveling again. The only thing that kept her from saying, let's just stay and hope the major never figures it out, was the fact she would be traveling with Swift who would treat her well.

The corncakes she'd made earlier sat on a flat rock. "Eat, then we will leave," she said to Swift, taking him by the arm and leading him to his place by the fire.

"Have you had food?" he asked, picking up a corn cake and sniffing it.

"Yes, and I have my extra set of clothes packed." She ran her hand down the leather dress Woman Speaks Softly insisted she wear. And the supple knee-high moccasins Moon Woman gave her. The footwear felt as if she had nothing on her feet, but kept her from feeling the burrs, rocks, and sticks.

Swift's gaze started at her feet and stopped at her eyes. "You are of the Whistling Water Clan of the Raven People now."

She liked that she belonged and was welcomed. "I think I'm going to like being a Raven People."

A warrior stepped into the tipi, spoke, and everyone started moving quickly.

"What's wrong?" Freedom asked.

"The army is on their way here. We must go." Swift grabbed the leather pouch she'd put her things in and her hand.

Two beautiful horses stood in front of the tipi. Both had leather bags draped over their wooden saddles.

Swift shoved her pouch in one and then grabbed her by the waist, lifting her onto the same horse. "Why aren't we using the horses I gave you?"

Swift didn't answer, he swung up onto his horse and they headed quickly out of the camp the same direction they'd came in.

Once they were in the trees, he set his horse at a trot and she followed. They traveled in silence at a trot for over an hour before Swift slowed his horse and settled alongside of her.

"We are using my horses so no one can recognize the dead man's horses." Swift said, staring forward.

"But the village? The people. The army will find the horses there." Fear tightened her chest. She didn't want to bring trouble to people who would soon be her new family.

Shaking his head, Swift said, "Wolf Tracker took the horses away from the village last night. He is taking them high into the mountains."

That eased her mind a bit. "But won't someone tell the army I was in the village?"

He shook his head. "It would harm everyone for one to say such a thing. All were told last night to not mention you."

"Then we don't have to worry about bein' seen?" she asked.

He shook his head. "The person who told the major about the body and said he had a dark woman with him, had to have seen you together." Swift studied her.

"I was in Milestown with Ben. He beat up an old man who was helpin' me get a stage coach ticket to go home. Then there was the woman at the boardin' house." She couldn't think of anyone else.

"We will stay away from towns." Swift said, with authority.

"Good idea. How long do you think we'll be travelin'?" She remembered it had taken she and Ben almost two weeks to get to Milestown from Shady Gulch. But they'd swung out of the way to see his friend— "I know who told the major. A man named Foster. We spent the night at his soddy." Her insides twisted remembering that night. "He was a nasty person and Ben…" she couldn't tell Swift how her husband had offered her up to the man.

Swift put a hand on her arm. "It was not good?"

"No. I promised Foster's wife, she's Indian, that I'd come get her. Her husband treated her terrible. Just like mine." Anger replaced the shame and disgust. She glanced at Swift. "It's probably a bad idea to try and find Mary and bring her with us?"

"We must stay clear of this man if he is the one accusing you." Swift held her gaze. "We must travel fast and get as far from the Army and our village as possible. When we have traveled five days, we can slow down."

She nodded and fell in behind his horse as he kicked it into a trot.

Many miles were between them and the village, and all Water Runs Fast could think about was making Sun Eyes his wife. They had traveled two nights and three days only sleeping for a few hours before moving on. Tonight, they had settled beside a small stream and made camp.

"Will we only eat pemmican and biscuits this whole trip?" Sun Eyes asked.

"Until we are two more days away." He handed her a tin cup with water. She had insisted they could drink from a cup and not his water pouch.

Her gaze met his. "Your mother and aunt said we should be cleansed by a sweat lodge before we come together as husband and wife. How can we do that while traveling?"

Was the talk about the sweat lodge a way to tell him she was still not ready to become his wife? He would answer her directly and see if she persisted it was necessary. "This is true if we were at the village."

She watched her hands, holding the cup. "Would

washin' in the stream be the same?"

His body tightened at the thought of running his hands all over her. "We would be cleansed." They'd talked while riding side by side. She'd told him how she'd only felt pain at the touch of the man she'd wed and she wasn't sure she'd be able to become Water Runs Fast's wife.

He'd promised they would go slow and if anything hurt, he would stop and they could wait.

Her gaze raised to his face. "I would like to cleanse in the stream and lay with you tonight." She stood, spread their blankets one on top of the other on a grassy spot beside their belongings, and then undressed.

Water Runs Fast was pleased to see she wore nothing under the dress. She came to him in the way an Absarokee woman would. Before he could blink, she walked to the stream and stepped in, sucking in air at the coldness of the water.

He shoved the biscuit in his mouth and chewed as he untied his leggings and breach cloth and walked naked to the stream.

While he'd seen her body unclothed many times, this would be the first time her gaze saw all of him. He knew he was a strong man and that a woman wanted a strong man to protect her and her children.

Sun Eyes was bent at the waist splashing water on her body, with her head toward the middle of the stream.

He walked up behind her and put his hands on her hips. She shot upright and spun in his arms. Their bare bodies touched for the first time and her eyes widened. While her body shook from the cold, he was used to it. Since he was small his mornings started with a dip in the nearest stream, snow or no snow. The icy water made the Absarokee men strong.

Her cold hands grasped his upper arms as her breasts pressed against his chest. They were so firm, yet soft. Her nipples were hard nubs. He grasped her round bottom in his hands and held her close, pushing his hard length against her.

Her eyes widened, but she smiled and wrapped her arms around his neck, pressing her body closer. His hardness was now captured between their bodies and so close to the area he wished to enter. His body quivered with the need to make her his.

Her lips brushed his. He forgot his need for a moment to taste her mouth and settle into the knowledge her power would make him stronger.

When their mouths parted, both panting, he said, "We must cleanse." He released her arms from his neck and she settled on her feet in front of him.

He cupped his hands and trickled water over her body, following each rivulet with his hands, washing away the water and any dirt or sweat. When he had washed her from her head to her feet, he stepped back and held out his arms.

A grin spread across Sun Eye's face and her golden rays flickered moments before she splashed water onto his chest and with as much attention to each inch of his body as he had done with hers, she cleansed him. She held his throbbing length in her hands, much longer than necessary. He was about to tell her to move on when she did, putting a hand between his legs and grasping his sack. His length wept from her touch.

She cleaned the tip and finished cleaning him before linking her hand with his and leading him to the blankets she'd prepared.

Freedom wondered at how she'd been so bold to touch every inch of Swift's magnificent body. After he had cleansed her so gently and warmed her from the inside out, she'd wanted to reciprocate. At first, she'd tentatively touched his man parts, knowing Swift would allow her anything she wished. She'd barely even seen Ben's. He'd just stick his length out of his drawers and shoved it in her. Freedom tossed that thought away. She would never be able to enjoy Swift's hands on her, if she kept remembering the hurt Ben caused her.

She stopped at the bed she'd made from their blankets. Craving his hands on her again, she looped her arms around his neck, pulling herself up to kiss his chin and press her breasts against his strong chest. She'd loved the way it felt earlier in the stream. The sensation of rubbing her nipples across his firm skin had sent tingles all the way to her toes. She enjoyed the sensations that coursed through her body at Swift's touch.

His hands cupped her backside, kneading with just enough pressure to excite her and not hurt. His action also pressed her woman's curls against his hard length. Running her hands up and down his length while washing him had filled her with a power she'd never known.

His head lowered and their mouths met. He no longer held back when their lips touched. His tongue delved into her mouth, and their tongues danced the dance she hoped they did while lying on the blankets.

As if he heard her thoughts, Swift gently lay her down, with his body over hers. She kept her legs locked together. Her mind knew they couldn't couple if she didn't open to him, but her body was saving her from the pain.

He didn't try to spread her legs. He continued to kiss her, while his hands ran up and down her sides, something skimmed across the sides of her breasts and she moaned with delight.

His lips left hers. His hair that had made a curtain around their faces as they kissed, tickled her neck and shoulders before one nipple tightened and grew wet. He suckled her as a babe would do. At first, she wasn't sure what to think. But the sensations of his actions and the disappointment when he stopped had her pulling his head to her other breast.

He latched onto it and her body arched as his hand rested on the curls at the juncture of her legs. The two acts had the area where his hand lay, throbbing. Her body had never felt so alive, and yet, so wanting. She didn't understand all the sensations, but she knew this was something it would only do for Swift. The man who would soon become her husband.

Before she even realized she'd spread her legs, he filled her. He held her tight in his arms and peered into her eyes. "Do I hurt you?" he asked, his eyes filled with concern.

Wonder at the fullness and sensations pulsing in the area that before had hurt, stunned her. She shook her head. "You feel right."

He smiled, kissed her lips, and moved in and out in a rhythm her body responded to. There was no pain. Only the most marvelous sensation of her body being pulled tight like the string on a fiddle bow. Swift plucked her inner strings, making her body quake and spark.

He paused, his arms banded around her, and his seed spilled.

Her body clamped around him, shuddered, and she floated on the clouds.

Water Runs Fast felt his woman's body embrace him and draw his last seed from his sated body. He wrapped his arms around Sun Eyes and kissed her eyelids. The moonlight on her face revealed a smile as sweet as a baby's and as fulfilled as a cougar with a full belly.

He rolled to his back, drawing her onto his body. He remained inside, enjoying the warmth, moisture, and tiny aftershocks.

Her head rested on his chest. Her arms hung over his body, lifeless. But she was alive. Her heart raced, beating against his chest and her breath was still unsteady.

He kissed her head and pulled a blanket over them. While he wouldn't mind enjoying her body more, she was tired.

~*~

Freedom woke because the ground under her wiggled. Why would the ground wiggle? She moved her head. Smooth, firm skin rubbed her face. She wasn't lying on the ground. She was on top of Swift. The night before came rushing back.

He'd coupled with her and she'd enjoyed every second. This was why newly married women beamed. She had been thoroughly loved last night. A smile tugged at her lips. Swift was her husband. He'd made her body hum, her breasts ache to be suckled, and he'd taken her to the clouds. The memories started her body heating. She kissed his chest, slid her hands down his arms, and linked their hands.

He stirred. "Sun Eyes you need your sleep," he said in a sleepy voice.

"I want to do it again, to prove it really wasn't a dream," she said, kissing his neck and finding his lips.

His body moved under her.

She rubbed her core against him and soon felt his hardness grow.

He grasped her waist, slid her up his body, and suckled her breasts. She slid her hands through his hair and held on as his tongue and teeth teased her breasts and made her woman parts throb. When she couldn't stand it any longer, she slid her body down his. Swift's hard length slipped inside, seating so deep she sucked in air from the awareness of his filling her. They rocked together until her body spasmed, Swift called out, and they collapsed together once more.

Chapter Twenty

Now that she was a real wife, one who enjoyed her husband's touch and lying beside him, Freedom rejoiced at the end of each day. No matter how much distance they'd covered, when she lay down next to Swift, her body would forget about the stiffness and her soul would soar among the stars. They'd been pushing for distance between them and the village and fort for over a week. This was the first day Swift hadn't kept them moving from first light until dark.

Dismounting, she discovered she'd started her monthly bleeding. While she hadn't wanted it to come because she'd learned from Moon Woman and Woman Speaks Softly that Crow men felt they would be injured or harmed if they spent time with a woman who was bleeding. It was as if the woman losing blood meant they would as well. But she was glad to see the flow because it meant all the times Ben had entered her, she'd not become with child. That had been a fear at the back of her mind since she and Swift had come together. She didn't know how Swift would deal with raising a child not his own. It could have come between them, because even though she loathed Ben, she would not have parted with her child.

Swift grasped the reins of her horse and sniffed. He peered into her eyes. She could see the questioning in them.

"I have started my monthly," she said, continuing to go about her usual evening tasks. Freedom placed their blankets one on top of the other in a spot that looked well cushioned with grass. She knew they would not come together this night or the next several because of her condition, but when Swift picked up his blanket and placed it far away from hers, tears formed in her eyes.

"Your mother told me you would think my condition would weaken you, but I didn't think you would disown me," she said, unsure if she should approach him or stay her distance even though at this time of the month she wished to be held and comforted. Something she never received from her first husband. She had hoped Swift would be different.

Water Runs Fast stood beside the blanket he'd placed on the ground three horse lengths from Sun Eyes. He didn't like her sleeping alone, but he had been raised to believe when a woman was bleeding her condition could cause any warrior near her to be injured if going on a raid or hunt. While their trip wasn't a raid, he needed to be of strong body to make sure they both arrived at Shady Gulch safe.

"If my mother told you then you know it is so." He had planned to have Sun Eyes cook tonight. But he could not eat the food she had touched. He went to their belongings and pulled out two leave bundles of pemmican and the hard biscuits made of ground roots.

Placing one bundle of leaves, one biscuit, and the metal drinking vessel she liked on a rock between them, Water Runs Fast said, "Here is your food." He nodded to the stream a short distance from them. "You get water there."

Sun Eyes marched over to the rock, snatched the tin vessel in her hand, and strode to the water without a word.

The hurt he had seen in her usually sparkling eyes made his chest ache. He rubbed at the center of his chest with the heel of his hand and tried to remember back to when he was a child and his father was still alive. Had his father stayed away from his mother during her bleeding time? His memory saw her staying in a hut with other women. His grandmother had cooked for his father, sister, and himself. After several days his mother returned and his father welcomed her to his bed.

He stared at the lone figure of Sun Eyes and his body reacted. She'd walked to the stream and removed all of her clothes, she stood in the stream washing.

The body he knew well by now, drew him like a bee to a flower.

It wasn't dark yet. They were no longer in trees. While he enjoyed the sight, he did not want another arriving and see her this way.

"Sun Eyes come. Put your dress on." He stood at the edge of the water. If he leaned out, he could grasp her arm, but years of hearing the tales, he kept his hands to his side.

"You want me out, come and get me," she said, not looking at him.

"I cannot, but I do not wish another to see you."

His words must have settled over her anger.

She glanced around, splashed once more, and walked toward him.

His gut told him to step back but his heart grasped her dress and held it up for her to duck into.

"Not this one. It needs cleaned." She walked by him to the pack and pulled out the dress she'd worn when they arrived at the village. Standing beside the pack, she pulled on the women's leggings, the thin under dress and then her outer dress. She wore all the layers he did not understand. She folded up something, raised her skirt and placed it between her legs, before she sat and tied the moccasins on.

All the time she was dressing, Water Runs Fast watched. He may not be able to touch, but he saw no reason to not look at his wife.

"Would you like me to make you hotcakes?" she asked.

He shook his head. "I cannot eat anything you prepare while you are bleeding."

She glanced at the food he'd placed on the rock and made a face. "Well, I can eat what I make. Please build a small fire."

While she dug in their supplies, he found old dried buffalo dung and long dried grass.

He twisted the grass, putting it in the hole he'd dug with his knife. Then he used his knife and a flint to make sparks and catch the grass on fire. Small flames crackled along the grass and he added the buffalo dung.

By this time, Sun Eyes had the hot cake batter

mixed and placed a heavy pan over the fire on rocks he'd placed for her pan.

She poured the batter in the pan and the smell made his belly talk.

Sun Eyes peered up at him and smiled. "It sounds like your belly would like this better than that." She pointed to the pemmican and biscuit still sitting on the rock.

Did he need to worry about the stories of men becoming weak because of their woman's condition? Afterall, Sun Eyes was his talisman, the person to guide him to help his people.

She flipped the hot cake and pulled a plate closer to the fire. "Would you like the first one?"

He'd heard stories of how some women's beauty and hold on a man could make him do wrong. He'd never believed those stories, always himself being strong against a woman who tried to take him down the wrong path. Now, looking into her eyes, smelling the food she'd cooked, and knowing he would give in, he understood those stories.

She slid the hot cake onto the plate and poured more batter in the pan before picking the plate up and offering it to him. "I've never seen a man grow weak from his wife's monthly. I don't know why the Absarokee believe this way, but I'm pretty sure, you'll be fine eatin' food I prepared."

Water Runs Fast took the plate and sat. Maybe because Sun Eyes wasn't Absarokee he didn't have to worry. He liked the idea of holding her, even if they couldn't come together.

~*~

Freedom was pleased when after Swift ate, he

walked over and put his blanket back with hers. It appeared she'd made him think about the silliness of her making him weak. She walked down to the creek and washed the plates and bowl she'd mixed the batter in.

The sound of horses came from across the creek. She glanced up and her heart stopped. A group of cavalry men were riding their direction. She finished washing the dishes and stood, walking back to their camp.

Swift stood by their horses, his hand near his bow and quiver.

The horses walked through the creek where she'd been moments before and stopped twenty feet away from the small fire that was burning out.

"What are you two doing out here on the prairie?" the man who appeared to be in charge asked.

Unsure if she should speak or Swift, she said, "We're headed to Dakota Territory. My family is expecting me."

The soldier stared at Swift. "Why are you traveling with this Injun?"

"He has scouted for the Army and knows the way," she said.

"You're a strange match, a darkie and an Injun." The man dismounted and handed the reins of his horse to the seated soldier next to him. He walked into their small camp, walked by the blankets placed together, and up to Swift.

"Who are your people?" the soldier asked.

"Whistling Waters clan of Absarokee," Swift said, crossing his arms. "You are of the Seventh Cavalry from Fort Keogh. I have scouted for Colonel Miles."

He shook his head. "Custer should have listened to the Crow scouts. We told them there were many striped-feathers and Lakota waiting for them."

The soldier stared at Swift then spun back to her. "How did you get to Montana Territory?"

"I was escorted out here to see if I would like it. I don't and wish to go home." She wasn't sure if he was fishing for her to say by her husband who was dead.

"Why did you come?" He walked closer to her.

Swift moved as if to step between them. The creak of saddle leather stopped him.

"I was offered marriage, but the man didn't suit me once I arrived." She shrugged. It was as close to the truth as she was going to say.

"Didn't suit you? That's kind of uppity for a darkie." The man towered over her.

"Perhaps I prefer my 'kind'." She dropped her gaze, reverting back to the actions she'd learned as a child in the South. Don't argue with a white and don't stand up to them.

The man laughed. "We could take you to Milestown. You could take a stage from there." He glanced at Swift. "Save you from traveling with an Injun."

Swift did step between them then. "Taking her to Milestown would be backtracking."

Freedom sucked in air. Why had the man wanted to take her back? She was glad Swift knew the country so well. She swallowed the anger she felt toward the soldier and said, "I believe I'll get to the train station in Bismarck quicker with my guide."

The man glared at Swift, who crossed his arms, still standing between the two of them.

"I can assure you, you will regret traveling with a heathen." The soldier remounted his horse and waved his hand. The group turned and trotted back the way they'd come.

Swift watched them until they were small specks and then started gathering their things.

"What are you doing?" she asked, following him around.

"They will come back. We will not be here." He put all their belongings on the horses and then put the leather pouches he had given her for shoes on their way to the village on the horse's hooves. But not before putting wads of grass in the pouches.

"What are you doing," Freedom asked.

"Making sure we cannot be followed."

Chapter Twenty-one

After the arrival of the soldiers, Water Runs Fast was more careful about not leaving any tracks or sign of a camp. He wasn't sure if the arrival of the cavalry was because he'd eaten food prepared by Sun Eyes while she was bleeding, but he was happy when she announced she was done and they could return to touching.

They had traveled through farming country the last two days, skirting the towns but following the long metal tracks of what Sun Eyes called a train. She told him this would bring them to her friends.

The people who saw them traveling together stared, but they didn't appear to be hostile.

"There it is!" Sun Eyes exclaimed and grabbed his arm as a cluster of buildings appeared ahead of them. "I thought I'd never see this place again." She smiled at him and her eyes shone like beams of sunshine.

Her happiness made him wonder if she would

leave this place to return with him to his people. He'd not questioned her returning with him before. He had brought her back to her people because she said they would make sure Major Litchfield didn't harm her. Keeping her safe was the only reason he'd made this trip. He wanted her alive and would do anything including leave her here if need be, but his heart would never be happy again and his vision would never be fulfilled.

Before town, she veered to the right, circling the buildings and riding up to a church.

She dismounted and motioned for him to do the same. "Come on. Savannah will want to meet you."

He slid off his horse, tied both horses to the post in front of the house and walked up to the building with Sun Eyes.

She knocked on the door and waited, a smile on her face. No one answered. She knocked again, her smile fading. "Maybe she's at the church."

Water Runs Fast untied the horses, following her to the church.

Sun Eyes stepped inside and scanned the building. Again, there was no one. "She must be over at the boarding house. If it's Wednesday, Lark is in Bismarck carrying papers for his brother's bank." Her smile returned. "Come on."

He followed her down the street and up to a large home. His worry grew. How could she be happy living in a tipi compared to this structure. It was larger than the long house that had room for all of the people in the village.

She ran up the steps and stopped. She glanced over her shoulder. "Tie the horses and come on." She held out a hand to him.

Water Runs Fast tied the horses to the hitching rail and joined her in front of the door.

This time she didn't knock. Sun Eyes pushed the door open and yelled, "I'm back!"

A tall yellow-haired woman with her hand on a bulge in her dress stepped out of a door to their right. Her face lit up. "Freedom! Oh, my word! We've been worried sick about you." The woman pulled Sun Eyes into an embrace. He saw tears in the woman's eyes.

An older plump woman hurried down the long room toward them. "Freedom? Did I hear Freedom is here?" She also pulled Sun Eyes into an embrace.

He stood inside the door watching as a smaller woman with yellow hair also arrive and embrace his wife. She was clearly loved by these women. How had she thought the man who beat her would care for her more than these people?

The pounding of someone running, had a woman appear from steps to the upper part of the house. "Freedom? I thought sure you were dead." This woman had dark hair and her face wasn't as open and happy as the others.

"I'm alive, thanks to Swift." Freedom slipped out of Belle's embrace and walked back to the door, grasping her husband's hand. Well, her husband in her mind and his.

Her friends all stared at her husband, then started asking questions so fast she couldn't hear a single one.

"Mrs. Dearlin', do you happen to have anythin' we can eat? I'm sick of hotcakes, pemmican, and a hard biscuit the Crow Indians make." She smiled at the woman who had become like a second mother to her.

"Of course, I do. Come sit in the kitchen. Liesa, run over and tell Beau and Jules, Freedom is here." The older woman led them down the hall to the kitchen.

Swift pulled a bit on her hand as she led him deeper into the house. She wondered if he'd ever been in a house. She glanced over her shoulder. His brow was wrinkled and worry glistened in his eyes. She squeezed his hand, making him look at her. She smiled and hoped he understood he was safe here.

Savannah was glowing. Her belly was protruding, telling the world she was with child. Freedom smiled at her friend as she motioned for her and Swift to sit at the end of the table.

After they were seated, Darie set glasses of water in front of them, and then Mrs. Dearling placed plates of roast beef, bread, and jam on the table within reach.

The back door burst open and Beau stopped just inside. Jules pushed him out of the way and the two men strode toward her.

Swift shot to his feet, ready to defend.

"It's all right, Swift. They are my friends." Freedom put a hand on his arm, lowering him back to his seat and stood, giving Beau a hug and then Jules.

Beau took a seat to her right and Jules to Swift's left. Everyone else sat down around the table.

"What happened?" Beau asked. "We planned to come looking for you if we didn't receive a letter from you this month."

Freedom had put food on her plate. She put the fork down as tears burned the back of her eyes. She peered around the table. "You all tried to tell me about Ben. I should have listened." Tears streamed down her face. "Once he had me far enough away from here, he changed." She swiped at the tears. Beau handed her a handkerchief. She scrubbed the tears from her face and blew her nose before continuing.

"He was awful." She glanced around at each of the women who had been badly hurt by a man before Beau took them in. The sympathy in their eyes told her she didn't need to say more.

"How did you get away?" Belle asked.

Freedom smiled at Swift. But she didn't want to tell the others what had happened to her. "Water Runs Fast, only I call him Swift, came along."

"Ben just let you go with this man?" Jules asked, his gaze boring into her.

She shook her head. This was why she'd made this journey back to these people. To get their help. But she couldn't say, couldn't tell them how bad her decision had been.

As if he realized her pain, Swift, grasped her hand and stared at Beau. "I left my hunting party to dream. Instead, I heard a cry and found a man whipping this woman."

Everyone at the table gasped.

Freedom squeezed her eyes tight. She didn't want to see their disbelief.

"I stop him. He attack Water Runs Fast. I fought back. He die by my knife."

A hand touched her chin and she opened her eyes. Swift peered down at her and smiled.

"She tell me her name is Freedom. But all I see is the sunlight in her eyes. She is Sun Eyes to me."

A collective sigh from the women had Freedom studying her friends. He had won them over.

She glanced at Beau. He was frowning.

He studied the two of them and asked, "Are you here because Major Litchfield is looking for you?"

Freedom blinked her eyes and stared at him. "How did you know?"

"That was the only reason I agreed to you marrying Ben. He'd told me he was Major Litchfield's son. I figured he would be like his father. The major has a reputation for being fair."

"But Ben told me he didn't like his father and the things he did." She gasped. "He was the complete opposite of his father."

"We hear a man tell Major Litchfield Sun Eyes killed his son. She say you were her friends and would help her be safe." Swift's gaze landed on each person at the table.

"We will help," Savannah said. Then she turned to her brother. "If this Litchfield has a reputation for being fair, once he hears how his son treated Freedom and that Water Runs Fast was only saving her, he'll understand."

Freedom studied Beau. He didn't look as convinced.

"Do you think there is a way you can help us?" She glanced at Swift. "We have to go back to the village. They need us."

He smiled. The worry that had made his features so stern now relaxed.

Beau stood. "Eat and get cleaned up. I'll go talk with Tuck and see if we can't come up with something by the time Lark gets back from Bismarck."

She'd been right, it was Wednesday. "There's something else Lark has to do when he gets back."

Everyone stared at her.

She smiled. "He has to marry Swift and I."

Their faces all fell.

"Freedom! Y'all have known each other less time than you knew Ben and…" Savannah glanced at Swift and back at her.

"Just because a man saves you doesn't mean you have to marry him," Belle said, nodding toward Beau.

"We are already husband and wife by my people," Swift said. He stood. "We do not need your word if we are to live at the village."

Freedom stared at all the shocked faces. "It's true. By the Crow customs, we are married. I wanted to make it true by our customs."

Jules stood. "Come. I'll take you to get a bath." He motioned to Swift.

She knew Jules wouldn't hurt her husband, only talk to him. And in a much kinder way than Beau when he was upset. "It's all right. Jules will show you where to get cleaned up. I'll be right here when you return." She kissed his cheek and he stood, following Jules out of the room.

"How are you married by their customs?" Liesa asked.

"He is a strong man," Savannah said.

Belle just stared at her, and Mrs. Dearling huffed, moving to clear the table.

Freedom told the three woman she'd lived with about how kind and caring Swift had been, taking care of her when she couldn't take care of herself and how he'd not taken advantage of her as her husband had.

By the time she finished, Darie and Mrs. Dearling had a steaming tub of water ready for her to soak in.

~*~

Water Runs Fast followed the man the color of Sun Eyes out of the home and over to his horse.

"Do you have clean clothes?" Jules asked in a way he'd not heard before.

Water Runs Fast glanced down at his leather shirt and leggings. Sun Eyes had insisted he put on the shirt when they started seeing more people. "These will do. I am not dirty."

"If you aren't dirty, what is the smell?" the man made a face.

This man was insulting him, acting as if he were an animal. "I bathe each morning as the sun rises."

"In hot water?" Jules asked.

"No. Only the weak use hot water. Cold water makes Water Runs Fast strong." He puffed out his chest. He'd been washing every morning of his life in cold water to make his body stronger.

"Hot water cleans better. Come on. While you are scrubbing, I'll bring you clean clothes." The man pointed to Water Runs Fast's long hair. "What about a haircut?"

He stopped and glared at Sun Eye's friend. "A Crow warrior's strength comes from his hair. It will not be cut."

Jules put up his hands in surrender. "As long as you wash it when you take a bath."

Why did this man like cleanliness?

The man stopped at a small building on the edge of town. "This is the bath house. I'll pay for the bath and go get you clean clothes."

"You find leggings and shirt of leather?" he asked.

"I'll see what I can do." Jules walked into the building.

Water Runs Fast followed and was surprised to see a small man with different color skin than he'd seen before. His eyes were different and he spoke even more strange than Jules.

The little man took money and hurried around a wall made of Army tent material.

"He be gettin' your bath ready. When he calls you back, take off your clothes and get in the water. I'll be back."

Water Runs Fast didn't wait for the little man to return. He stepped behind the tent wall and was surprised. The steam curling up from the water in the tub reminded him of the sweat lodge. Perhaps this was the white man's sweat lodge.

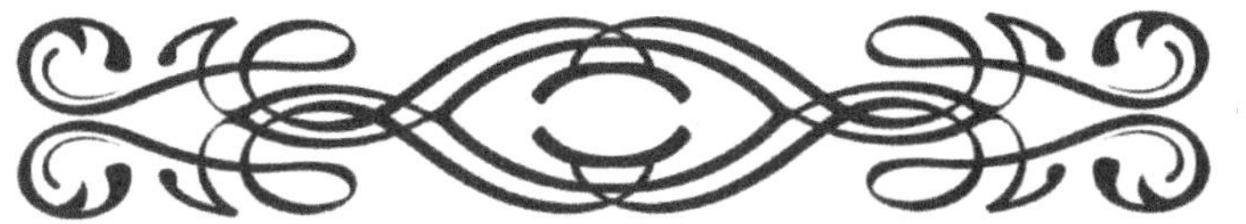

Chapter Twenty-two

Freedom felt better than she had the last two months. Her body and hair were clean and smelled of lilacs from the fancy soap Savannah had given her before she'd stepped into the tub. She wore one of her old dresses that she'd been unable to take with her when she'd left.

Sitting at the kitchen table, Liesa was on one side brushing and braiding her hair. While she was dressed in her usual clothes, she wanted Swift to see she still wore the braids of his people and the moccasins. She'd never had anything that was so comfortable on her feet.

"Do you think Beau, Tuck, and Lark will be able to figure out how to contact the major?" she asked no one in particular. She trusted Beau would know what to do, and she and Swift wouldn't be wanted by the army soon. But until then, she worried for both their safety.

"I'm sure once they all put their heads together thangs will be set to right," Savannah said, sitting at the end of the table, sipping tea.

"I hope so. I can help Swift's people. Teach them better ways to cook and use the supplies the army gives them. I can show them how to make clothes from cloth since they will no longer have buffalo hides and the other animals are becoming scarce." She sighed. "Their whole way of life has been changed since the army put them on a reservation." She felt for the Crow, Cheyenne, Sioux, Arapaho and the other tribes Swift had told her about who were on reservations and some of them weren't even on land they'd lived on before.

"Are you sure you want to go back and live with Indians?" Liesa asked.

Before she could answer, the front door opened and footsteps hurried down the hall.

"It is you!" Lottie Mae pulled Freedom into a hug. "We've been so worried about you." She held her back and looked at her. "Marriage has been good?"

A sound in the hall caught Freedom's gaze. Her heart lodged in her throat and her eyes scanned her husband from his moccasin clad feet up his trousers, to the white shirt pulled tight across his chest and sleeves rolled up to his elbows, showing off his muscular forearms. His shiny black hair hung down his chest and arms, stopping half way. He'd used the bear grease and made the long bangs at his forehead stand up.

She stepped out of Lottie Mae's embrace and walked over to Swift. "This marriage is goin' very well." She smiled up at Swift. He smiled at her, but his usual good humor didn't shine in his eyes.

Lottie Mae stared at Swift and then down at Freedom. "This isn't the man you left here with."

"It's a story I don't feel like repeatin' right now."

She glanced at Swift and decided it would be best if they had some time alone. "We'll be in the parlor." She slid her hand down to grasped his and led him down the hall to her favorite room in the boarding house.

Once they were in the room, she faced him and asked, "What's wrong?"

The hand that she didn't hold, moved up and down. "These are not my clothes."

"You look handsome in them," she said and that made his frown even deeper. "What did I say wrong?"

"You would like me better if I dressed as a white?"

"No. I said you look handsome in the clothes. You are also strikin' in your own clothes." She ran a hand up his forearm. "I like how this shirt," she ran her hand across his chest, "shows how strong your chest is. Your leather clothing hides your body."

His eyes lit as her hand continued to caress his chest. He placed a hand over hers, stopping her movement. "I would think you prefer that the Absarokee only wear leggings in the warm weather."

"Oh, I do. But here, the people, especially the women, are not used to seeing men without shirts."

He put his arm around her drawing her close. "I will wear this for you, now. When we leave, I will wear my clothes."

"Thank you." She kissed him and he drew it out.

"Ahem."

Before Freedom could see who stood in the doorway, Swift had her tucked behind him and he faced the door.

"We need to talk," Beau said.

Freedom stepped around her husband and grabbed his hand, leading him over to the settee. "What about?"

Behind Beau stood Tuck, Jules, and Lark. She hadn't realized it was getting that late in the day that the train from Bismarck had arrived.

Lark walked past the others and put his arms around her. "It's good to see you. Savannah has been worried sick. We've prayed for you every night."

"Thank you." She grasped her husband's hand. "Water Runs Fast, this is Reverend Lark Webster, Savannah's husband. And that," she pointed to Tuck who was eyeing Swift critically, "is Sheriff Blake."

Swift nodded to each of the men. She drew him down on the settee beside her. "Can you help us?"

Lark and Tuck stood while Jules and Beau sat in the only other chairs available.

"We've decided it would be best to send someone to talk with Major Litchfield," Beau said, watching Swift.

"But that would be a month before we hear anything." Freedom glanced at her husband. "We can't be away from the village that much longer. Swift's mother, aunt, and nieces depend on him."

"We're thinking about all of us, well Tuck, Jules, you two and myself going as far as Milestown," Beau said. "Tuck and I'll go on to the fort and talk to the major while you, Jules, and Water Runs Fast wait for us to return with the answer from the major."

"Won't I need to tell him how I was treated?" Her face heated thinking about telling someone she didn't know how his son had beat her.

"We'll see what he says first," Tuck said. "Could be he already knows the type of man his son was. Which would make it easier for you. If he didn't, we'll have to find people to tell him."

Freedom knew of three people who could tell him. "There's the man in Milestown who offered to buy my stage coach ticket for me when I told him I was gettin' away from a mean husband." Her chest tightened. "I hope he's still alive." She told them about Ben hearing the man ask about a ticket to Shady Gulch and beating the man to find out where she was. She peered into Beau's eyes. "He took the money you gave me and wouldn't give it back. As far as I know it was on him when he died." She glanced at Swift. "He wouldn't let me go back and get it." She rocked sideways, bumping her husband's arm, "Or my shoes. He didn't want us to be found with the body."

"Is there anyone else who could tell the major how you were treated?" Beau asked.

"He stayed away from people other than Milestown. The woman at the boarding house can tell you how he dragged me out of there." A thought struck. "Mary! He did take me to a soddy in the middle of nowhere. A friend of his…" She glanced at Swift then to Beau. "The man we think said I killed Ben. Foster was his name. His wife, Mary, was scared to death of Ben. That's when I really started to realize what kind of a monster he was." She shuddered. "I promised Mary I'd come back and get her. Foster treated her as bad as Ben treated me."

Beau nodded. "We'll do that after we get the major to excuse you from his son's death."

Maybe all of this will do some good for Mary. The woman deserved a better life than she had.

"When do we leave?" Swift asked.

"The day after tomorrow. I have some things to clear up with my deputy," Tuck said.

"And we'll have to see if Manfred and Lottie Mae can help in the saloon while Jules and I are gone." Beau glanced over at his business partner who nodded.

Freedom scanned each one of the men present. "I'm sorry I dragged all of you into this."

Lark shook his head. "We all had bad feelings about the man you married. But he knew what to say to make us think you would be happy with him."

"He did have two sides to him. When it got him what he wanted he could be as smooth and nice as a gentleman. But most of the time he relished bossin' people around and hurtin' them when they didn't do his biddin'."

Swift's arm wrapped around her shoulders. She'd found a good man. She planned to show him how much he meant to her.

"We'll leave Friday morning at first light. According to Tuck, if we head straight toward Milestown, we should be there on Monday." Beau stood. "Jules will get the supplies together. Let him know what you'll need."

"We have everything we need with us," Swift said.

Jules stood and studied him. "You only have two small pouches. We have four days travel to make."

Freedom smiled. "Those two small pouches held everything we needed for ten days. You can just get enough food for all of us."

Jules stared at her before he and the others left the room.

Water Runs Fast was glad when the men all left. While they believed they could help Sun Eyes, he did not believe they would help him. But as long as she was free, he would be too, even if he were locked up behind bars or hanged.

"Why do you look so grim?" Sun Eyes asked.

"These men will help you. I am certain."

"But you don't think they will help you?" She put her hands on either side of his face.

He liked when she did this and he could stare into her beautiful eyes.

"You listen to me. They are my family and because they are, they will help you because I love you."

"Anyone who knows you loves you," he said. Meaning every word. His mother and sister had opened their arms to her as did the man who tried to help her in Milestown. She was a person who was instantly liked.

She pressed her lips to his and drew back when he started to take the contact to a more intimate encounter. "And everyone who meets you loves you. By the time we get to Milestown, the others will have learned more about you, and they will work as hard to keep you free as they do me." She stood. "Come on, we have to find out what they are going to do about sleeping arrangements." She walked to the door of the room, leading him. A glance over her shoulder and she said, "Men aren't allowed to sleep in the boarding house."

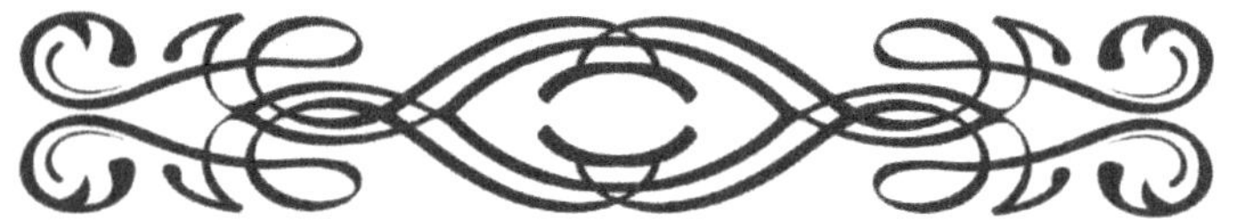

Chapter Twenty-three

Freedom was disappointed when at supper Mrs. Dearling announced they weren't married in the Lord's eyes and therefore, Freedom would sleep in her room and Water Runs Fast would sleep in a room Beau paid for in the closest hotel.

The uncertainty in Swift's eyes, told her he wouldn't use the room unless she was with him. He would be uncomfortable walking into the building alone.

She put a hand on his leg under the table to show solidarity with him. She'd sneak out of the boarding house and join him at the hotel.

After that announcement, Mrs. Dearling went on to say Lark had agreed to marry them the next day. It would just be friends, with dinner at the boarding house afterwards.

"I would like the weddin' with only friends present, but I want a picnic." Freedom glanced at Swift.

"I want this weddin' to be different than the last. I want this one to be a day we don't forget."

"Where do you want the picnic?" Darie asked. She and Mrs. Dearling were the only ones at the boarding house.

Freedom stared at Swift. She loved the spring where Lottie Mae and Manfred were building their house. But it also held the memory of picking the wrong man the first time. Swift smiled at her, his head cocked sideways slightly. Celebrating their wedding in that spot would be the perfect way to prove to herself, she'd made the right decision this time.

"I'd like to have it at Lottie Mae and Manfred's place." She glanced at Swift. "We could go talk to them after supper."

He nodded.

"Are you sure? That's a piece to go for a picnic," said Mrs. Dearling.

"It's not that far. We can rent two wagons from the livery and everyone go out at the same time." Freedom smiled. She liked the idea of celebrating out in the open and knew Swift would like it better too.

"It has been beautiful weather, but getting hotter each day," Darie said.

"All the better to have the picnic in the shade of the trees by their spring." She faced Swift. "It's a beautiful place you'll like."

He smiled. "With you all things are beautiful."

When she glanced around the table the two women were smiling at Swift. This time she didn't have any objections or worries. He was the man for her.

As soon as dinner finished, she grabbed Swift's hand. "Come on, let's go ask Lottie Mae and Manfred."

She glanced over at Mrs. Dearling. "When you take the dinners to the saloon, would you ask Beau about getting the wagons?" The other women were working at the saloon. And now that they were down to just Belle and Liesa, Mrs. Dearling took their meal over to them, and they took turns eating in the backroom.

"I will and I'm sure he'll be pleased to do it." The older woman smiled and waved her hand. "Go talk to the Albrechts. I'll leave the light on in the parlor for you, Freedom." The stern look Mrs. Dearling cast her direction, was a sure implication that she'd better sleep in the boarding house tonight.

Freedom sighed. She didn't want to leave Swift alone in the hotel, but she didn't want to disappoint Mrs. Dearling either.

Her steps were slow as they left the boarding house and walked down the street toward Manfred's Blacksmith shop.

"Why are you taking tiny bird steps?" Swift asked.

She glanced over at him. "To spend more time with you."

He stopped and tipped her face upward. "Then smile and do not act as if you are walking to your death."

Freedom laughed. "I'm sorry. I was feeling sorry for myself because I can't join you at the hotel tonight." She linked her arm in his and they continued walking.

She nodded at the few people they met. Most stared but didn't say anything.

At the blacksmith shop, Swift stopped and stared. "Your friend lives here?"

"In the back."

"This is funny place to have a picnic. And we can

walk. There is no need for wagons."

Freedom laughed again. She sobered at Swift's confused expression. "They live here now, but where I want to have the picnic is that way." She pointed north. "Manfred has property that they are building a house on."

Swift smiled. "I would like being far from town."

"I thought as much." She walked down the side of the shop to the new door Manfred had put on the back of the building that allowed Lottie Mae to enter and leave without having to walk through the dirty work area.

She knocked on the fresh wood and waited.

The door opened and Manfred ducked his head to see who they were.

Water Runs Fast saw the large man in the doorway and instinctively moved to protect Sun Eyes. He'd never seen one with such wide shoulders and his head was above the door until he ducked down.

"Freedom! It is goot to see you!" the man said with the same excitement as the others.

It was clear his Sun Eyes meant a lot to a lot of people.

"Manfred! You look as big as ever," she said and the man laughed. His laughter rumbled around inside the building and out the door.

"Come in. Lottie will be happy." The man stepped back.

Freedom caught Water Runs Fast's hand and led him into a small room with two chairs and a small table. The man took up most of the room.

"Manfred, let's take our guests across the street to the park. This room is too small to entertain." The woman with the red hair shooed them all out of the building like they were small children playing where they shouldn't.

At the park, the woman and Freedom sat on a seat for two. He and the large man sat on the ground in front of them.

"Why did you two come to see us?" the woman asked.

"Lark is going to marry us—" Sun Eyes started.

"I thought you said he was your husband." Lottie Mae said, her gaze landing on him.

Water Runs Fast returned the woman's scrutiny.

"We are in the eyes of the Crow, but I'd like to be in the eyes of God. So Lark is marrying us tomorrow, and we'd like to have the wedding and a picnic afterwards at your property." Sun Eyes smiled at the woman and then the man.

"That is wonderful idea!" the large man said, smiling.

"I agree," the woman said, smiling at her husband.

Swift could see the two were happy together. He glanced at Sun Eyes. Her love of these two people glowed in her eyes. She reached out her hand and he captured it. "I want this marriage to Water Runs Fast to last until my death and I want the memory of our marriage here, in Shady Gulch, to be happy."

"You already look happier and more content than the last one," Lottie Mae said, her glance settled on Water Runs Fast. "You have made my friend the happiest I have ever seen her. While I'm going to miss her, I'll know she is happy and you are taking care of her."

"Her happiness makes my heart sing." He smiled at

Sun Eyes.

"Where are you staying tonight?" the large man asked.

Sun Eyes wrinkled her nose. Water Runs Fast thought it was cute, but didn't say so, knowing she was showing her irritation at the sleeping arrangements.

"Mrs. Dearling says because I'm not married in God's eyes, I'm sleeping in the boarding house and Beau rented a room for Water Runs Fast." She squeezed the hand still holding hers. "I'd rather stay with him at the hotel. He's not going to like being there alone."

He glanced at his wife. Did she think he was scared to sleep alone in a building? "I have slept in barracks with soldiers as a scout. I do not fear sleeping in a building."

"Then I'm scared of sleeping alone." She gave him a half smile.

The couple laughed.

"I think she just wants an excuse to stay with you tonight," Lottie Mae said.

Water Runs Fast puffed out his chest. He was happy she wished to be with him always. "I will make it happen."

"You'll have to tell us how you do it," the woman said, smiling. "I'm guessing Mrs. Dearling could use help in the morning with the food for the picnic?"

"If you don't mind," Sun Eyes said, still smiling at him.

She liked the idea of him helping her stay with him this night.

"I'll be there as soon as I get Manfred's breakfast ready." The woman stood. "We'll let you two go plot

Freedom's escape from the boarding house."

The big man laughed and gracefully rose to his feet, taking his wife's hand. "I will see you both tomorrow." The two walked back to the shop.

"They are nice people," he said, helping Freedom to her feet.

"They are. And they are a wonderful couple." She put her hands on his shoulders. "How are you getting me out of the boarding house?"

"You walk in, blow out the light, and walk with me to the hotel." He nuzzled her neck. "We will be together always."

Freedom liked his comment and marveled at his plan. It was so simple, she grinned at the simplicity, and how, as long as the light went out, Mrs. Dearling would think she was upstairs in her bed.

They walked back to the boarding house and not one light was on, there was light coming from the kitchen and the parlor.

"I don't think we'll be able to douse the light and leave," she said.

Swift stopped on the porch and drew her to him. "Tell me of your marriage ceremony," he said. "Why does Mrs. Dearling say you cannot sleep with me?"

"It is the way of our people that the man and woman cannot have come together until after the preacher has said the words that bind them. This will be the ceremony tomorrow." She could see he was thinking about what she'd said.

He nodded. "As the missionaries have tried with our people. But it is when the bodies come together that the two are truly bound together. Words before only say how to treat each other."

"Ben said the words and behaved the opposite. The words mean little to me. Your actions and feeling your love means more." She stepped close enough their bodies touched. Having a wedding would make her friends, and her family when she wrote them, happy. For her, knowing Swift loved her meant more than all the words Lark could say at the ceremony in the morning.

"We will make your friends happy. You will stay here this night." His arms embraced her and he brushed his lips across hers. "Tomorrow night, we will come together again."

"You don't mind sleeping in the hotel by yourself?" Not that she thought he'd be scared, but more uncomfortable.

"I would prefer you by my side, but can wait." He released her.

"Be here for breakfast," she said to his back as he strode away from her.

He stopped at the street and said, "I will be here at first light."

Freedom watched until he dissolved into the dark night before she entered the boarding house. Voices in the kitchen drew her down the hall.

Mrs. Dearling and Darie were making a cake.

"I don't need a cake," she said.

They both spun from where they'd been hunched over the table and stared at her.

"Everyone else will enjoy it on the picnic," Mrs. Dearling said. "You should go on up to bed and get a good night's sleep."

"I can help. I'm the one putting you to all this trouble." She walked further into the room and sniffed.

"Is that chicken frying?"

"We are getting the food ready for tomorrow. That way we won't have to worry about it in the morning," Darie said.

Freedom smiled. Those were the most words the young woman had ever said to her at once. The girl had come to them a year ago. She'd been so traumatized by her attack she hadn't talked for months and had refused to go to church or about town. It seemed she was slowly returning to herself. This was the wonderful work Beau, Jules, and Mrs. Dearling did with damaged women.

That reminded her of Mary. "If all goes well, when Beau returns, he'll have an Indian woman with him. Mary has a mean husband and would like to get away from him. I told her I'd help her and Beau would take her in."

Mrs. Dearling studied her. "We take in any woman who needs help."

"I know. She's a sweet woman. About my age and her family gave her to this man who is cruel. She said she can't go to her family or she'll be punished for not staying with him."

The older woman tsked. "That's not good. We'll take her in with open arms."

"Thank you. I'm tired. I think I will go to bed. See you in the morning." Freedom walked down the hallway and stopped at the open door, staring out the screen door. Her heart and body wanted to walk out the door and be with Swift. However, her head knew that to show respect to Mrs. Dearling she should remain in her room. In her short time with Swift, she'd realized doing what gathers others respect is more important than her own wishes.

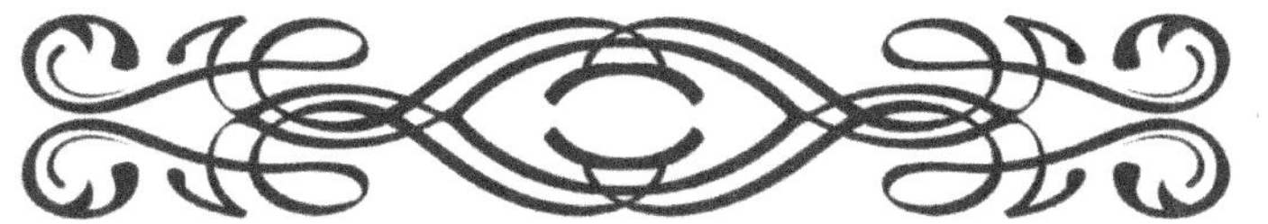

Chapter Twenty-four

The church had small bunches of wildflowers tied to the ends of the pews when Freedom walked in wearing a pale orange dress with long sleeves and lace that Savannah had brought over to the boarding house that morning.

Freedom hadn't been able to talk to Swift all morning. Mrs. Dearling had Beau take him to breakfast at a café to keep him away from her. They were all treating this wedding as if it were her first, which she found endearing, but also aggravating.

Finally, walking up the aisle of the church, she saw Swift. He stood with his hands to his side, watching her approach, dressed in the same clothing he'd worn the day before, only with a fancy suit coat over the shirt. It had to be one of Beau's jackets.

Freedom stopped beside Swift. He smiled and grasped her hands.

Lark read through the usual wedding promise.

They both said "I do" at the proper times.

"I now pronounce you Mr. and Mrs…" Lark stared at them. "I'm not sure what to call you."

"Mr. and Mrs. Swift," Freedom said.

"You may kiss the bride," Lark said to her husband.

Swift held her head and brushed his lips across hers. Their friends cheered, and he grasped her hand, turning them to face the people who were present.

Mrs. Dearling dabbed a handkerchief to her eyes.

Freedom laughed. She couldn't remember being this happy.

"The wagon is waiting to take us to Manfred's place," Beau said, by way of rounding them all up.

At the wagon, Swift picked her up in his arms and placed her on the hay that someone had put in the back of the wagon, no doubt, for padding.

Lark helped Savannah into a four-seated buggy. Jules helped Mrs. Dearling into the back seat and sat beside her. Beau climbed up onto the seat of the wagon and Tuck mounted his horse. Manfred helped Lottie Mae, Darie, Belle, and Liesa into the back of the wagon before plopping onto the seat next to Beau.

Freedom smiled at everyone and hugged her husband.

The wagon lurched forward and Swift's arms circled around her, pulling her tight to his side. Those in the back of the wagon sat facing one another, their backs against the sides of the wagon. Lottie Mae sat beside Freedom with Belle, Darie, and Liesa facing them.

"This was a fun idea, having a picnic," Lottie Mae said. "We don't get out here enough. This house has to be finished by January.”

“Why don’t you stay out here and work on the house?” Swift asked.

“Because we need the money Manfred makes at his blacksmith shop and this weekend and week we’ll be helping at the saloon.” Lottie Mae glanced at her husband’s back. “I wouldn’t do it if Manfred wasn’t going to be there.”

Freedom understood. She never wanted to set foot in the saloon again. She loved Beau and everyone she worked with at the saloon and was thankful it and Beau had been there when she needed something to do to stay alive, but she didn’t care to dance and sing and serve drinks ever again.

“Why does it have to be finished by January? I would think you’d want it done before the first snow,” Belle said.

Lottie Mae’s pale cheeks splashed dark red. She leaned forward, motioning for everyone else to do the same.

Freedom slipped out of Swift’s arm and leaned forward like the other women.

“I’m with child but haven’t told Manfred yet. I plan to tell him while we’re out at our place,” Lottie Mae whispered.

Everyone started congratulating her in whispers.

“It’s quiet back there. Are you all torturing Water Runs Fast?” Beau asked.

Darie, Freedom, and Liesa giggled. Belle rolled her eyes, and Lottie Mae said, “It’s women talk. The stuff you always leave the room when we talk about it.”

Beau glanced over his shoulder. “Water Runs Fast would you like to join Manfred and me at the front of the wagon?"

"No. I am happy," Swift said, putting his arm around Freedom's shoulders. They exchanged a gaze, and she couldn't wait until she was carrying his child.

By the time they arrived at Manfred and Lottie Mae's place the sun was beating down and they were all hot and thirsty.

Mrs. Dearling handed out jars of lemonade.

Lottie Mae and Manfred showed Freedom and Swift their framed-up house. Freedom was happy for her friend. "This is going to be comfortable and just the right distance from town."

"I love it here and can't wait to start a family." Lottie Mae's eyes sparkled.

Freedom took the hint. "Let's go see if they need help." She tugged on Swift's hand, leading him back to the bustle going on by the spring. She wanted Lottie Mae to have the time to tell her husband the good news.

Beau, Jules, Lark, and Tuck had set up a table using the lumber for the house. Savannah sat on a bench also made from the lumber. The other women were setting the food on the table.

"Ja! Ja! Ja!" Shouted Manfred from inside the structure.

Freedom caught Swift's gaze and they smiled.

"Land sakes, what has gotten into that man?" Mrs. Dearling asked.

Manfred stepped out of the door carrying Lottie Mae. They both had smiles as bright as the noon sun. "We will have child!" Manfred said before kissing his wife.

Everyone congratulated the couple. Mrs. Dearling had tears streaming down her face for the second time today. Freedom hugged the older woman. "Your family is growing. First Savannah and Lark having a child and now these two."

"It is a blessing. I can't wait to be a grandmother." Mrs. Dearling studied her. "I won't get to hold your children."

"We'll come visit and you are all welcome to visit us any time you want." Freedom studied her husband, shaking hands with Manfred. He would bring her here whenever she wished. Of that she was certain.

Everyone calmed down and dug into the cold fried chicken, bread, preserves, pickles, and cake. The sun had started to cast cooler beams by the time everyone loaded back up into the buggy and wagon.

This time however, Manfred insisted Lottie Mae ride in the back seat with Mrs. Dearling and Jules had to ride in the wagon. As was Jules way, he quietly did as requested and sat beside Freedom on the ride back to town.

"I would like to say, this wedding is more suited to you," he said in a quiet voice.

Across from them, Belle sat between the two smaller women, Darie and Liesa. The smaller women leaned their heads on Belle who also had her eyes closed. They had to be thankful Beau had closed the saloon today and tonight for them to all be at the wedding and picnic.

"Why is it more suited?" Freedom asked as Swift gently squeezed the hand he held. She glanced at him, smiled, and returned her attention to Jules.

"You arc happy this day, instead of uncertain. It be easy to see this man, he cares for you." Jules nodded to Swift.

She motioned to the women across from her. "I hope they find love soon, and you and Beau. You all deserve to have someone who loves you in your lives."

"Someday. My friend and I, we have women to help before that happens."

"You don't want to wait too long. You both deserve happiness too." She leaned against Swift. She'd found her happiness.

"Oui. The day will come." He leaned back and pulled his narrow-brimmed hat over his eyes.

Swift wrapped both his arms around her, pulling her back against him. "Rest. We will have a long journey tomorrow."

She was willing to rest now, so when they settled into his hotel room later, she would be ready to complete this wedding ceremony.

Water Runs Fast heard pieces of what Sun Eyes and the dark man, Jules, said. She wished her friends to all have the happiness she did. That warmed his chest along with the way she'd looked at him when her friend talked about being with child. Sun Eyes wished to carry his children. This would make his mother and all the band happy. There was nothing more revered in their people than children. It meant they would go on and their stories would be told.

He would do whatever it took to make sure he and Sun Eyes never parted. Not only did he wish to have children with her, but he wished to have her always by his side. They had to make the major understand that his son had been a mean person.

Beau and the sheriff said they would all ride hard until they reached Milestown. Then it would be a matter of waiting while those two went on to Fort Custer and talked with the major.

He wasn't sure how the people of Milestown would like having two brown-skinned people and an Absarokee in town for however long it took Beau and the sheriff. He and Jules would have to be vigilant.

Following the buggy, the wagon lumbered into town. Both stopped at the blacksmith shop. Manfred hopped off the wagon and plucked his wife from the buggy. Everyone waved and said goodnight.

The wagon rumbled down a street and over, stopping in front of the hotel.

"Water Runs Fast, this is where you and Freedom get off," Beau said.

"*Ahóoh*," he said, sliding out the back and reaching in, picking his wife up like a child.

"We'll be here at first light with horses. Be down here and ready to go." Beau slapped the horse's rumps with the reins and the wagon moved on.

He glanced down at Freedom. It might be best if she walked into the hotel. He didn't want someone accusing him of kidnapping her.

Slipping his arm out from under her legs, he settled her feet on the ground. "*Áxxaashe Ishté*, wake my Sun Eyes," he said quietly into her ear.

"Swift?" She reached out and he captured her hand.

"We are at the hotel. You need to walk." He waited until her eyes opened and she stared at him.

"We're back in Shady Gulch?" she asked, looking beyond him at the building.

"Yes. I thought it best if you walk rather than me carry you to the room." He grinned, thinking if not for the trouble they were already in, it would have been fun to do.

"Yes. That would be best." She grasped his hand and they walked in together.

The man behind the tall table watched them.

Water Runs Fast walked by the man and up to the stairs. He had tucked the key the man gave him last night into his pocket. Sun Eyes was still sleepy as they climbed the stairs to the second floor.

He kept one arm around her as they walked down the hall to his room. A turn of the knob and the door opened. He saw no need to lock the door. They had only blankets covering their homes at the reservation and no one entered or stole from them.

One look at their belongings scattered about the room and he growled.

"What is it?" Sun Eyes asked. Her body straightened. "Who would do this?"

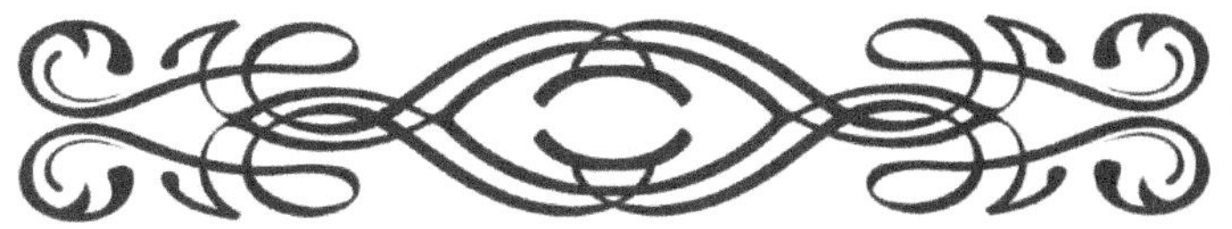

Chapter Twenty-five

Freedom stared at their meager belongings flung about the room. "We had nothin' of value, why would someone do this?" She walked over and picked up her extra set of underclothing and straightened.

Anger tightened Swift's face and burned in his eyes.

She put a hand on his arm. "Let's clean it up and see if anythin' is missin'."

His arm vibrated under her fingertips. "Water Runs Fast!" She made him look at her. "Close and lock the door. Do not go lookin' for trouble." Under her breath she said, "We have enough."

He must have heard her because the door closed, and he knelt on the floor helping her pick things up.

"Do you see anythin' missin'?" she asked.

Swift shook his head. "No. I have nothing a white man would want. Did you have anything in your clothing?"

She shook her head, thankful she had rejected Beau's offer of money. He'd come to get her things before the wedding to put them in the hotel room. While taking her things he'd handed her a pouch with money. She'd refused, saying she'd lost the other money he gave her and didn't want to lose more. And she surely would have, had it been in this room.

When everything was packed back in their leather parfleches, she turned her back to her husband. "Would you please help me out of this dress?" She glanced over her shoulder and was pleased to see his eyes light up.

Once she stood in only her chemise and drawers, she began undressing him.

"This is not fair," he protested.

"What?" she asked, kissing his powerful chest.

"I wear nothing and you…" He pulled the tie on the front of her chemise. The garment slid down her shoulders.

She shimmed and the underclothes slid down to her waist, hanging up on her drawers. "Is this better?"

Swift didn't say a word, he swung her up into his arms and placed her on the bed. Running his hands down her body, he rid her of the rest of her clothing.

Her body responded to his touch. It was a sensation she craved. Her husband knew every inch of her body and used it to his advantage. She squirmed under him, trying to get closer. She wanted to feel him in her but he was drawing out the entry.

"*Áxxaashe Ishté,* I wish to have children with you. Is this your wish?" he asked, whispering in her ear.

The heat of his breath on her ear and neck added to the pressure of his maleness poised at her welcoming opening.

"Yes, I want to have your children as well. Strong Absarokee children." She captured his lips and he entered. Her body erupted in waves of sensations as he deepened the kiss and took her breath away.

~*~

Morning came too soon for Freedom. They'd coupled twice during the night and had been ready to go a third time when Swift looked out the window and said they needed to get ready.

Her stomach rumbled as she dressed in a riding skirt, again, supplied by Savanah. If her friend hadn't inherited a large sum of money and used it to help everyone in Shady Gulch, Freedom would have been ashamed to accept all of Savannah's gifts. But she knew it was Savannah's big heart and her ability to help others that endeared her to everyone.

"You are hungry." Swift handed her a leaf bundle of pemmican.

"How do you always have so much of this with you?" she asked, unfolding the leaves and taking a bite before putting on her moccasins.

He grinned. "My mother believes in always being prepared. She makes many bundles and saves them."

She shook her head and stood, grabbing the pemmican and one of the leather pouches with her clothing.

Swift was dressed and grabbed the rest of their belongings. They walked down the stairs. He stopped at the counter where the clerk stood.

Swift set the key on the desk. "It is a good thing you give keys to rooms. If it not locked, people walk in and throw things around."

The clerk's face turned white. "I don't—"

Swift glared at the man.

Freedom said, "Mr. Gentry will hear about how you treat your customers." She slid her arm through Swift's and they walked out of the hotel.

Tuck, Beau, and Jules rode up leading the two horses Swift and she had ridden into town.

She waited for Swift to tie on the pouches he had before handing him the one she held. He tied hers on and helped her onto her horse before he swung up onto his horse. He wore his leather shirt and leggings, looking every bit the Absarokee warrior he was.

They headed west with the sun on their backs.

Tuck lead the group, leading a pack horse. Jules rode beside him. Beau dropped back and rode beside her. Swift was on her other side.

"Did you get a chance to get anything to eat?" Beau asked.

She held up the pemmican.

He twisted, reached into his saddlebag, and produced a square brown parcel. She had no doubt it would be a preserve sandwich on Mrs. Dearling's delicious bread.

Freedom took the parcel and unwrapped it. Her mouth watered. It was exactly what she'd thought. She glanced over at Swift. His eyes were on the sandwich.

"Do you have another one in that saddlebag?" she asked.

Beau produced another one. She handed it over to Swift. "Thank you."

"You know Mrs. Dearling. She thought leaving this early without a proper breakfast was silly. But we really need to cover as many miles as we can. We have to get to Major Litchfield before he sends more soldiers out looking for the two of you."

She nodded. Though the words made it hard for her to swallow the bite she'd just chewed.

He urged his horse forward and rode alongside Tuck.

Freedom glanced at Swift. "Did you hear what he said?"

Her husband nodded. "It is true. We must get back and tell the truth."

The sandwich filled her stomach but she didn't enjoy the taste as much.

~*~

They rode until dark. Water Runs Fast would have kept on going if not for the way Sun Eyes had nearly fallen off her horse twice as her eyes closed and her body slumped. He'd finally pulled her off her horse and held her on his lap as the three men ahead of them continued on.

The men were her friends, yet, they seemed to be more intent on getting to Milestown than seeing to her needs. He had stopped with her when she'd needed to stretch her legs and relieve herself. They had caught back up when the group had stopped after looking back and not seeing them behind.

Now as they set up camp, it was plain they were setting up their side of camp. That was fine with him. He would rather have conversations with his wife than the three men. They may be helping them but he knew it was only for her and not him.

Sun Eyes woke up when they stopped. Now she scurried around putting down their blankets and gathering supplies from the packhorse to make a meal.

Jules walked over to her. "Need me to fetch

water?"

"Please." She handed him the canvas bucket.

Water Runs Fast walked over and crouched beside her. "Do you wish my help?"

She smiled. "Mrs. Dearling sent along a stew for tonight. All I have to do is heat it up and make biscuits." She continued stirring the contents of a bowl.

He stood. The sheriff and Beau leaned against their saddles talking quietly. Water Runs Fast walked back over to his blankets and sat down, watching his wife cook. He couldn't wait to get back to the village and return to the life he knew.

Chapter Twenty-six

Milestown stretched out in front of them. Freedom was as anxious to get to the town as she'd been the first time she'd ridden toward it. Then she'd wanted to find help to get away from her husband, this time it was to find a way to save herself and her husband.

The three nights they'd spent on the way here, she'd felt Swift pulling away from her. She wasn't sure if it was because she and the other three men talked while he sat over on their blankets or if he believed they were all planning to give him to the soldiers. When she'd tried to talk to him, he said nothing. And once again, she was wondering about her choice of a husband.

But this one she was willing to fight for. She knew part of his behavior dealt with living differently than the people he traveled with. She was ready to get this over with and get to the reservation where she and Swift could start their new life together.

Beau led them onto the main street and stopped in front of a hotel. "Let's get rooms. Tuck and I will head for the fort tomorrow morning."

Tuck remained on his horse. "I'm going to check in with the sheriff. See what he's heard about any of this." He handed the packhorse rope to Beau and rode down the street.

Swift dismounted and was by her side before she could swing her leg over the horse. She didn't know why he was all of a sudden showing interest in her, but she liked it.

"I will be with the horses until you have the rooms," Jules said, standing beside their horses.

"Should we stay as well?" Freedom asked.

"No, only one needs to watch the horses," Beau said.

"I will stay too," Swift said.

Freedom studied the two men standing with the animals. She shook her head and followed Beau into the hotel.

The man behind the counter at the base of the stairs smiled at Beau. His smile faded at the sight of her.

"I need four rooms for tonight and two of those will be needed until I get back in a week," Beau said, pulling his wallet from his inside jacket pocket.

"Who will be using the rooms?" the man asked.

"Myself, my partner, a sheriff and this woman and her husband." Beau grasped her elbow, drawing her forward.

The man cleared his throat. "We don't rent rooms to her sort."

Beau studied the man. "You would turn down the rent of two rooms for over a week because my friend is different than you?"

Freedom didn't want Beau to get in trouble because of her. "Maybe the woman who rented me a room before would have space for all of us?" she suggested.

"I'd rather do business with someone who isn't so simple-minded." Beau led her out of the building.

"What happened?" Jules asked.

She figured he'd known Beau long enough to see how upset he was.

"The man didn't like the looks of me," Freedom said.

Jules nodded. "We've been getting stares."

"If I can find the boarding house that Ben dragged me out of, that woman may take us in." Freedom scanned the street. "If you can get me to the stage depot, I'll know which direction to go."

Beau nodded and they walked down the street, leading their horses.

Swift stayed close to her as if he feared someone would reach out and grab her. He said in a low voice, "We could camp out of town."

She shook her head. "I'd rather be here where we can hear things and get word from Beau easier."

Beau stopped in front of the stage depot.

Freedom pointed to the side street. "Down there two blocks and then left."

They walked down the side street where there were less people. She glanced down one of the streets and her heart nearly stopped. "That's him!" she said loudly and dropped the reins to her horse and ran down the street.

The old man who had tried to help her sat on a box

at the back of a building just like when she'd met him before. She ran up to him and stopped. Catching her breath, she said, "I'm so happy to see you're alive."

The man looked up. He squinted then glanced at something behind her. "Your man banged me up pretty good." His narrow face pointed over her shoulder. "Did you finally get away from him?"

She spun around and was relieved to find her companions behind her. Facing the man, she said, "Yes. I'm free of him. These are my friends and my new husband."

The man's eyebrows rose. "I'd a thought you'd have sworn off husbands after that one."

She nodded. "I would have if Water Runs Fast hadn't saved me."

Beau stepped forward and held out his hand. "Beau Gentry. I'm happy to meet you Mr.?"

"Hobkins. E.W. Hobkins." The man stood and shook hands with Beau.

"Freedom told us how you tried to help her. Would you be willing to go to the sheriff's office here and have him write down how her husband attacked you?" Beau asked.

The man stared at Beau then at each of them, his gaze landed on Freedom. "You the woman the army is looking for?"

She started to open her mouth, but Swift stepped in front of her. "She not kill man. I did."

The man's eyes widened. "I take it there's more to the story?" He focused on Beau. "You look like a lawyer. I suppose you want me to tell the sheriff how the man attacked me when he discovered I was getting' a ticket for his wife?"

"Yes. We want to prove to Major Litchfield that while Freedom didn't kill his son, the man was whipping her when Water Runs Fast came upon them. He tried to stop the man and they fought." Beau put his arm around Freedom. "We want the major to see what kind of a person his son was as we state the facts to him."

The man studied Freedom. "He really was whipping you?"

She nodded and swallowed. "Because I tried to get away." It was hard enough to tell people she knew, but if telling this man would save Swift, she would find the courage to say the words. "I had become unconscious from the pain when Water Runs Fast found us." She shuddered. "Because I had asked you to purchase a ticket on the stage, my husband had kicked and beaten me every night. I was trying to get away from him during the night when he caught me and whipped me."

"She should not have been beaten or whipped. She is a good woman." Swift stood beside her, frowning at the man.

"Miss Freedom, I wish I had been able to purchase that ticket and get you on the stage." He glanced at Beau. "I'll go tell the sheriff and I'll have Andrew at the depot go over and tell him what he saw. No one should end up in a noose over that man's death."

"Thank you!" Freedom hugged the man. "We're going to see if Mrs. Dudley has rooms for us until Beau and Sheriff Blake come back from Fort Custer."

Mr. Hobkins grinned. "I happen to know she was looking for boarders. There were some railroad surveyors staying there who left just yesterday."

"Sounds like we'll be in luck. Thank you, Mr.

Hobkins." Beau shook hands with the man. Jules and Swift did the Absarokee greeting of grasping forearms.

"I'll head straight over to the sheriff," he said as they led their horses down the street.

Freedom had a feeling everything would be fine for the first time since the warrior rode into the village and said the army was looking for her.

~*~

The woman at the house started to make a fuss about Water Runs Fast, Sun Eyes, and Jules staying at her home until Beau pulled out his wallet and paid for the four rooms for a week.

"I do have one other boarder, but I'm sure he won't mind sharing meals with you." Her gaze landed on Water Runs Fast and she shuddered.

He had been on the end of this kind of scrutiny before. He had long ago learned to pretend he didn't see it. But when her gaze flit between he and Freedom and her face scrunched in distaste, he grabbed Sun Eyes' arm to pull her back outside.

"It seems all the men you pick are forceful," the woman said.

He dropped his hand and peered into Sun Eye's face. Did she think him no better than the man he'd saved her from?

"That is something else," Sun Eyes said, linking her hand with his. "Would you be willing to tell the sheriff how my last husband dragged me out of here?"

The woman glanced at Beau. He held out a ten-dollar bill. She snatched the bill from his hand as quickly as it appeared and nodded. "I could tell the sheriff how mean your last husband was."

"Thank you," Sun Eyes said.

While he wanted to be sure all the people who had met the cruel man told their stories, he wondered at Beau paying the woman. She should tell the sheriff because it was the right thing to do.

"Could you show us to our rooms before you go see the sheriff?" Beau asked.

Mrs. Dudley leaned the broom she'd been holding against the wall and stopped at the bottom of the stairs. "Are you each in need of a room? You asked for four."

"Freedom and Water Runs Fast will be in one room. Jules will need a room, I will need a room, and Sheriff Blake will need a room," Beau said.

The woman's face lit up at the mention of the sheriff. "I'll put the sheriff in the room downstairs. Follow me."

Water Runs Fast followed everyone up the stairs. At the top the woman opened two doors. "You two men can use these rooms." She moved down the narrow hall and opened the door on the end. "This is the biggest room and has a bed for two," she said.

Freedom entered and spun back to the door. "This will be wonderful. Thank you."

Water Runs Fast walked into the room. It had a big bed like the room in the hotel where he and Sun Eyes slept after the wedding ceremony. The same white vessel for water sat on a tall table with parts that slid out. A colorful rug covered the middle of the floor and two chairs sat by a small round table at the window. He crossed the room and looked out the window. They were at the front of the house, looking out onto the street.

The sheriff rode his horse up the street.

"Sheriff Blake is coming," he said.

The woman twittered and hurried out of the room.

Water Runs Fast faced his wife. "How long must we stay here?"

She put her arms around his waist. "Until Beau returns. He hopes no more than a week."

He sighed. Living among so many white people would be hard.

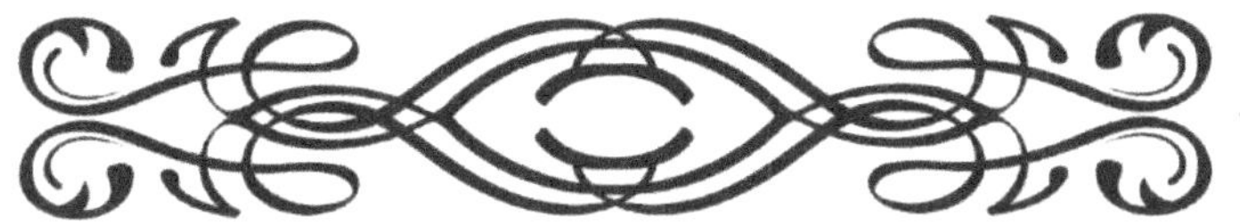

Chapter Twenty-seven

Freedom looked around the table in Mrs. Dudley's boardinghouse. The woman was a good cook. They had all sat down with the one other boarder. A man who it appeared was a salesman. Of what, she didn't know. He never really came out and said what he pandered.

The fried ham, sliced potatoes, and canned green beans had tasted wonderful.

"I could help you with the dishes if you'd like?" Freedom offered when the woman started clearing the dishes away.

A wistful expression flit across the woman's face before she said, "You are a guest. Enjoy some time in the parlor."

Beau rose as did Jules and Tuck.

Freedom glanced at her husband. "Would you like to take a walk?"

"I would. But I do not think it is a good idea." He sighed and stood, holding out a hand to her.

They walked into the parlor. Tuck and Jules had started up a card game. Beau sat in a chair, reading a newspaper.

She hadn't had a chance to talk with Tuck since he'd come back from the sheriff's office. He'd been shown his room and then he and Jules had taken the horses to the stables. When they'd returned, dinner had been announced.

"Tuck, what did you learn at the sheriff's office?" she asked.

At that moment the other boarder walked in.

"Mr. Fine, would you like to join us in a game of cards?" Tuck asked the man.

"No. I prefer to just read for a bit before I go to my room." The man sat down in the other cushioned chair and opened up a book he'd brought in the room with him.

Swift's antsy motions irritated her almost as much as the salesman's sly glimpses of them.

"Do you know if there is a park nearby?" she asked anyone in the room who could answer her.

"There is one about three blocks down and one block to the north. We walked by on our way back from the stables," Tuck said.

"You shouldn't go out walking after dark," Beau said.

She sighed heavily and stood. Everyone but Mr. Fine also stood, like gentlemen. "I'm goin' to see if there isn't somethin' I can do to help Mrs. Dudley. I'm bored."

One step out of the room and she felt someone behind her. She spun around and bumped her nose into her husband's chest. "What are you doin'?"

"I wish to go for a ride with you."

She put a hand on his arm. "We can't go tonight. The horses are tired and I'm tired. Perhaps tomorrow." She nodded to the room. "Either go in there and talk with Beau or go to our room. I'll be up soon."

He nodded and strode to the stairs.

Her heart ached for how he must feel. He would be back at his village doing what he always did under the stars if not for saving her. She wondered at his love for her, that he would endure so much.

She walked into the kitchen. Mrs. Dudley had her back to the door. "Are you sure there isn't somethin' I could help you with?"

The woman jumped and whirled around. Water dripped from her hands. "What are you doing sneaking up on a body?" The woman looked upset but not mad.

"I'm sorry. The men are playin' cards and visitin'. I was bored. Let me help you." She grabbed a towel and picked up a dish, drying it.

"I won't give you back any money, you offering to help," the woman said.

"That's fine. I only need somethin' to do." She dried plates and stacked them on the table.

"What happened after your last husband dragged you out of here?" the woman asked.

Freedom told her story of how he'd beat her and whipped her and how Swift came along. She didn't say anything about the killing.

"So you left him for the Indian?"

The disbelief in the woman's voice stopped Freedom cold. "Would you stay with a man who beat and whipped you?"

"I'd rather that than sleep with an Indian."

Freedom threw the cloth down on the table. "Water Runs Fast is more compassionate and carin' than my first husband ever was. I prefer him to that brute. Good night, Mrs. Dudley."

Her sight was hazed over with rage as she marched down the hall to the stairs. She bumped into someone at the bottom of the stairs.

"Are you all right?"

She didn't know the voice. Shaking her head, she cleared her vision and found the other boarder, Mr. Fine, holding her by her arms. Freedom took a step back, putting space between them.

"I'm fine. Excuse me." She tried to walk by him to the stairs.

He stepped in front of her. "Are you the darkie who killed Major Litchfield's son?"

"I did not kill anyone." Her voice rose and the sound of feet on the stairs behind her caught both their attention.

Swift had a hold of the man by his jacket collar. "Do not touch my woman."

Beau set Freedom to the side and walked up to Mr. Fine. "What exactly do you do?"

The man's face was becoming white from Swift's grip on his clothing.

"Swift, leave him loose," Freedom said.

Her husband released the man, who would have fallen to his knees if Beau hadn't grabbed the front of his jacket. "Let's have a talk in the parlor." Beau glanced over at Freedom. "You go up to your room."

"You aren't goin' to hurt him?" she asked.

"No. Just ask him some questions." Beau and Tuck escorted the man into the parlor.

Freedom clutched Swift's arm. "Are you coming with me?"

"No. I must hear." Water Runs Fast eased by his wife and strode into the room where the men had been relaxing before. The air rippled with distrust.

He walked over to stand beside the men he'd ridden into town with. They were his comrades. They all wanted to see that nothing happened to Freedom.

"I happened to have heard you ask Freedom if she was the *woman* who killed Major Litchfield's son." Beau crossed his arms. "What do you know about that?"

The man glanced at each one of them, his gaze remaining on Water Runs Fast. "I know that a brave showed up at the village of the Crow Whistling Waters clan with a colored woman about the time someone showed up at Fort Custer saying they'd found Ben Litchfield stabbed to death and the last time the man had been seen, he'd had a colored woman with him."

"How do you know so much about this?" the sheriff asked.

The man reached in his pocket and pulled out a shiny object, like the one the sheriff wore on his clothing.

"You're a Pinkerton?" the sheriff asked.

"What are the Pinkertons doing messing around with something like this?" Beau asked.

"I happened to have been delivering information to the fort for the railroad and Major Litchfield told me about the death of his son and asked if I could try and locate the woman accused of murdering him." The man stared at Water Runs Fast. "I'm assuming you are the brave who rode into the camp with the murderess."

"She did not kill him. I did." Water Runs Fast took a step toward the man. "I stabbed him when he attacked me for stopping his whipping of Sun Eyes."

The man's eyes widened. "What do you mean whipping?"

Beau sat in the chair he'd been in before and motioned for them all to sit.

Water Runs Fast could not sit. He paced the floor, recounting why he'd been alone along the river and what he had encountered and what had happened.

The man, Pinkerton, studied him. "You only stabbed him once?"

Reaching down to his moccasin, Water Runs Fast pulled out his knife. "With this knife."

"Put that away," the sheriff told him.

Water Runs Fast slipped the knife back into his moccasin.

"Why did you ask him if he'd stabbed only once?" Beau asked.

The Pinkerton man studied Water Runs Fast. "There were three stab wounds and the knife that had been used lay beside the body. The man who reported it to the major said Ben had been stabbed three times with his own knife."

Water Runs Fast shook his head. "Only once. I wrap Sun Eyes in blanket and carry her away. She want to go back for shoes and money, but I told her bad to be found with dead white man."

Again, the man, Pinkerton, studied him. "What money?"

"I not know. She say get her home." He shrugged.

"It was money I'd given Freedom in case the marriage didn't work out. I told her not to let Ben know she had it and if she needed to come back to Shady Gulch to use it." Beau studied him. "She told me after a man here tried to purchase her stage ticket back to Shady Gulch, Ben took the money from her. We met the man today who told us when he asked about the ticket, Ben had been in the depot and beat him to find out where Freedom was staying. Which was here. You can ask Mrs. Dudley about how Ben dragged Freedom out of here." He glanced at Water Runs Fast. "The man went to the sheriff to give his account of how Ben beat him up and took the money. If you would like to hear from Freedom what happened to her after they left Milestown, Water Runs Fast can go up and get her."

He didn't want Sun Eyes to have to tell this man how she'd been beaten. But if Beau thought it would help convince the man, he would fetch his wife.

"No. That's not necessary. I'm wondering about the three stabs if this man says he only stabbed Mr. Litchfield once. And there was no money found on the body when it was brought to the fort."

"Who brought the body to the fort?" the sheriff asked.

"Amos Foster. A friend of Mr. Litchfield's who had gone to the man's cabin to visit and found no one there. He'd backtracked from the cabin to Milestown and found the body."

Water Runs Fast shook his head. "The rider from fort came same night we arrived at village."

"Foster is the man Freedom said treated his wife badly. They stopped at their soddy on the way to Milestown. So the man would have known they weren't at home." Beau glanced at Water Runs Fast. "Did she tell you anything else about the man, Foster?"

"Only she did not like him. He was mean to his wife and he did something Sun Eyes did not like." He glanced toward the door. Maybe they did need Sun Eyes here to tell them about this man. "I will get her."

Before anyone said differently, he bounded up the stairs and to the room he would share with his wife. He opened the door. She stood from a chair where she'd sat, staring out the window. He was glad she had not undressed.

"There are questions about Foster," he said.

Her eyes widened. "What kind? Why do you need to know?"

He crossed the room and drew her to her feet. "The man downstairs is called Pinkerton. He is looking for us for major."

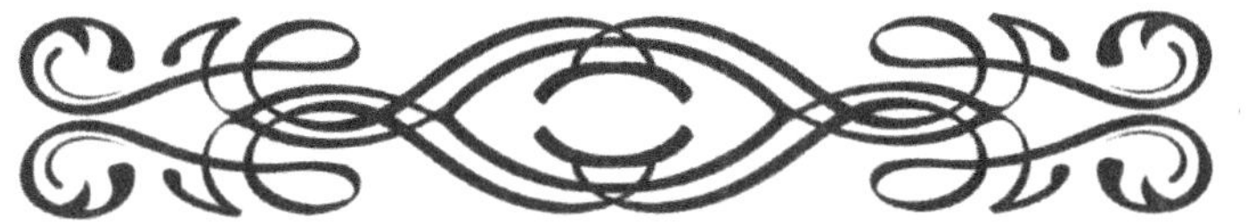

Chapter Twenty-eight

Fear gripped Freedom's chest and made it hard to speak as her throat tightened. "He can't take you away from me."

Swift put his arms around her. "I think he believe us."

She peered up into his face. He was relaxed. More so than she'd seen him for days. She nodded. "Then I will talk to him."

They clasped hands and walked down the stairs and into the parlor, side by side.

The man Swift called Pinkerton, and she knew as Mr. Fine, sat on the couch. Jules, Beau, and Tuck sat in the other chairs facing him. Jules rose and placed a chair between his and Beau's. She sat and Swift stood behind her, a hand on her shoulder.

"Freedom, this is Mr. Fine, who you met at dinner. It turns out he's a Pinkerton investigating Ben's death for Major Litchfield," Beau said.

She nodded and glanced at the man. She hadn't forgotten the way he'd grabbed her and accused her of killing a man. Returning her gaze to Beau, she asked, "What did you want to ask me?"

"Do you know for certain that the man standing behind you only stabbed Mr. Litchfield once?" the Pinkerton asked.

"I can't say for sure. I had passed out from the pain of the whip slicin' my back open." She stared pointedly at the man. He had the good sense to flinch at her description of her torture. "But since meetin' Water Runs Fast, I have never found him to tell anythin' but the truth."

"And did you insist on going back to the body?" the man asked.

"Yes. I needed my boots, and Ben had taken the money Beau gave me to get back home. Ben had figured out I had money after he beat up poor Mr. Hobkins." She smiled wanly at Beau. "I was so sure that marryin' Ben and gettin' out of the saloon was all I wanted. I should have listened to all of you who warned me about him."

"How much money did you have?" Mr. Fine asked.

Freedom shook her head. "I'm not sure. I think close to twenty dollars. I hadn't spent any of it."

"I gave her twenty dollars," Beau said.

The Pinkerton stared at Beau. "There wasn't any money found on his body. His father said his son often came to the fort asking for money to purchase supplies."

Freedom glared at the man. "He had my money when Water Runs Fast saved me."

"What can you tell us about a man named Amos

Foster?" Mr. Fine asked.

Her body shivered at the man's name. "He had a soddy out in the middle of a prairie about five days from Shady Gulch and two long days from here. He had an Indian woman for a wife. He treated her as badly as Ben treated me." She glanced at Beau. "You need to try and find Mary before you go back to Shady Gulch. She needs your help."

He nodded.

"Why did you shudder at the man's name?" the Pinkerton asked.

Her chest squeezed, shoving all the air out of her lungs. She was in a room with five men, one of those her husband. She didn't think she could talk about what all had happened at that soddy.

Swift's hand moved up and down her upper arm as if showing her he was there and wouldn't judge. She glanced at the other men present. Beau and Jules would be furious. And Tuck, he was so forward with women, she didn't like talking about it with him present. She swallowed. Fear and shame warred with wanting the man to understand how vile her husband had been.

It would be easier to tell this man she didn't know than the ones she did. Freedom put her hand on Swift's and scanned the faces of the men who came with them. "It would be easier to tell this part if you all would leave the room."

Beau's face and ears reddened as his face scrunched in anger. Jules stood and put a hand on her shoulder. Tuck glanced at the Pinkerton man and Beau.

It was Swift who protested as the other men rose to leave. "I wish to hear this."

She shook her head. "No. You don't. It isn't

somethin' I can talk about with those of you here who know me. I would never be able to look you in the eyes."

The others had left the room, but Swift remained. "I do not wish to leave you alone. Your story is hard and full of sorrow. You will need my strength."

She peered into his eyes. "I do need your strength, but I will need it after I tell the story. Please, return when I call for you."

He slowly walked to the door and disappeared.

Mr. Fine studied her. "What could you not say with the other men present?"

She drew in a deep breath and brought back the fear, shame, and anger she'd felt that night in the soddy. She told about Mary's fear of Ben, how Freedom had stopped whatever he had planned for the woman and of Foster's attempt to bed her while her husband lay next to her. She stared down at her hands, clenched together. "I slapped him after my husband, Ben, went outside telling Foster if he wasn't man enough to take me, it wasn't his problem. Foster came at me with a knife. I told him I'd rather be dead than have him touch me. He went outside but later told me he'd have his way with me another time."

Mr. Fine leaned forward, bringing his hands into her view. "And your husband did nothing to stop this?"

She shook her head and wiped at the tears trickling down her cheeks. "Foster said Ben told him he could bed me." She stared up at him and glared. "He called me a whore. I had bedded no one until Ben. He had no right to call me that and to think he could give me to any man who came along."

"Did you stab him before Water Runs Fast came

along?”

"No! I'd dreamed about it. Mary gave me a small knife, but there was never a chance. I just wanted away from him, not to kill him. The knife was for protection, but he found it the first night after Milestown when he beat me for trying to get away."

"It sounds like you married a mean man." Mr. Fine said.

She laughed almost hysterically. "He didn't show this side of him until we were several days from Shady Gulch. He told me he hadn't planned to marry me, but my friends had insisted I couldn't leave with him without marrying. He had planned to use me for bedding and taking care of him. He didn't care for me. Thought I was a clean darkie." She started laughing. "And I thought I was in love. I've learned the difference between an infatuation and love."

"You're in love with Water Runs Fast?" The Pinkerton studied her.

The rage and humiliation dissolved as she thought of all the things Swift had done to show her how much he cared about her. "Yes. We belong together."

"Do you believe this Foster would have killed his friend?"

She stared at the man. From what she'd witnessed of the two, she wouldn't have put it passed either one to have killed the other. "Yes. They said they were friends, but their actions were more like two dogs keeping their distance but at the same time helping each other take down a meal."

The man nodded. His gaze went to the door.

She glanced over her shoulder.

Swift stood inside the room. His gaze landed on

her. He crossed the room in three strides, dropping to his knees beside her chair. "He has upset you."

"Mr. Fine didn't. The memories upset me." She glanced at the Pinkerton. "May I go?"

He nodded.

Swift helped her to her feet and escorted her out of the room. At the bottom of the stairs, she saw the other three men striding down the hall. She figured they would go in and ask Mr. Fine what he had learned about Foster.

Right now, all she wanted to do was fall asleep in Swift's arms.

Water Runs Fast followed Sun Eyes up the stairs and into their room. Her face was drawn, her eyes red, and her usual happiness smothered by the memories she'd had to relive.

"You did not have to talk to the man," he said, closing the door and crossing the room to take her in his arms.

"I did. He had to see the other man, Foster, had more reason to kill Ben than you or I." She leaned her head on his chest. "Can we talk about something else?"

He put his finger under her chin and raised her face to his. "How about no talking?" Capturing her mouth with his, he enjoyed the sensations the meeting of his lips to hers brought to his body.

She wrapped her arms around his neck, pressed her body to him, and hummed.

He ran his hands up and down her back, pressing her closer. The clothing between them angered him. He wanted to be skin to skin. Shoving away from her, he grabbed the bottom of his shirt and drew it over his head.

Locking gazes with her, he saw fear in her sunshine eyes.

"What did I do *Axxaashe Iste*?" He held out his hand, palm up.

When she didn't take his hand, he dropped to his knees and gazed up at her. "I would never hurt you. *Ah-badt-dadt-deah*, the one who created us all, has brought us together to care for each other and the Absarokee."

"I just told Mr. Fine about all the anger and hurt I received at the hands of two men." She shook her head. "I would rather die than go through that again."

Now he knew the Foster man had hurt her as well as the man he'd stabbed. His anger grew inside for this man. He shoved it down, deep in his belly to use when he saw the man. Right now, he had to make Sun Eyes believe in him and his love for her again.

"Sit on the bed." He remained on the floor.

She studied him and sat on the bed.

He crawled over and untied her moccasins, caressing each foot after he'd removed the footwear. He moved his hand up her legs, caressing and staring into her eyes.

"Would you allow me to remove your dress?" he asked, standing.

She nodded.

He unfastened the split skirt and it dropped to her feet. She stepped to the side. Picking up the skirt, he hung it on a hook on the wall. Back in front of her, he slowly unbuttoned her shirt and slid it down her arms. He placed it on top of the skirt.

She stood before him in the thin clothing she called underclothes. He still saw no need for the garments but smiled at the way they barely hid her dark nipples and black curls between her legs.

"Would you like to go to bed clean?"

Her eyes lit up, and he walked to the table with the pitcher of water and poured some in the bowl. He placed a cloth in the water and when he turned around, she stood beside him, bare.

Water Runs Fast smiled and slowly moved the cloth over her face and down her neck and shoulders. He rinsed the cloth in the water and cleaned every inch of her body down to her toes.

When he finished and she stood, glistening with water drops in front of him, he lapped at the droplets and she moaned.

Freedom held onto Swift as he took her humming body over the pinnacle and the stars of heaven flashed in her mind. Cradled in his arms, his body filling her, she knew he would never hurt her.

She fell asleep, dreaming of the children they would make and being by this man's side always.

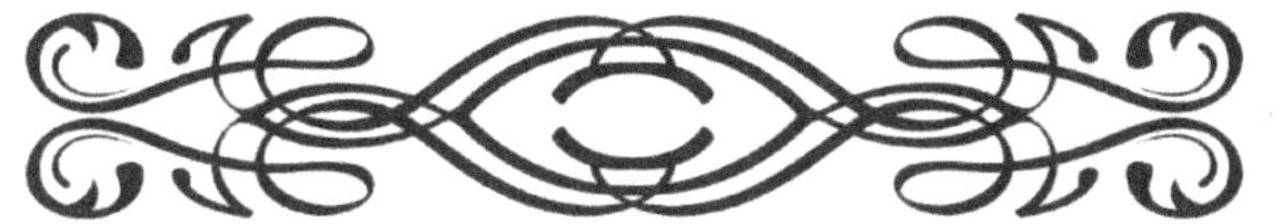

Chapter Twenty-nine

Opening her eyes, Freedom smiled at the cheery glow of sunshine warming the room. She reached over.

The other side of the bed was empty.

A quick scan of the room revealed she was alone.

She sat up, forcing her mind to wake when something bumped at the door. Wrapping her fists around the top of the blanket, she pulled it up to her chin and stared at the door, hoping it wasn't Mrs. Dudley.

The door opened and Swift walked in carrying a tray. He smiled seeing her. "Mrs. Dudley say you like meal in bed." The confusion marring his handsome face put a smile on her face.

"I've never had breakfast in bed." She waited for him to place the tray on her lap and walk back to close the door before she dropped the blanket to pick up the cup of coffee.

Swift faced her and his eyes lit up at her sitting so

immodestly. When Ben looked at her that way and he'd taken off her clothes, she'd felt ashamed. Swift's hungry eyes only heated her body and made her heart light.

"Have you eaten?" she asked.

He nodded. "Beau, the sheriff, and Pinkerton have left for the fort."

She was glad Mr. Fine would go with them. He could tell the major what kind of a son he had and that it was possible Foster killed Ben.

"I'm glad Mr. Fine went with them. What are we goin' to do all day?" She smiled and picked up a piece of toasted bread.

"I would like to leave the town." He sat on the edge of the bed.

"I'll put on my ridin' skirt when I finish eatin'." She liked the idea of getting away from the staring eyes and out of the boarding house. Mrs. Dudley took them in when the hotel wouldn't, but Freedom had the notion it was only because Beau paid for four rooms when they were only using two for the rest of the week. Less work and more money for the woman.

"There is no hurry. We have all day." Swift nuzzled her neck.

"You keep doin' that and I won't get anythin' to eat." She smiled and leaned her head, exposing more of her neck for him.

She barely finished her toast and cooked egg before Swift whisked the tray away and laid down on the bed beside her. "When we return to the village, we will have a home all our own. Because you do not have a mother in another village, we will remain with the Whistling Waters clan and not have to move in with your family."

Freedom studied him. "You mean had you married a woman from another village you would have had to leave your mother and aunt even though they need you?"

He nodded. "It is how our people do not mix family."

She understood the reasoning behind the men and women of other clans marrying. It was on the same principal as her mother and father had talked about with the plantation owners pairing the strongest slaves from other plantations together to make stronger workers. The plantation owners had been wrong to use the slaves like cattle, breeding to make a stronger herd. She'd always thought of that when realizing she was free to marry whomever she wanted.

"Could you pick who you married?" she asked.

"Sometimes. If the woman I had picked was approved of by my mother and aunt, yes. If not, they would pick the woman they found suitable." He shrugged and skimmed a finger down her shoulder to her breast. "I am much happier I found the woman of my visions and they cannot say no to my vision and the medicine man's approval."

She leaned toward him, settling her breast in his hand. "You have mentioned the vision before. Can you tell me more about it?"

He weighed her breast in his hand and stared into her eyes. "When I was but a boy, I learned my spirit is the water. All of my vision quests have been high in the mountains where the streams and rivers begin from melted snow. When I was ten summers, I fasted four days and climbed naked to the highest mountain. Where the snow was melting and forming a stream that met with other streams and continued down to the big river, I fell to my knees exhausted. I stared into the water and soon lifted out of my body, following the sound of gurgling water. In a meadow alongside the large river, I found you. We talked. You told me of ways to feed my people and make their lives better." He released her breast and captured her chin. "We talked of becoming one when I was a man and you were a woman. I told you I would wait for you and you disappeared." He peered into her eyes. "I woke up and found myself back at the snow melt, but I knew you were my vision. I returned to the village and told Antlers On Wrong." Swift leaned closer and brushed his lips across hers. "You have already taught me how to make you happy. Soon we will both teach my people how to be happy living on the reservation."

Her heart swelled that he believed in her, but she also worried she would not be able to fulfill this promise he felt she had made to him in his vision. "What if I can't help the Absarokee?"

He grinned. "You will. My vision has said so." He rolled to the edge of the bed. "Come. We will ride in sunshine and smell fresh air."

Freedom slipped out of bed and dressed with her husband grinning and watching. It was apparent while the Absarokee women were covered while out in public, their men enjoyed their nakedness while alone.

Once she was dressed, they carried the tray down to the kitchen and found Jules in the parlor.

"*Bonjou*," he said, glancing up from writing on a paper.

"We're goin' for a ride," Freedom said, letting the

other man know they were going out.

"Be careful. I walked to the store this morning for this paper and envelope. The stares, they were not friendly." Jules stood, extending his gaze to Swift.

"We're both feelin' cooped up. We'll stay away from people." It had been a while since she'd needed to be wary of another person's fear. The sense of survival that had lain dormant when they'd left the south and moved to Chicago had flared since marrying Ben.

"Stroll straight north. Less houses and people," Jules offered.

"Thank you." Freedom started for the door.

"You should wear a hat," Jules said.

"I'll be fine." She smiled over her shoulder and followed Swift out onto the porch. A deep breath and she understood her husband wanting fresh air. Even though they had stepped outside, the air was still filled with cooking, animal, and human dung odors. There was no fresh air while they were in a town of this size.

Water Runs Fast glanced down as Sun Eyes hooked her arm through his. He'd noticed the men and women in town walked this way. It was a strange custom, but he would walk such with his wife as he enjoyed any time she touched him. He hurried through the streets to the stable where they had left the horses. He'd walked over with the sheriff this morning to get his and Beau's horse while Jules and Beau talked.

There was something about the brown-skinned man and the big white man he did not understand. As they approached the stable, he asked, "How did Beau and Jules become brothers?"

Sun Eyes slowed their pace and said, "They grew up together and have been together since leavin' their homes in New Orleans. They act like brothers most of the time, but sometimes in the bar when there are decisions to make, they can quarrel." She thought a moment and laughed. "Like brothers."

He grunted. There were warriors in the village he considered brothers. Never had he considered a white man a brother. Even when he had scouted with the army there had not been a white man who tried to friend him.

They stopped at the stable.

Two men stood at the opening. "Look at that, a darkie and an Injun," one man said, jabbing the other man with his elbow.

"And they're strutting along as if they belong." The other man walked toward them. "What you two want here?"

Swift tucked Sun Eyes behind him. "We are here for our horses."

"If you have horses you stole them," the first man said, stepping up beside the other man.

"They are my horses. The best from my herd. Move." Swift made a motion as if to grab the knife handle at the top of his moccasin.

"There now. There's no need for trouble. Marvin and Tom, you move on. This man has two horses stabled here." The man who owned the stable walked out of the barn.

"No Injun owns a horse. They only steal them," one of the men tossed as they walked away.

"I'm sorry those two troublemakers were standing here when you walked up," the owner said. "You'll find your horses in the corral out back."

Sun Eyes stepped out from behind him and the

man's eyes narrowed.

"We will be gone a few hours," Sun Eyes said.

The man nodded and walked to the side of the building.

When they followed the man to the corral, Sun Eyes whispered, "He likes you better than me."

That was the impression he had as well. "Stay here," he told her as he picked out the head ropes for the two horses. The horses came right up to him as if they were ready to leave the town as well. He caught them and Sun Eyes opened the gate for him to lead the horses out.

"Could you ride without a saddle?" he asked.

"I did as a child. I don't see why I can't now." She took the reins of her horse.

Water Runs Fast helped her onto her horse. He swung up onto his. He faced his horse to the north and headed out of town at a fast walk. The sound of Sun Eyes' horse following behind made him smile. She was an Absarokee in all ways.

As soon as they passed the last house, he urged his horse into a run. He glanced over his shoulder and was happy to see Sun Eyes leaning over the neck of her running horse, a grin on her face.

He slowed and stopped when they were concealed in the trees along the river.

Sun Eyes caught up to him. She breathed heavily and laughed. He helped her off the horse and she wrapped her arms around his neck.

"I haven't ridden like that in a long time. It was fun!" She kissed him on the lips before releasing his neck.

He enjoyed her playfulness. "Come. Sit by the

water." Grasping her hand, he led Sun Eyes to a large boulder in the shade beside the river. They climbed up on the rock and sat facing the water.

"Listen."

She closed her eyes, tipped her face upwards, and said nothing.

"Hear the birds talking?" he whispered in her ear.

"Yes," she said quietly. "The water talks, too."

That she also believed the water talked pleased him. She was his mate in all ways.

Another sound caught his attention and the birds stopped singing. He put a hand on her arm. "Someone is near," he whispered. "Stay. I will see."

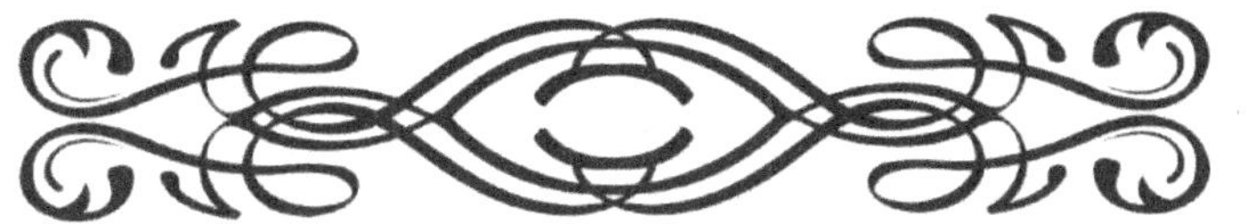

Chapter Thirty

Freedom watched Swift slip off the boulder and duck behind a tree. Within seconds, she could no longer see or hear him. What had he heard? Her heart started pounding, making a noise in her head that made it hard to concentrate on the sounds around her. Could it be the two who had made disparaging remarks at the stable? She hoped not. The thought of Swift going up against two adversaries rippled fear up her spine.

He'd told her to stay, but her feet started edging to the side of the boulder. Her mind clicked in. She had no idea what direction he went, and if she left this spot, he would think someone had taken her.

A quick glance at the horses who continued to eat grass, calmed her a bit. The horses didn't seem disturbed by who or what had caught Swift's attention. But to keep from being seen so easily, she slipped off the boulder and sat with her back against it, staring into the trees where Swift had disappeared.

A flash of red caught her attention to her left. Peering hard at the trees, she tried to catch another glimpse and see who it was. Nothing.

She sighed and relaxed against the warm rock. Her eyelids drooped down, but she held them open, knowing it wouldn't be wise to not be alert.

The sound of a loping horse caused Freedom to twist her head to make sure their two horses hadn't come loose. They stood with one back leg cocked, their eyes closed. Had it been the person she'd seen wearing red?

"*Áxxaashe Ishté*!" Swift said, not far from where she sat. His voice held a trace of fear.

She stood and spun around. He stood on the other side of the boulder.

"You are safe." He hurried around the rock and pulled her into an embrace.

"I stayed here, but thought it best to not sit in the open on top of the boulder." She nuzzled her face against his shoulder.

"There was a man. I did not see him clearly. He rode away on a horse." Swift held her away from him. "We must be careful. We are among many enemies."

"Do you want to go back?" she asked, not excited about spending long hours in the boarding house, but knowing it was their safest place to be right now.

"No. We will ride more." He grinned. "Not so fast."

"I enjoyed running the horses, but I would like to ride slow and talk with you." Riding more was better than going back to town.

Swift helped her onto the horse and gracefully swung up on his horse. They meandered through the trees following the river upstream.

"Did the man look like either of the two who caused trouble at the stable?" She preferred to know who was following them and if he might be up to no good.

He shook his head. "This man was not the same body as those two. He was shorter, wider. Moved through the trees like wolf."

She shuddered. A man who moved through the trees like a wolf sounded dangerous.

They talked of more pleasant things and soon turned around as the sun moved from above them toward the west. The horses walked out of the trees. She could see the outline of the town in the distance.

The joy of the ride returned to reality. They would spend the remainder of the day inside. There was one activity they could do. However, she'd be embarrassed when she locked gazes with Jules or Mrs. Dudley if they locked themselves in their room and enjoyed one another's body. She sighed.

"You do not wish to return to town?" Swift asked.

"No, but we can't stay out here until dark. Jules will worry." That moment her stomach growled. "If we do this tomorrow, we need to bring a picnic along."

Swift agreed as they slowly neared Milestown. They entered the same way they'd left. A few more people milled about the houses than had this morning. Some children stopped playing and watched as they walked their horses down the street.

At the stable, Swift helped her down and released the horses into the corral. He placed the headstalls on a post on the side of the corral and they walked into the building.

The owner was cleaning out a stall. He leaned on the pitchfork and watched them walk up to him.

"Our horses are back," Swift said. "Please give them feed. We will be back in the morning to ride."

The man nodded. "Them two from this morning were in here asking where you went. You might want to keep a lookout when you're out there riding."

Swift nodded.

"We think someone else followed us today," Freedom said. She felt it would be good to let someone know about their interloper.

"Not them two that was here?"

"No. One man. He had on red." She glanced at Swift to see if he was going to add to her comment.

He glanced at her and then studied the man. "He moved through trees like wolf. You know someone like this?"

The owner shook his head. "Can't say as I've come across someone like that. I'll keep an eye out though." He stared at Swift. "If he moved like a wolf, I'd say it was one of your kind."

"No. He was not an Absarokee. Absarokee wolf would not be seen." Water Runs Fast glared at the man. This was a white man who moved through the trees as if he did it a lot. He knew to keep his footsteps light and use the trees and bushes to hide behind.

Water Runs Fast held out his arm and Sun Eyes smiled at him as she slipped her hand through the crook.

They walked back to the boardinghouse like this. He with his eyes forward ignoring the people around them and his wife smiling and nodding at people. Why she tried to be friends with people who did not care to be their friends fascinated him. She found no one an enemy. Having witnessed her whipping and hearing others had treated her poorly, he didn't understand how she could be so open to those who showed hostility.

At the boardinghouse, Jules stepped out of the fancy room as soon as they walked through the door. Relief softened the man's face.

"You rode a long time," Jules said.

Sun Eyes smiled at him. "It was good to get out of town and enjoy the sunshine and fresh air." She glanced up at Water Runs Fast. "I'll go see if Mrs. Dudley has somethin' cool for us to drink."

He watched her walk down the hall and motioned for Jules to return to the room. When they were both seated, he peered into the man's eyes. "Why does Sun Eyes, Freedom, smile at everyone?"

The man in front of him smiled, revealing white teeth and wrinkles at the corners of his eyes. "Miss Freedom has the good grace to not hold a grudge against everyone for what a few bad folk have done to her."

Water Runs Fast shook his head. "She has scars. It proves she is strong. But she will be hurt if she is not careful of people."

"She can tell a good person from a bad most of the time." Jules frowned. "That Ben, he fooled all of us."

"What about Ben?" Sun Eyes asked, carrying a tray with glasses and a pitcher of something with a brown color.

"I said he fooled us all," Jules said, standing and taking the tray from her.

Water Runs Fast watched this exchange between the two. The man had stood and took the tray away.

She'd carried it this far, why had he taken it? Especially, since now she was pouring the drink into the glasses.

Sun Eyes smiled at him as she handed him a glass. "This is sweet tea."

He sipped and wondered at the way the drink made his tongue feel. He'd tasted few things that tingled his tongue. Honey was one.

Sun Eyes handed a glass to Jules and sat down with her own glass. "There was a man watchin' or followin' us."

Jules set his glass down and studied her, then him.

Water Runs Fast could see the man was about to tell them what they didn't want to hear.

"You two should stay here, in this house, until Beau and Tuck return." Jules turned his gaze on Water Runs Fast.

"We will not be captives. We will come and go as we wish." He stared back at the man.

"I thought maybe you could wait about half an hour tomorrow and then follow us? See who he is," Sun Eyes said.

He liked the way his wife thought. They could get the man caught between them and see who he is and why he followed them. "That is a good idea." Water Runs Fast studied Jules. The man didn't act as interested in helping as he should. He was a friend of Sun Eyes, if not him.

"It's not a good idea to back someone into a corner. This man could be dangerous." Jules glanced at Sun Eyes but his gaze remained firm on Water Runs Fast.

"It is best to know one's enemy, even if it means a fight." He remained with his gaze locked to Jules' gaze.

Sun Eyes snapped her fingers to get their attention. "Gentlemen, there will be no need for a confrontation or fight." She smiled, sipped her drink, and said, "We just want to get a look at him."

Chapter Thirty-one

The following day was as warm and sunny as the day before. Freedom decided wearing a hat would be a good idea. She'd noticed a couple of spots on her face that were tender from the sun's rays the day before. The only problem, she didn't have a hat and she didn't have any money.

Jules was once again in the parlor writing when she came upon him after breakfast. He and Beau always had money. She'd ask him for enough to purchase a hat at the mercantile. She didn't need anything fancy, just a straw hat with a wide brim.

She stepped into the room and Jules glanced up. While it was one thing to think about asking him for money, it was another to come out and do it. She smiled and walked over to the desk.

"Freedom, what are you thinking so hard about?" Jules asked, setting his quill down and staring up at her.

"It was hot when we went ridin' yesterday and I

left all my fancy hats with the ladies at the boardin' house. I won't need them at the reservation." She looked up from the desk where Jules' hands rest and into his face. "Is there a chance I could borrow enough money to purchase a straw hat for my ride today?"

He grinned. "Your new husband has no wallet I've noticed."

She didn't like the implication that she'd go wanting by living with Swift at the reservation. "He will provide for me well. But in town, he lacks what is needed to provide. He doesn't like it here and doesn't plan to stay any longer than necessary."

"I didn't mean for you to become upset." Jules pulled a wallet from his inside jacket pocket. He handed her a five-dollar bill. "This should purchase a hat and anything else you need."

Swift walked through the door. He strode across the room and stared at the money she held in her hand. "What this?"

"Money. I need a hat before we ride today. I showed you the redness on my face from our ride yesterday."

"No money. Use bear grease." He took the money from her hand and held it out to Jules. "Sun Eyes no longer your sister. She my wife."

Freedom removed the bill from Jules hand and nodded for him to leave the room. He didn't need the hint. He was already headed to the door.

She faced her husband. "While I can smell like bear grease when with the Absarokee because they are used to it, I won't walk around this town smellin' like a stale bear when people are already starin' and wonderin' about me." She put a hand on her husband's chest. "You have to admit you like how I smelled of flowers the night of our wedding."

His eyes grew round and a smile lingered on his lips before he gave one crisp nod. "I thought we were in a spring meadow."

"Women who live in town like to smell good. Do not get mad with Jules for helpin' me out. He knew you would not like it. I had to talk him into givin' me the money." Freedom tucked the bill in her skirt pocket.

"You are going to get hat alone?" he asked, a frown wrinkling his brow.

"No. Mrs. Dudley has to do some shopping. I'll go with her and when we get back, you and I can go for our ride." She stood on her tiptoes and kissed his cheek. "We won't be long."

"What I do while you go with Mrs. Dudley?" He put an arm around her, drawing her body next to his.

"You can get to know my brother Jules better." She smiled. Jules had had a funny expression on his face when Swift called her his sister.

Swift nodded. "I have wanted to speak with him."

Now she was worried. What could he want to discuss with Jules? "What did you want to speak to him about?"

"Nothing for you to worry about." He kissed her lips and released her.

She dropped to her feet and stared as he strode out of the room. Unsure if leaving him to question Jules was a good thing, she wandered to the kitchen in search of Mrs. Dudley.

~*~

Jules had gone upstairs to his room. Water Runs Fast stood outside the door. He remembered Mrs.

Dudley and Beau hitting their door when they wanted to tell them something. He raised his hand and banged the side of his fist on the door.

"What is wrong?" Jules said, opening the door.

"I would like to speak with you," he said, slipping around the man and into his room.

"Did you and Freedom fight?" the brown-skinned man asked.

"We are not enemies. We do not fight." The man was crazy if he thought he would fight the woman he loved.

"She is getting the hat?" Jules shut the door and sat down on a chair by a small table. The room and bed were smaller than the one he and Sun Eyes slept in.

"She goes to store with Mrs. Dudley." Water Runs Fast sat on the bed. "She said to wear bear grease in town make people stare more." He didn't understand what was wrong with smelling like bear grease. He used it to make his hair stand up in front.

"Women like to smell good." Jules faced him. "You may take Freedom to live with your people, but she's still gonna want to live with some of the things she's used to."

He nodded. "She has strong medicine and must live her way to not lose it."

"Strong medicine?" the other man asked.

Water Runs Fast explained how she'd come to him in a dream and had promised to help his people.

Jules nodded his head as Water Runs Fast spoke. When he finished, Jules said. "I've witnessed her strength. But as strong as she is, she is also delicate in many ways."

It was his turn to nod. "I have seen her weakness

and her heart that is as fragile as a dried leaf."

~*~

Freedom ignored the stares of the other women in the mercantile. She walked to the back where straw hats were piled on a shelf. Plucking one off the top of the pile, she tried it on. It was a good thing there was a leather strap to tighten under her chin. The hat was too big, but she didn't think there would be much difference in any that she tried.

The store clerk was helping another woman and Mrs. Dudley was in line behind her.

Freedom left the hat on her head and wandered along looking at some men's dress shirts. It would be cooler for Swift to wear a cotton shirt like this rather than his heavy leather shirt. The five dollars Jules gave her would pay for both easily.

She wasn't sure of his size and held up shirts until she found one that looked as wide as his shoulders. With the shirt draped over her arm, she walked toward the counter where Mrs. Dudley was now making her purchases. The woman faced her as the clerk went to fetch an item for her.

Freedom held up the shirt. "Do you think this will fit my husband?"

The woman shrugged. "What would I know about your Indian husband."

The snide remark shot heat to the tips of her ears and had a scathing remark burning the tip of her tongue. But she held it. This woman could throw them out and where would they stay as they waited for Beau's return?

The clerk returned and finished Mrs. Dudley's transactions. She spun on her heel and headed for the door. Freedom wanted to call out to the woman to wait for her but didn't want the woman to know she feared walking the streets alone.

She tugged the hat from her head and placed it and the shirt on the counter. The clerk didn't touch either item.

"That will be a dollar."

She held out the money.

The man stared at it. She dropped it on the counter.

He picked it up by the corner and placed four silver dollars on the counter.

Freedom scooped those up and into her skirt pocket, plopped the hat on her head and draped the shirt over her arm. The clerk had wrapped Mrs. Dudley's purchases.

She stepped out of the store with the same uneasy, disappointment she'd felt when she was small in the South and in some areas of Chicago. She had a heart, mind, and faith just like the white people, why did they treat her as if she were less than human?

Her mind on the way she'd been treated, Freedom stepped out onto the board walkway and turned the direction of the boardinghouse. Musing over how no one at the reservation treated her any different, she squeaked as a hand grasped her arm and pulled her into the alley.

The face she saw sent waves of fear rushing through her body. She opened her mouth to scream and a dirty hand clamped over it.

"You keep your mouth shut or I'll make sure you can't yell." Foster's nasty breath made her gag.

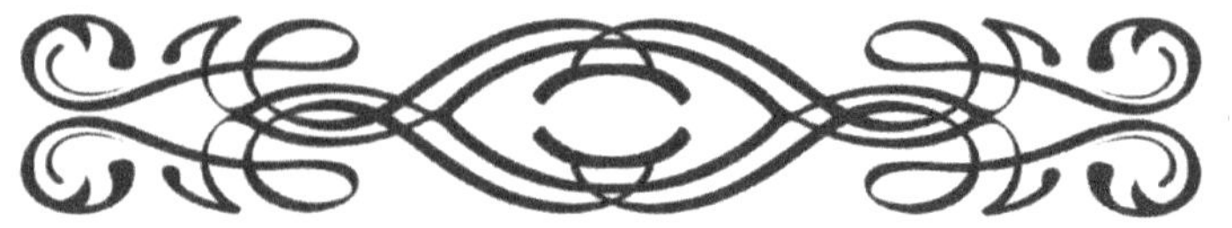

Chapter Thirty-two

Mrs. Dudley walked through the front door. Water Runs Fast stood up from the stairs where he'd been sitting, waiting for the women to return.

"Where is my wife?" he asked.

The woman shrugged. "I showed her how to get to the mercantile. I figured she was smart enough to find her way back here."

He grabbed her by the upper arms. "Which store?"

The woman's eyes were as big and round as one of her small plates. Her mouth opened and closed but no words came out.

"Water Runs Fast, let go of Mrs. Dudley," Jules said behind him.

He released the woman. She started to slump to the floor. He grabbed one arm and Jules grabbed the other. They walked her into the fancy room and put her on the chair for two.

"Why were you holding her by the arms?" Jules

asked, propping the woman up with soft squares.

"She left Sun Eyes at the store." Something was wrong. He could feel it. "There is trouble." He walked to the door.

"You can't go alone. Wait." Jules pulled on a string around the woman's neck and a small vessel appeared. He opened it and held it under the woman's nose.

Her head rocked back and forth before she shoved his hand and the vessel away.

"Get that out of my nose," she demanded, opening her eyes and staring at Jules. "What did you do?" She grabbed at the object in Jules' hand and sat up straight, getting as far from him as she could.

"Mrs. Dudley, which mercantile did you and Freedom visit?" Jules asked.

"Smythe and Jordan." She pressed deeper into the chair.

Jules stood and strode over to Water Runs Fast. "Come on. Let's go find her."

He headed to the door and strode down the street toward the busy part of town with Jules keeping up with him stride for stride. Once they hit the wide street with many businesses side by side, Jules took the lead. He could read better than Water Runs Fast. He spent a few years in a missionary school, but he spent most of his time there wishing to be back with his family.

"There it is," Jules pointed and picked up his pace.

Water Runs Fast pushed through the doors ahead of Jules. There had been no sign of Sun Eyes as they walked to the store. He walked up to the long table where a man was talking with a woman.

"Where is woman who came here to buy hat?" he asked.

Jules walked up beside him. "There was a woman with my coloring who came in with Mrs. Dudley. Can you tell us when she left?"

The man sputtered a minute. "She bought a hat and shirt and left here a good thirty minutes ago."

Water Runs Fast had no idea how long that was, but from the look on Jules face, it was too long. "She has been gone long?"

"Long enough she should have been back to the boardinghouse." Jules walked to the door and stopped outside. "Let's go get the sheriff to ask if anyone saw her." He strode into the street.

"Why not ask ourselves," Water Runs Fast said, keeping up with the man.

"Because no one would talk to us." Jules glanced over at him. He knew what the man meant.

No one would tell a brown man and an Indian what they wanted to know. His chest tightened with worry for Sun Eyes. What happened to her? He had a thought. "I will talk to the man at stable." He didn't wait for a reply. He ran down the street, ignoring the people moving out of his way. It just made his journey faster.

~*~

Pain sliced through Freedom's jaw. She opened her eyes and found herself slung over the pack on a mule. She tried to shift her weight and discovered her hands and feet were tied. The motion of the animal pushed something sharp into her right hip. She tried shifting and something else poked into her ribs on the left.

The trees and birds singing were too cheery for the problem she was in. She closed her eyes. How had Foster found her? And why had he knocked her out and hauled her out here? Her stomach churned. Swift would tear the town apart looking for her. If he were thrown in jail, she'd have no one to help her. She had to get out of this on her own. And keep her wits about her.

A clump of trees and then a rock looked familiar. She knew where she was. He'd taken the same path she and Swift had the day before. Twisting her neck and raising up a bit to see the back of Foster, she knew who had been watching them yesterday. He had on a black and red plaid shirt. It looked like the same one he'd worn when she'd met him over a month ago.

Where was Mary? Her stomach landed in her throat. Did he kill her? She hoped not. Beau had promised to help her.

She rode on another mile enduring the gouging in her side and hip. She didn't know what he'd do if he knew she were awake. But the longer he kept moving the harder it would be for anyone to find her.

Deciding it was better to try and get away while she was closer to town than further, she called out, "Stop, please!"

The animals stopped. She kept her head lowered, not wanting him to see she was interested in what he was doing.

The creak of leather and a heavy thud had her thinking he'd dismounted. His moccasin clad feet came into view as soon as his body odor hit her nostrils.

He grabbed one of her braids and raised her head up, kinking her neck. "What makes you think I take orders from the likes of you?"

"It wasn't an order. It was a plea." She tried to talk and not inhale his smell. Even the bear grease was a welcome scent to this man's. "Something is poking me in the side and the hip. Could I sit up?"

The man dropped her head and pulled out a knife. He cut the rope tying her hands to the side of the pack and then went around to the other side. She rubbed her wrists and started to push up to raise her body, when hands gripped her sides and pulled her off the animal and onto her feet.

The jarring of her feet hitting the ground shot pain through her jaw. He'd hit her hard when she'd struggled with him in the alley.

His hands remained digging into her sides and he didn't move.

She heard sniffing. What was he, some kind of dog? His touch and sniffing repulsed her but she didn't want to be knocked out again. She steeled herself to not flinch or gag.

His hands loosened and moved up her side. She spun out of his grasp, but her feet were still tied together and she couldn't step away.

"Don't you try to run from me. I got you now and you're mine." He grabbed her arm, tugging her toward him.

Thank goodness her tied feet didn't allow her to step forward. She grasped a strap on the pack and remained standing rather than falling at his feet. "I'm not yours. I'm married to Water Runs Fast."

The man stared at her. "No. I killed Ben so I could have you. And now, I do. You're mine."

She shook her head. "What about Mary? You are her husband. You can't have two wives."

His face grew red and his mouth twisted into an angry smirk. "She left me. I showed her the money I took off Ben and then went back out lookin' for you. When I went home, she was gone and so was the money." He narrowed his eyes. "What did you tell her when you was there?"

"That she could do better than you." The second the words came out, she knew she'd said too much.

"And I suppose you think you're better than me?" He yanked on her arm and this time she couldn't hold onto the pack strap.

Her body fell forward, and she landed against his chest.

His arms wrapped around her like a noose and she went limp, making it harder for him to do anything. She'd learned this as a child that going limp made a body feel heavier and much harder to control.

He finally dropped her to the ground. She hit hard but it was a relief to being close to him and fearing what he might do.

"We'll stay here for the night." He walked to her feet and sliced the ropes. "Get up and start setting up camp."

She'd rather work than lay across the back of a pack animal or be next to the man.

Freedom didn't realize until he shouted at her that making camp meant she unsaddled and unpacked the horse and mule, took them to water and staked them out as well as set up the camp and cooked while he leaned against a tree and watched her, grinning.

Chapter Thirty-three

The stable owner said the two men who had bothered Water Runs Fast and Sun Eyes the day before, hadn't been in today. But a man had left his horse and a pack mule with him for only a couple hours before he came back out of breath, wanting his animals fast.

"What did man look like?" Water Runs Fast asked.

"He wore pants like yours, a red and black shirt, short brimmed leather hat, and smelled like he hadn't bathed in years." The stable man followed him to the corral. "Why are you asking about Marvin and Tom?"

Water Runs Fast studied the man. He had been good to them so far. "My wife, the woman who was with me yesterday, is missing. She went to buy hat with Mrs. Dudley and not come back."

The man's eyes softened. "She may have decided to look for something else."

He shook his head. "No. Sun Eyes didn't need anything else. She wanted hat to go riding again today."

He rubbed his hand up and down the middle of his chest. "Something wrong. I feel this." His horses came over to him. He caught his and Jules' horse. They would go looking for Sun Eyes.

"Good luck finding her. She seemed like a nice girl," the stable man said, after helping him saddle Jules' horse.

Water Runs Fast mounted his horse and led Jules' as he made his way back to the wide street and the sheriff's office. He hoped Jules had talked the sheriff into helping them look for Sun Eyes.

The two men stood on the walkway in front of the office. From the way Jules motioned with his hands the sheriff wasn't going to help.

"We go," Water Runs Fast said, tossing the reins of Jules' horse to him.

The other man mounted his horse. "The jackass won't do anything to help. He thinks she ran away knowing Major Litchfield will want charges brought against her."

Water Runs Fast glanced over at the man as he headed back to the edge of town. "What is charges?"

"Make Freedom pay for the death of his son." Jules stared forward.

"She did nothing. I will tell this major so. Come, we must find her." He told Jules about the man with a packhorse that sounded like the man who had been watching them the day before. "We look for tracks outside of town."

They rode to the edge of the town and then started north. Water Runs Fast kept his gaze on the ground. His heart stopped as he noted tracks of two unshod horses. The one behind made deeper indentions. It was a pack animal and could have more than a pack on it. "This one. We follow." He pointed the nose of his horse along the edge of the tracks and urged the animal into a trot. The lawman would not help them, but they did not need his help. He would find Sun Eyes and take revenge on the man who took her.

~*~

The darkness descended much too quickly for Freedom's liking. She knew once she no longer had tasks that needed done, the man would either attempt to bed her or tie her up. She hoped for the later but had also come up with a plan to get away from him. Though stabbing him would make her look like she had killed Ben and if she stabbed him in the wrong place he could die and not tell Major Litchfield the truth—he'd killed Ben.

She picked up the tin plates and utensils and walked out of the circle of light the fire cast.

"Where you going?" Foster asked, jumping up from where he'd lounged since he told her to make camp.

"Wash the dishes in the river." She held the dishes up.

He shook his head. "They don't need cleaned."

She glared at him. "These dishes were disgusting. I scratched all the rancid food off with a rock. I'm cleaning them proper."

"Then I'm coming with you. Wouldn't want you to think you could duck out through the trees and get away." He picked up his rifle and followed her.

Not the scenario she'd had in her mind but at least she could clean the dishes. A thought came to her as she crouched beside the water, scrubbing the plates. While she couldn't swim in her full skirt, she could say she wanted to bathe and get out of the yards of fabric and let the current take her downstream, where she'd climb out and hope to find help.

But the current would take her further away from Swift. She sighed, long and drawn out. There would have to be another way, even though the thought of drifting away on the current hounded her.

"Them's clean enough. Come on back to the camp." Foster grabbed her by the arm, hauling her to her feet. The dishes clattered to the ground.

"Let go. I dropped them." She ripped her arm from his grip and picked up the dishes. When she straightened the horses nickered.

"Get along." He pushed her in front of him, prodding her with the end of the rifle as they walked back toward the firelight.

Her gaze darted to the horse and mule when she stepped into the light. They stood quietly but their ears were straight up and twitching as if trying to catch a sound.

She walked over to the pack and tucked the dishes away. "Would you like more coffee?" she asked, thinking of something to keep him occupied.

Foster didn't answer. He stood just outside the firelight, staring into the darkness beyond her.

She took that as 'no' and pulled a blanket out of the pack. Freedom wound herself up in the blanket and sat with her back leaned against a rock. She'd managed to slip a knife into her boot while washing the dishes. It wasn't anything like what Swift carried but it might do enough damage to get away from the man if he tried anything.

Foster waited a long time before he entered the firelight, leaned his rifle against a tree, and walked over to the fire and poured himself a cup of coffee.

Freedom lowered her eyelids to feign sleep when movement by the tree where Foster had leaned his rifle caught her attention. The weapon was gone. She hid a smile in the blanket and prayed it was Swift and not someone else.

Foster turned his back to her as he peered at the tree where his rifle had been.

Someone grabbed her under the arms and dragged her behind the rock. She held her surprise and stared into the eyes of her husband. He pressed a finger to his lips.

She put an arm around his neck and whispered in his ear. "We need him alive. He killed Ben and took the money."

Swift nodded and disappeared into the trees.

"Damn darkie what did you do—" the man's voice stopped abruptly. He had to have spun back around and found her gone as well.

His footsteps approached.

"Are you looking for this?" Jules asked from across the way.

Water Runs Fast waited for the man to charge Jules before tackling him. He wanted to make sure the man wasn't close enough to Sun Eyes to cause her any harm.

"Why you no-good Injun. I shoulda killed you when I had the chance," the man yelled as Water Runs Fast sat on his back, holding him down.

Jules brought rope and tied the man's hands and feet.

"You can't do this. You're just a darkie and an

Injun. Damn whore. I didn't even—"

Jules shoved a piece of cloth from his pocket into the man's mouth.

Water Runs Fast had wanted to hit the man to make him quiet but Sun Eyes had wanted the man awake.

She appeared from behind the rock and ran to him, flinging her arms around his waist. "I knew you'd find me."

He held her close, enjoying the way she clung to him. "When Mrs. Dudley came home and did not know where you were, we went looking." He glanced at Jules over Sun Eyes' shoulder. He had the man turned over on his back.

"Did he hurt you?" He leaned back, scanning her face. The firelight wasn't as bright as he would have liked.

"He hit me in town." She touched her chin and side of her face. "My jaw hurts."

Anger whipped through him like a cold winter wind. He unhooked her arms from around his waist and took two steps toward the man tied in rope.

"No! Don't!" She ran to stand between him and the man. "We need him just as he is. We need him to tell the truth to the major."

"What is this?" Jules asked.

Sun Eyes grabbed Water Runs Fast's hand and led him around the fire, putting distance between her husband and the man. She motioned for Jules to join them. "We need to get him to the fort. He told me he killed Ben and took the money." She smiled. "Mary stole the money and left him. She has to be on her way to Shady Gulch."

Water Runs Fast stared at her. "He is the one to take your man's life? Not me?"

She smiled. "Yes. Beau said Ben had been stabbed three times. You said you only stabbed him once. Foster came along, saw Ben's injury, stabbed him two more times and took the money. Then he went on to the fort and told them I did it."

Water Runs Fast was happy his wife would not be in trouble for killing her man. "We will go now."

Jules held up a hand. "We can take him to the jail in Milestown and telegraph the fort to let Beau and the major know we have the killer."

"Will that get this all over with sooner?" Sun Eyes asked.

Jules nodded.

"Then that's what we should do." She glanced at him. "Are you alright with takin' him to the jail?"

He studied her. "Will he be there when major arrives?"

"Why wouldn't he?" she asked.

He glanced at Jules. "He would not help us find you."

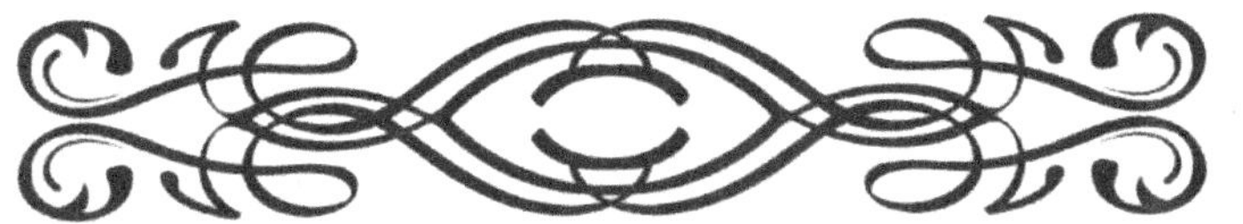

Chapter Thirty-four

The ride back to town didn't take as long as the ride away had felt. Freedom's head throbbed as they rode up to the sheriff's office.

Jules dismounted and strode into the building.

Swift slid off his horse and came over to lift her down. "Are you well?" he asked.

"My head hurts." She leaned against him.

Foster hung over the packsaddle the same way he'd carried her away from town.

Jules and the deputy walked out of the sheriff's office.

"Ma'am, I'll need your statement to hold this man," the deputy said.

She nodded and wished she'd answered instead. The motion ignited the pain.

Swift walked her into the building and sat her in a chair then walked back out. Within seconds, he and Jules escorted Foster into the building and through a door. The three men returned to the office.

"I'll take the horses to the stable and come back," Jules said.

She didn't nod this time. Swift did and stood behind her.

The deputy pulled out a piece of paper and dipped a pen in ink. "Tell me what happened?"

Freedom started with Mrs. Dudley leaving her alone at the store. Swift's hand on her shoulder gripped harder when she said Foster hit her, knocking her out. She pointed to the area.

The deputy stared at her, "That looks nasty. You might want to go see Doc Terry when we're done."

Swift's grip loosened, and she leaned her head against his arm. "I woke up and realized we were in the trees along the river. He suggested we, well, I make camp for the night." She drew in a breath and her stomach roiled. She drew in deep breaths to stop the nausea. "He told me he stabbed Ben Litchfield and took the money, my money, that was on him." She used all her energy to remain focused on the deputy. "He went to the fort and told the major I'd killed Ben. It was revenge for when I'd met him earlier and struck down his advances." She should have been embarrassed but she was too ill to care.

"You had met this man, Foster, before?" The deputy studied her.

"When I was with Ben Litchfield, my husband."

The man's gaze flit up to Swift. "I thought he was your husband?"

"He is now. After Ben died, Water Runs Fast came along, doctored me, and we became husband and wife." She was so tired. "Is that all? I think I should see a doctor."

Swift swept her up in his arms. "If you need more. We are at Mrs. Dudley's."

Jules walked into the building. "Where are you going?"

"Doctor. Sun Eyes is unwell." Swift spun back to the deputy. She held down the bile rising in her throat. "Make sure Foster is here when Major Litchfield comes."

He turned back around and walked out of the building with Jules behind him. Freedom glanced back at the worried expression on her friend's face.

"Why don't you send a telegraph while I see the doctor," she said, sounding as healthy as she could muster.

Jules put a hand on Swift's arm stopping him. He peered into her eyes. "Did he do more than hit you?"

She understood his meaning. "No."

He nodded and strode down the street.

"Do you know where the doctor is?" she asked Swift weakly.

"I will find him."

She had no doubt her husband would.

Water Runs Fast strode down the street until he found a man sitting on a bench. "Where is doctor?"

The man pointed the direction he was headed. "Down there about three blocks and turn left. Can't miss it."

He glanced down at Sun Eyes. Her eyes were closed and her breathing even. "What is a block?"

The man said, "Go down three cross streets."

He nodded and strode down the street, counting the roads to cross the one he walked on. He headed the direction the man had moved his hand and soon saw what looked like the letters he knew to mean doctor.

Water Runs Fast kicked the door.

A tall slender woman answered. "How may I—Oh my heavens, bring her in here."

He followed the woman into a room with a tall long table.

"Set her down. What happened?" The woman tied on a white cover like Mrs. Dudley wore.

"A man hit her here." He motioned to the darkening of Sun Eyes' skin on the side of her face.

"Did he just do it?" the woman lit a lantern and held it close to Sun Eyes' face.

"No. It was earlier today. We found them. She said her jaw hurt then at the sheriff office she said head hurt and now she is asleep."

The woman looked up at him. "Who are you?"

"Water Runs Fast, her husband." He stood beside the table and picked up one of Sun Eyes hands.

The woman smiled. "Have a seat in the other room."

He stood where he was.

"I can't help your wife if you stay in here in my way."

He nodded and walked into the other room. But he didn't sit. He walked back and forth, looking out the window and returning to the door where his Sun Eyes lay hurting.

A soft knock and Jules walked through the door. "How is she?"

"Woman doctor with her." He tipped his chin to the other room.

Jules put a hand on his shoulder. "She'll be fine.

I'll go make sure Mrs. Dudley didn't put anyone in our rooms. You come back there as soon as you can bring Freedom. I sent the telegraph and all we can do now is wait and make sure Foster stays in jail."

Water Runs Fast nodded. He didn't want the man getting out and harming Sun Eyes again.

Jules left as quietly as he'd arrived.

Plopping onto a chair, Water Runs Fast put his hands in his face and prayed to *Ah-badt-dadt-deah*, the one who made all things. If the vision he was given was to be fulfilled he needed Sun Eyes by his side. And to help with a whole heart, he needed her in his life.

~*~

The room was cold. Freedom felt hands moving across her face. She opened her eyes and stared up into the inquisitive eyes of a woman with blonde hair.

"Who are you?" she asked, realizing she lay on a hard, long table.

"I'm Dr. Terry. Your husband brought you in and said you'd been hit on the side of the head." The woman straightened and peered down at her. "Why did you become unconscious?"

"I don't know. Maybe from the pain? My head hurt as if someone were tryin' to crush it. Then my belly started squirmin' and feelin' like I could vomit." Freedom put a hand to her jaw. "It feels like the strike from the man knocked my jaw loose."

"Let me see." She grasped Freedom's chin and moved it about.

"Ugh. Now my belly is roilin' again."

"I would say bedrest and nothing solid to eat until that jaw doesn't hurt." The doctor offered her a hand.

Freedom sat up. "Can I ask you a question?"

The woman smiled. "Yes."

"How did you become a doctor?" She'd never known a woman to be a doctor.

"I went to a school for doctors. There were only a few women in my graduating class, but doctors are needed out west and towns are willing to take anyone who can give them something for their aches and pains."

"I'm glad you were able to find a job. Do you ever travel to reservations?" She thought it would be a good idea to have a doctor come check the Absarokee once in a while.

The woman smiled. "I was sent to a reservation when I first graduated. What reservation are you asking about?"

"The Crow Reservation by Fort Custer. My husband's family lives there." Freedom didn't know if they would even listen to a doctor but it was worth a try.

"If you think a doctor is needed, you can send a telegraph from the fort." Dr. Terry helped her down off the table and told her to stay. She walked to the door. "Your wife is ready to go."

The doctor backed up, and Swift strode into the room. His gaze scanned from her feet to the top of her head.

"You are well?" he asked, stopping in front of her.

"Better."

"She isn't well. She needs rest and foods that don't require chewing." Dr. Terry peered at Swift. "Do you understand what I'm saying?"

He nodded. "I will tell Mrs. Dudley."

"Is that where you're staying?" Dr. Terry asked.

"Until Major Litchfield takes away man who hurt Sun Eyes."

The doctor had a confused expression wrinkling her brow.

"It's a long story. I'm Sun Eyes, or Freedom, my real name. Water Runs Fast named me Sun Eyes." She smiled at her husband and he held out his arm.

She slipped her hand through the crook at his elbow and said good-bye to the doctor. Out in the cool night air, she shivered.

"I carry you. We go faster," he said.

"I'd rather walk slow. It jars my jaw and head less," she replied and he slowed his pace.

The boardinghouse appeared as she was about to ask Swift to pick her up. Her legs were wobbly, her belly churned, and her head throbbed.

He opened the door, and Jules appeared from the parlor.

"How are you?" he asked.

She slumped against Swift. He swept her up in his arms.

"Doctor say she eat foods no chew," he said and packed her up to their room.

Freedom sank onto the soft bed, dreaming her husband undressed her and covered her with the blankets before kissing her forehead.

Chapter Thirty-five

Down in the fancy room, Water Runs Fast told Jules what the doctor had said and asked when they would know if the major and Beau would return here.

"We should hear back from them in the morning," Jules said. "We can take turns checking at the jail to see they keep Foster in and watching Freedom."

"Why they not keep man? He killed and he stole Sun Eyes." He didn't understand how a white man's law would allow someone the likes of this Foster to not pay for their crime.

"It depends on if the sheriff believes Freedom's statement."

The uncertainty in Jules' eyes had Water Runs Fast thinking maybe seeking revenge would be the better course. "Sun Eyes tells truth. We saw how he treated her, heard what he told her. She would not lie."

"We know that. We have to make sure the sheriff knows that. Or get Foster to admit what he did." Jules eyes lit up. "I have a plan. I'll work on it tomorrow. Go to bed."

"I should take food to Sun Eyes." He took a step toward the kitchen.

Jules put a hand on his arm. "Let her rest. You can take her something to eat in the morning."

Water Runs Fast nodded and followed the man up the stairs. Jules entered his room and Water Runs Fast walked to the door of the room he shared with Sun Eyes. He stepped into the dark room and slipped out of his clothing. Naked, he slid into bed beside his wife.

She muttered and rolled toward him.

He smiled and his heart sang as he drew her into his arms and held her as he fell asleep.

~*~

The weight of an arm across her chest was the first thing Freedom became aware of as sleep slipped away and the warmth of sunlight flickered on her face.

She knew by the scent it wasn't Foster. It was her husband, Swift. She twisted her neck and studied his face, resting on a pillow by her shoulder. Her nose wrinkled at the bear grease he used to stand up his forelock, but she had slowly grown used to it. The mild scent along with earthy undertones was a smell she was becoming to love as much as she did the man.

He'd found her yesterday when she'd been sure she'd have to find her own way back to town. And he'd taken her to a doctor and carried her up to bed. She pressed her lips to his forehead.

His eyes fluttered open. A smile tipped his lips. "You are better?"

"So far." She touched the side of her face Foster had hit. It was sore and her jaw ached when she tried moving it. "I'll be back to normal soon."

He ran a finger over her lips. "I wish to kiss you but fear I will hurt you."

She smiled. "I can see how much you care in your eyes. That will have to do until my jaw is healed."

He nodded. His arm drew her closer. "If I am careful, I could show my love another way." The heat in his eyes had her heart quickening.

"You know another way?" she asked.

He rolled to his back, bringing her with him. She lay on top of him, hips to hips, chest to chest. His hardness pressed at her center.

She moved her legs, opening for him and was rewarded with a gentle trip to a place where her body hummed with pleasure.

A knock on the door had them both staring at it.

Freedom rolled off of her husband and stifled a giggle in the blankets.

Another knock sounded. "Are you two coming down to breakfast?" Jules asked.

"In a few minutes," Freedom replied as Swift rolled out of bed and headed to the door. "Don't open that!" she said, not wanting Jules to see her husband naked and her hiding in the sheets.

Swift spun back toward her a huge grin on his face.

She threw a pillow at him. When he started to chuck it back at her, she reminded him of her jaw.

They washed up and dressed quickly. Freedom had a lot of questions to ask Jules.

At the kitchen, Jules was seated at the table. Two chairs had plates sitting in front of them. One had a huge breakfast and the other had scrambled eggs. She knew the eggs were for her. Freedom sat in front of the eggs and her stomach growled.

Mrs. Dudley turned from the cookstove with a coffee pot in her hand. She filled the cups in front of both she and Swift. He sniffed the drink, wrinkled his nose and took a sip. The cup thumped on the table.

Freedom added two scoops of sugar to her coffee and slipped a bite of eggs into her mouth, barely chewing before swallowing.

"Have you heard from Beau?" Swift asked Jules.

She glanced from one man to the other. What had they said to Beau?

"No. Major Litchfield received my telegraph. He said Beau and Pinkerton Fine had not arrived, but he would set out today and catch them along the way." Jules smiled at Freedom. "I sent a telegraph last night while you were with the doctor. I told him we had the man who killed his son."

"You sent it to just the major?" she asked, wondering why Swift had asked about Beau.

"I sent it to both Beau and the major." Jules put preserves on his biscuit.

Her mouth watered and she wondered if chewing a biscuit would hurt her jaw. She plucked a biscuit from the platter on the table and spread preserves on a half. Opening her mouth halfway, she bit and chewed. The pain wasn't worth eating. She sighed and handed the biscuit to her husband.

He took the offer and shoved the whole thing in his mouth and chewed. At least he was getting something satisfying. She continued to eat her eggs.

"I'll go check on Foster," Jules said, scooting back from his empty plate.

"Why are you checking on him?" she asked.

"Jules think sheriff not believe you." Swift frowned.

She faced Jules. "You think, he thinks I'm lying?" Her chest squeezed. "He has to keep that man in jail. He told me he is a killer." She raised a hand to her chest. "He would kill again if he could get away with it."

"I know. That is why Water Runs Fast and I will take turns hanging around the sheriff's office. To make sure Foster doesn't get out."

Jules strode out of the room.

Freedom studied her husband. "What are we going to do when you aren't at the jail?"

He raised an eyebrow and she felt her face heat.

Mrs. Dudley picked up Jules' dirty dishes. "I thought you were under doctor's orders?"

"She is to rest and eat soft foods," Swift said.

"I know," Freedom said. "You know English but I don't know how to speak Absarokee. You can teach me." She smiled and was excited to understand what Swift's mother and aunt said when they thought she couldn't understand them.

Swift frowned. "There is no village to teach you."

"Village? We don't need the village." She stood and led him into the parlor. They both sat on the settee. "What is this?" She started with parts of the body. She asked and he said the word. She repeated it until Swift said she pronounced it correctly.

They had spent several hours with her learning Absarokee words when Jules returned. "It's your turn," he said, taking off his hat. "When I told the sheriff the major was on his way to speak with Foster, he seemed to agree keeping the man locked up was a good idea."

He shrugged. "I still think we need to watch."

Water Runs Fast nodded. He'd enjoyed teaching Sun Eyes how to speak Absarokee. She was a quick learner. Sitting outside the sheriff's office would not be as fun.

Sun Eyes grasped his hand. "Be careful."

He nodded and strode out of the house and down the streets to the sheriff's office. There was a chair by the door of the building. He walked inside.

The sheriff glanced up. "What are you doing here?"

"I am to watch man in jail." He walked to the door to the rooms with metal bars. Opening the door, he peered at the man lying on a narrow bed. His arm rested across his eyes. Water Runs Fast closed the door, pivoted, and walked back out to the chair. He sat down, crossed his arms, and watched the people in the street.

The sun had moved over the buildings next door when the sheriff stepped out of the building. He glanced at Water Runs Fast. "You're still here?"

The man could see he was sitting in the chair.

"I'm going to get something to eat. My deputy should show up soon. He'll be bringing food for the prisoner." The sheriff walked down the street, talking to the people he passed.

Water Runs Fast remained on the chair. He would have liked to stand and stretch his legs, but he attracted less attention sitting still.

Two boys ran up to him. "You a real Injun?" one asked.

He ignored them. They were not like Absarokee youth. If they were, they would know by looking he was an Indian. There was no need to ask.

One of them pranced up and down in front of him as if he rode a horse. The third time he went by he stuck out his hand and made the sound of a rifle shooting.

Water Runs Fast shot to his feet. The two boys screeched and ran away. He smiled and sat back down.

The deputy he'd met the night before walked up carrying a basket. From the smells the basket had food inside. "You taking up being a deputy?" the man asked.

He shook his head. "I not like being in one place all the time."

The man laughed. "I do plenty of walking to check on businesses at night." He entered the building and Water Runs Fast remained on the chair, scanning the people passing on the street and the walkway.

He narrowed his eyes as the two from the stable walked across the street toward him.

"What do we have here?" the smaller of the two said.

"Looks like an Injun taking up sitting at the sheriff's door. What's wrong, you afraid someone is going to hurt you?" the larger of the two made as if to grab him.

Water Runs Fast lunged to his feet and pulled his knife from his moccasin.

"We were just funnin' you," the smaller man said, backing away.

"You know how to use that?" the larger man asked, pulling a knife from the sheath on his belt.

"What's going on here?" the deputy asked, stepping out the door.

"This here Injun pulled his knife on us," the larger man said.

Water Runs Fast scowled at the man. He'd started

the fight with his comment. "I pulled my knife to your threat."

"Tom put your knife away and go on about your business," the deputy said.

The man slowly slipped his knife back in the sheath. The smaller man grabbed him by the arm, leading him away.

"You not need to help me," Water Runs Fast said, feeling as if he'd missed a chance at counting coup. The two were his enemy. If he could have tapped the man and neither one get hurt, he would have had another coup to add to his name.

"There will be no fighting in front of the sheriff's office. I'm on your side, but if you cause trouble, Sheriff Merkle will make you stay away." The deputy returned to the building.

Water Runs Fast sat down. He crossed his arms as he spotted Jules striding down the street toward him.

"I'll take over from here," the man said as he stepped up onto the walkway. "Everything go smooth?"

He wouldn't tell Jules about his encounter. It was of no importance. "The man is still in the jail. Do you wish I come before dark?"

Jules shook his head. "I don't think anything will happen at night. The deputy is sympathetic. He saw how shook up Freedom was and realizes she is telling the truth."

Water Runs Fast nodded and headed back to the boarding house. He liked the idea of spending more time with his wife.

Chapter Thirty-six

Three days had passed since Foster had captured Freedom and he'd been put in jail. Swift told her that each day Foster became more and more angry at being in jail. He made her promise to stay away even when he was sitting outside the sheriff's office. She could tell when he came back the first day from keeping an eye on Foster, and she'd asked him what he did while he sat there, that something had happened he didn't want to talk about.

She sat in the parlor, stitching a bonnet. She'd gone to the mercantile with Mrs. Dudley and purchased the fabric and sewing items with the leftover money from what Jules had given her for the hat she'd lost when Foster took her.

So much had happened since she'd first left Shady Gulch. While at the store, she'd also purchased paper, an envelope, wax, and a seal. Yesterday she'd sat in the parlor and wrote a three page letter to her family, telling them what had happened to her since she'd left Chicago. Swift had encouraged her to write and let them know she was living the life she was meant to live. When she'd finished, she'd dried the tears of regret, smiled, and sealed the envelope. Jules had mailed it for her on his way to relieve Swift.

Foot stomping and the front door opening, startled Freedom. She shoved her sewing into a leather pouch. She stood as Beau walked into the room. He was back and had to have good news. She ran across the space between them and stopped in front of him.

"Freedom. I have someone for you to meet," Beau said, releasing her arms.

She stepped back and knew immediately the name of the man in the military uniform. Her first reaction was to hide behind Beau, but the concern in his eyes had her keeping her feet planted.

"Freedom Meade Litchfield Swift, this is Major Litchfield," Beau introduced them.

She held out a hand.

The man studied her face before shaking. "I understand you were married to my son."

She stopped the shiver that started at the base of her neck. "I was. Until he died."

The man moved further into the room, his gaze remaining on her. "A Mr. Jules Matthieu sent a telegraph saying the man who killed my son has been caught."

Her body did shudder this time. "Yes. Mr. Foster—"

The major's eyes narrowed. He took a step toward her. "That's the man who said you killed my son." His voice said he thought she lied.

She flinched, but stood her ground. "I'd expect you to not believe me. Will you beat me like your son did to try and make me change the truth?"

The man had the decency to glance away. "I know my son had a temper."

"Temper? That's what you call kicking, hitting, and whipping me because I didn't do something the way he wanted." She laughed derisively. "I did not kill your son. But three days after our marriage, I wished I was dead because of the way he treated me."

"I'd like to make that up to you. I can either give you money to return to your family or you can live at the fort. Teach the immigrants in our platoon how to read and write." His offer sounded sincere. A lot like the man in Milestown who Ben had beat up.

Swift entered the room as the man made his offer.

"Major Litchfield, this is my new husband, Water Runs Fast. He is of the Crow tribe on the reservation near Fort Custer." She smiled at Swift. He studied her in a way she'd not seen before. What was he thinking?

"I believe you scouted for me several times," Major Litchfield said.

Swift nodded.

"I brought the major here to get a room for the night," Beau said. "After he talks to Mrs. Dudley, I think we should all go to the sheriff's office and settle the death of his son."

She couldn't agree more. "That sounds good. I'd like to get this over with."

Beau and the major left the room.

Freedom faced Swift. "You didn't tell me you knew Major Litchfield."

He shrugged. "Good soldier. Treat scouts good."

His gaze scanned her face. "You should go to your family. You will be happier there."

She stared at him. "What do you mean? I don't want to go back to Chicago. I want to live here, with you."

He shook his head. "You don't belong on a reservation."

"You don't belong on the reservation either. I won't go to the fort or Chicago unless you come with me," she added, wondering why he was trying to get rid of her.

"I was not asked to live at the fort."

"And you told me the fort wasn't a place for me to go." She put her hands on her hips.

"No one would hurt you. You are family of the major." His eyes showed no emotion.

What was he doing? Why did he want her to live away from him? "I don't understand. I thought we were going to live in the tipi your mother and aunt were setting up? We were going to help the Absarokee."

He scanned the room. "This is what you know. You belong in a home with chairs and beds. You can have that at the fort."

Beau and the major returned.

"Ready," Beau asked.

She wasn't through discussing this with her husband. But she did want to get the confession from Foster over with. "Yes."

Sun Eyes wrapped her arm around Water Runs Fast's arm. He glanced down at the determination in her eyes. He'd heard the major offer her the chance to live at the fort and teach the soldiers. She would be a good teacher, and she could live the life she knew. She belonged in a wood home with a bed off the floor and big stove to cook on. He could not give her that. He wanted her happy. She would soon grow tired of living the way of his people.

She strode with forceful steps all the way to the sheriff's office. The building was too small for so many people. He started to duck back out, but Beau put a hand on his arm. "You need to stay."

Beau and Jules stepped out of the building, but he noticed they remained just outside the door.

"I understand the man you have in jail killed my son, Benjamin," Major Litchfield said to the sheriff.

"He allegedly." The sheriff stared at Sun Eyes.

She glared back. "He told me he did."

Water Runs Fast's heart thudded hard against his ribs. She was a strong woman.

The major studied her. "When did he tell you this?"

"When he kidnapped me four days ago. Hit me so hard on the side of my head, I still can't chew food without it hurting." She pointed to the purple and yellow bruising on the side of her face.

"And you have a record of this?" the major asked the sheriff.

"She gave a statement when the Indian and darkie brought Foster in," the sheriff said.

"Darkie?" the major asked.

"Jules. The man outside with Beau." Sun Eyes narrowed her eyes on the sheriff. "Foster told me he finished off Ben and took the money Ben had taken from me. He was mad because his wife had run off with the money." Sun Eyes smiled. "I'm glad Mary ran away and took the money. He was as awful to her as Ben was to me."

"Why did this Foster take you?" Major Litchfield asked.

Sun Eyes glanced at Water Runs Fast then back at the major. "He said he killed Ben to have me."

The major looked shocked. "Why would he want you?"

She shrugged. "I don't know. But the night Ben and I stayed at the soddy with Foster and Mary, he, Foster, tried to…" she gulped. "I hit him, knocked him backward. He complained to Ben, who told him if he couldn't control me it was his problem." She stared the major in the eyes. "My husband was allowing another man to…" She shuddered.

Water Runs Fast couldn't let her stand there being disbelieved. He put his arm around her. "I was riding along the river when I heard a scream. I followed sound. Sun Eyes lay naked over rock. The man she say your son was whipping her." He stared the major straight in the eyes. He'd scouted enough for the man that the major knew Water Runs Fast did not lie. "I grabbed the whip. He turn on me with knife. We fought. I stab him, wrap her in blanket, and we leave with his horses and supplies." He stared at the major. "My people have not received all the food they were promised. I take food back to them."

"I wanted to go back for my shoes and the money Ben had taken, but Water Runs Fast refused. He feared we would be found with him and no one would believe us." Sun Eyes put her arm around his waist. It felt right.

"Why wouldn't anyone believe you?" the major glanced between them.

"Because I'm colored and he's Indian." She

motioned toward the sheriff. "It's why he doesn't believe me."

The major faced the sheriff. "Is this true? You don't believe them?"

"It is hard to think the two of them—" the sheriff stopped when the major glared at him.

Beau stepped back in the office. "My partner, Jules, has an idea."

"Have him come in here and explain it," the major said.

~*~

The sheriff escorted Freedom into a jail cell. "That's what you get for lying," he said, locking the door.

She sank down on the cot and put her face in her hands, pretending to sob.

"What about me. When you gonna let me out!" shouted Foster.

"I'm working on it," the sheriff said, walking through the door into the office.

Freedom peeked between her fingers to see what Foster was doing. He switched his gaze from the door to her. The nasty sneer that tingled the hair on the back of her neck graced his mouth.

"It's you and me locked up. Too bad he didn't put you in this here cell with me. We coulda kept each other company." He walked over and put his hands and arms through the bars that separated their areas. "He said somethin' about lyin'. What they think you're lyin' about? Me takin' you?" He laughed. "That Injun and darkie can vouch for that."

He narrowed his eyes. "You try to tell them I kilt your man?" He laughed again. "They'll never prove otherwise, not with that worthless wife of mine running off with the money."

She removed her hands and glared at him. "I'm glad she got away from you. The pain and humiliation you put her through. I should have told her to kill you and leave, then maybe Ben would still be alive."

He laughed. "She wasn't no match for me. I'd of kilt her first."

"But you couldn't have killed Ben if Water Runs Fast hadn't fought with him and stabbed him before you came along." She wanted him to say he killed Ben. Then the men standing on the other side of the door could hear him confess.

"I do have to thank your Injun for making him too weak to do anything but watch me sink my knife into him."

The door opened and an enraged Major Litchfield strode up to Foster's cell. "You will be hanged for the murder of my son."

Foster's eyes grew wide and round. He started to sputter when the sheriff walked through the door. "We heard it all." He walked over and unlocked Freedom's door. She walked out and through the door into the office.

Beau and Jules stood in the office. She didn't see Swift. "Where is Water Runs Fast?"

She knew before anyone said a word. The concern on Beau's face caused tears to trail down her face. "Why?"

"He said you should live with your family." Jules put a hand on her shoulder.

"He's become my family." She rubbed the tears off her cheeks and peered into Beau's eyes. "I know you need to get back to Shady Gulch and the saloon, but could you escort me to his village?"

"If he can't, I'd be honored to escort you anywhere you want to go," Major Litchfield said. "My offer stands to pay your way back to your family or to live at the fort."

"I don't want to live at the fort. I want to live at the Whistling Waters clan village." She faced the major. "And I would be honored to have you escort me there."

"We'll leave at first light tomorrow morning." He held his hat in his hands. His gaze left her face. "I'm sorry for what my son put you through. He had a mean streak in him since the day he was born. But he also learned how to use his charm to get what he wanted. It worked for him with his mother until her death, with an aunt, and later with other men and women he came across. I would like to give you the money he stole and more to show you I bear you no ill will."

A thought came to her. "Instead of money, how about a wagon load of supplies for the Whistling Waters clan?"

He smiled. "I'll have my sergeant get it ordered and loaded in a wagon. You'll ride into that village bearing gifts."

Freedom smiled. She'd not only show up and prove to Swift that she belonged with him, she'd also bring along food for the people.

Their people.

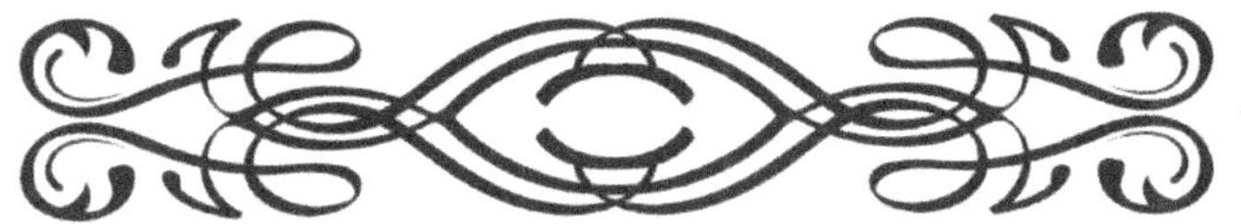

Chapter Thirty-seven

Six suns had passed since Water Runs Fast rode away from Sun Eyes. When he arrived back at the village without her, his mother, aunt, and Antlers on Wrong questioned him. They had all heard him out then told him he had walked away from his vision. His life would become a struggle for the rest of his days.

Sitting in the tipi his mother and aunt had erected for he and Sun Eyes, his heart believed their words. He missed her smile, her bright eyes, her laugh. She had been more than eyes that held rays of sun. She had been a beam of sunlight in his life.

The flap on the tipi opened. His nephew Two Missing Teeth stuck his head in. "Soldiers and wagon come!"

There had been no mention of supplies coming from the fort. His mother had said the agency man had told them again that there were not enough supplies to feed all the clans. They were dependent on what they could find to eat on the overhunted reservation land.

He ducked out of the lodge and strode to the area where he saw mounted soldiers and a crowd of villagers. Drawing closer, he recognized Major Litchfield. He was talking with Antlers on Wrong.

He approached the crowd, and they parted. Standing beside the wagon was Sun Eyes. His heart slammed against his ribs and began beating again.

She walked over to him. "Why did you leave?"

When he couldn't speak, only look into her sad eyes, she continued, "I talked the major into escorting me here, and since he'd offered to compensate me for his son's bad behavior, I asked for supplies for our village."

"Our?" His heart raced as his breath stopped. She called this village, our village.

"Yes, ours. You married me, and I'm not going to let you sneak away and not share your life with me." She stepped closer, and stretched on her toes to whisper in his ear. "Besides, our baby needs a father."

He wrapped his arms around her and peered into her eyes. "Our baby? First our village and now our baby?"

She smiled. Her eyes lit up like the noon day sun. "Yes. I would say he or she will put in an appearance in time for Thanksgiving."

"What is Thanksgiving?"

Freedom laughed. "It is a time when we give thanks. I'm sure you have a ceremony that is similar. Maybe we could combine them." She slipped her arms around his neck.

"Miss Freedom, we'll leave it in your capable hands to see that those in need get supplies." Major

Litchfield, saluted her and rode out of the village with his men behind him.

She faced her husband. "It looks like you're stuck with me."

"I have missed you," Swift said quietly.

She could see he had more to say to her. "Moon Woman, Woman Talks Softly, could you see that every family gets the supplies they need?" she asked the two women who were now her family.

They smiled and nodded as two boys about twelve climbed into the wagon and started handing items down to them.

Swift put his arm around her waist. "Come see our home."

"I would love to. And while we're there, I want to hear why you thought I'd be better off without you when my heart is yours." She had spent the last five days driving the wagon and worrying when she arrived, he would turn his back on her just as he had in the sheriff's office.

He led her to a new white tipi on the edge of the village. Holding the blanket aside for her to enter, he smiled. She returned the smile and gasped at the pile of buffalo hides on one side of the structure.

"Why do you have so many hides?"

"They are wedding gifts. My mother told the others you are not used to sleeping on the ground. They wished to make you a bed you can sleep in with comfort." He led her over to the pile. "Sit."

She did and found they were more comfortable than the hard ground.

He walked over to the opening, and slipped a stick through the blanket and a loop on the pole by the door.

He grinned. "This will keep others out."

"Why do we need to keep others out? We need to talk."

He nodded. "But I must see this child growing in you." He unbuttoned her dress, sliding it off her arms and helping her to stand to drop it on the ground at her feet.

"There isn't much to see, yet," she said as he drew her chemise over her head and sat her back down on the hides.

He placed his hand on her belly, moving it back and forth and up and down. His gaze caught hers. The love shining in his eyes was unmistakable. Her heart picked up speed and she leaned toward him, brushing her lips across his.

Freedom knew the second he took over the kiss and laid her on the hides that she was home and he would never let her go.

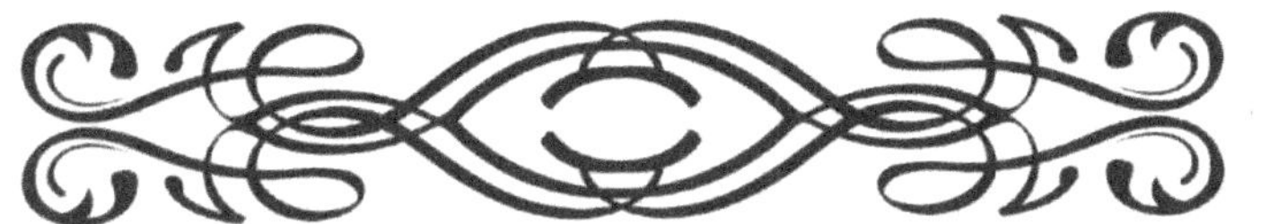

Epilogue

Freedom wrapped her baby boy into the cradleboard and covered him with a blanket her mother had brought when her parents came to visit in October before the baby arrived. She'd received a letter from them only a week before they'd arrived at the village.

It had been a tear-filled reunion with her being with child and her mother overjoyed to know she was happy. Her father and Swift had grown fond of one another the week her parents stayed with them. He had even agreed to bring Freedom and the baby to Chicago to see them.

Freedom knew this had been a grand gesture on his part, for they did not have the money for a train trip to Chicago. But that he had suggested it, made her happy.

Good news she'd learned a month after settling in at the reservation, Mary had arrived in Shady Gulch. Freedom had asked Swift if he could take her and the child to Shady Gulch in the spring. She wanted to let Mary see if she could find happiness, her friend could too.

Today, they were headed to the fort. Major Litchfield had written a letter on their behalf to the President, requesting a new Indian Agent be put in charge of the Crow Reservation. She and Swift had brought about proof that the previous Agent had been shorting the villages and selling supplies to settlers.

The new Agent was arriving at the fort, and they wanted to be there to greet him and see that he understood the needs of the people of the reservation. Major Litchfield invited them to stay with him whenever they went to the fort. He would be delighted to see the baby.

"Are you ready?" Swift asked, entering the tipi along with a blustery wind.

"We are." She picked up one of the buffalo hides from the bed. It would help to ward off the cold wind on their ride in the wagon they used to travel back and forth to the fort. The major had suggested they keep the wagon and use it for whatever needs they had.

Swift grasped her by the shoulders. "You are Absarokee. I thank *Ah-badt-dadt-deah* every time I look into your eyes that you shine your good light on us all. And have a heart big enough to forgive my foolishness."

Freedom's heart soared at his words. She'd finally found her family and was where she needed to be. "I am home with you."

About the Author

Thank you for visiting Shady Gulch. I hope you enjoyed reading about the lives of the women and men of this small railroad town. Freedom is the third woman from the Silver Dollar Saloon who finds the one man who loves her unconditionally. If you liked **Freedom**, please leave a review. It is the best way to let an author know you enjoyed their book.

All my work whether it's my romance or my mysteries have Western or Native American elements in them along with hints of humor and engaging characters. My husband and I raise alfalfa hay in rural eastern Oregon. Riding horses and battling rattlesnakes, I not only write the western lifestyle, I live it.

I love to hear from fans. You can find or contact me at:
patyjag@gmail.com
or my website – www.patyjager.net

Continue to the next page to find a listing of my historical western books or visit my website:

https://www.patyjager.net

Silver Dollar Saloon Series
Savannah
Lottie Mae
Freedom
Jules *(Coming 2020)*

Halsey Brother Series
Marshal in Petticoats – Gil's story
Outlaw in Petticoats – Zeke's story
Miner in Petticoats – Ethan's story
Doctor in Petticoats – Clay's story
Logger in Petticoats – Hank's story
Halsey Homecoming trilogy
Laying Claim – Jeremy's story
Staking Claim – Colin's story
Claiming a Heart – Donny's story
A Husband for Christmas - Shayla's story

Letters of Fate
Davis
Isaac
Brody

Other Historical Western Romance
Gambling on an Angel
Improper Pinkerton
For a Sister's Love

Historical Paranormal Romance
(Native American)
Spirit of the Mountain
Spirit of the Lake
Spirit of the Sky

Thank you for purchasing this Windtree Press
publication. For other books of the heart, please visit
our website at www.windtreepress.com.

For questions or more information contact us
at info@windtreepress.com.

Windtree Press
Hillsboro, OR

www.ingramcontent.com/pod-product-compliance
Lightning Source LLC
Chambersburg PA
CBHW070558170726
48291CB00003B/641